SUGAR COATED SECRETS

small town steamy romance

Pretty Georgia Peaches

Tara Gallina

For those afraid to stray from the version of love you've created in your mind, trust your gut and your heart to guide you, even if the path seems scary.
Take the chance, it might lead you right to where you belong.

Chapter 1

Sadie

Don't take the alley. Don't take it. A little rain never hurt anyone.

Thunder cracks, rattling through me as I hurry down the city sidewalk.

Make that a lot of rain.

I glance up at the evening sky, unable to see more than tall buildings, the windows aglow.

I can't believe I left my raincoat and umbrella at work. I knew rain was in the forecast. I showed up prepared, and yet I left everything behind—because I was in a hurry to beat the rain.

In my defense, I don't usually work this late, only on rare occasions. I don't like change. I don't like being unprepared, and I don't like anything potentially dangerous. Like alleys.

Atlanta might not be as big a city as Manhattan or Chicago, but to this small-town girl, it can be just as scary.

As an avid—obsessed—murder-show enthusiast, I know not to take a dark alley alone, even if it means getting home fifteen minutes faster and dry. I know this isn't the safest part of town, although it's not the worst. I know scary movies are made with openings like this, not that I watch horror flicks. Good old-fashioned serial killers and Dateline episodes are my thing.

Even my Uber driver warned me not to end the ride in this part of town. But we'd been in stand-still traffic for an hour due to an accident. I knew we'd be there for another hour, if not longer.

I had a choice. Brave the weather and walk the much shorter twenty minutes it would take on foot, or stay trapped in that Uber for two or more hours, while the driver made awkward small talk about dating in the city and not-so-subtly tried to gauge if I was single.

I made the smartest choice based on three facts:

- The weather app on my phone showed no rain for thirty minutes.
- I couldn't stand another second in the car with Mr. I'm-A-Great-Guy-And-The-Woman-Here-Are-Too-Picky.
- And I couldn't remember if I fed Detective Pickles this morning when I left earlier than usual for work.

A fat raindrop lands on the top of my head. I feel it through my hair and tense. My gaze locks on the alley in the near distance. I know it. Have passed it before. It would shave ten minutes off my walk. But it's dark, long, and not safe for a woman who's barely five-five, lightweight, and who looks twenty, even though I'm a couple months away from turning twenty-four.

Another crack of thunder has my feet shuffling even

faster. My earbud is still in my ear from the pretend call I took to get a break from the Uber driver.

I get my phone from the front pocket of my purse and call my bestie.

"Hey," Everleigh answers, a smile brightening her voice. "I was just thinking about you."

"Probably because I'm about to do something very out of character, so don't hang up."

"Why would I hang up? And why do you sound so serious?"

"In case I need you to call 911."

"Why would I do that, Sadie?" Everleigh asks, her tone now laced with concern.

I swallow deep in my throat and turn between the two buildings. "Because I'm walking down an alley alone to get home faster."

She snorts. "No, you're not."

"I am." I dodge a puddle and question the source. It hasn't rained yet today.

"Daire?" Everleigh shouts away from the phone. "Sadie's walking down an alley and she's alone."

"Why are you telling Daire?" It's not like her husband can do anything more than call 911 if I get into trouble. They live on his pecan farm two hours away.

"Yeah, right," his deep voice sounds in the background.

"I'm not kidding," Everleigh says. "She's taking a shortcut to get home faster."

Chills run over my skin, and I shiver. Is this alley colder or is my body responding out of fear?

A cat-sized animal scurries by. I squeal and jump away, bumping into the brick wall of one of the buildings.

"Why did you just scream?" Everleigh asks, her voice tense.

"It's okay." I exhale. "It was a rodent or something."

"Sadie, get out of the alley. Right now."

I glance behind me, considering doing just that when wind promising rain whips through the alleyway, cutting through my blouse as if to say, *here I come*.

"What is Sadie doing in an alley?" A familiar demanding voice sounds in the background of the call.

"Easton's with you?" For a moment, I'm distracted by images of Everleigh's smoking hot brother-in-law.

"Give me the phone," he snaps.

"Hey!" Everleigh squeals.

"*Hey*," I echo her. "Don't manhandle the pregnant woman." You can barely tell she's preggers, even at five months, but that belly is carrying precious cargo.

"Sadiecakes, what in the hell are you doing?" Easton barks.

"Sadiecakes?" Everleigh's voice stands out, her tone confused for obvious reasons. He's never called me that around her.

"I'm racing home before a downpour soaks me to the bone," I tell Easton and hop over a torn garbage bag, half the contents littered on the ground. My heel catches on a piece of...toilet paper?

I squeal and shake my foot trying to dislodge the gross, possibly used—because what is that brown smear?—piece of tissue. My stomach threatens to heave up the salmon and rice dinner I ate at the office.

"What's wrong?" Tension floods Easton's tone.

"Nothing. It's trash." Trash that attacked me. "It's disgusting."

"Take a deep breath and focus on your surroundings," Easton says in the calm voice he uses to soothe me when I'm in panic mode.

4

I manage to dislodge the toilet paper and sigh with relief. "I'm fully aware of my gross surroundings. Wet trash is so much worse than dry trash." My nose wrinkles, and again I wonder where the puddle came from. "I'm not cut out for this," I murmur, more-so to myself.

"Why are you alone? Where's Dash?"

My ex-boyfriend as of yesterday, who knows? He wouldn't be with me anyway. It's one of the reasons why I ended things. Easton doesn't know that, though. No one does. Yet.

"I had to work late," I answer his first question. "I always work late when my mom and stepdad are out of town. You know that." Did I mention they were leaving town when Easton and I spoke last week? Maybe I forgot.

A clatter sounds behind me.

I gasp and glance over my shoulder.

"What is it?" Easton asks, sounding as on edge as I feel.

"Two tall men have joined me, but they're far enough away that I'm not concerned." Not too much. "Could be nothing."

Easton growls. "I'm going to spank you so hard when I see you."

"Spank her?" Everleigh's voice sounds again and is filled with shock.

"I told you they've gotten close," Daire blurts in the background.

"Someone should spank her for giving us all heart attacks," Easton grinds out.

"No one is spanking me," I state firmly, and then glance over my shoulder again. "Why do men wear hoodies? It's not a look that says, 'I'm trustworthy.'"

"The men in the alley are wearing hoodies?" Easton asks, panic deepening his tone.

5

"It's okay. I'm almost to the end, and they appear to be going the other way now." Weird.

"Good. Regardless, get out of there as fast as you can," Easton orders. "Do you have your mace and your whistle?"

I almost laugh at how well he knows me. "Never leave home without them." I reach for the mace keychain on my purse. "Shit."

"What?"

"It's gone." How did I lose it? I stop and scan the ground.

"I swear, Sadie, if you stopped walking to look for it, I'll tie you up and spank you for days when I see you."

I swing back around and slam into a colossal man.

"Oh!" I stumble backwards and fall.

The man grips my arms, stopping me from landing on my butt. He pulls me upright.

"Th-thank you."

"It's dangerous to be out alone in a place like this. Terrible things can happen." His gravelly voice is as menacing as his size.

I can't see his shadowed face, but I think he's wearing a suit, which, for dumb reasons, makes him seem less dangerous.

No voices sound through my earbud anymore, and I can't feel the device. It must have fallen out.

"You can let go now. I'm okay." I try to slip free from his grasp.

His hold on me tightens. "I don't think so."

I reach for the whistle hanging from my neck, but my fingers meet a broken chain. Oh God. My heart drums in my ears as loudly as the thunder was a moment ago. What do I do?

"You need to come with me." The man drags me forward, my heels scraping the concrete.

"Stop! Let go! Help!" I cry, my throat too tight from fear to be loud and effective. I wriggle and jerk my body, unable to get away.

My heart pounds in my ears, drowning out all sounds. I force myself to calm down and recall what I learned in my self-defense classes. Squat. Break free. Run.

I drop to a crouch, taking him by surprise. His grip loosens enough for me to pull my arms free. My gaze is level with his groin. Another technique springs to my mind. My fist thrusts forward. A direct punch to his dick. Then I run as fast as I can. At the end of the alley, I turn right and scream for help, my voice cooperating.

A middle-aged couple walks out from a bar.

I wave to them.

They turn, and the man runs to me.

Panting, I grab his jacket. "Help me. Please."

"Are you hurt?" he asks, supporting me by my elbows.

The woman joins us. "She's terrified."

"Are you okay?" he asks again.

I catch my breath. "A man. He grabbed me." Glancing over my shoulder, I search for his massive form. A few people walk on the sidewalk in the distance, beyond the alley. No one is big enough to be him. "I don't see him."

"It's okay. You're safe now," the woman says in a gentle tone. To the man she says, "Call it in, honey."

He nods toward the bar door and brings his phone to his ear. "This is Detective Mason, I've got a possible attack."

"You're shivering." The woman removes her sweater. "Here, take this." She drapes it around my shoulders.

I pull it closed and notice my shirt. "It's ripped." The

7

lace sleeve is torn, and the satin bow at my collar is missing. "How?"

"It's okay. You're safe now," the lady repeats.

The punch of adrenaline leaves my system and exhaustion hits me like a truck. A fat raindrop lands on my nose. I glance up, and more droplets hit my face.

The lady puts her arm around my shoulder and ushers me toward the bar door. "Let's get you inside."

Low lights and chatter mixed with music greet us. People crowd around a big bar and high-top tables. She leads me to a booth near the front windows, away from the commotion. My body shivers like I'm freezing, even though I don't feel cold.

"Are you sure you're not hurt?" She sits beside me.

"I don't think so."

"My husband will make a report and ask you some questions. Afterward, you can go home. Is there someone you want to call to be with you?"

I nod and fumble to get my phone from my purse. Everleigh is the first person to come to mind. She must be so worried. I have to let her know I'm okay. But that's not who I call.

Chapter 2

Easton

I unlock the front door to Sadie's condo and guide her inside. With her arms wrapped around her body, she seems smaller and more fragile. I wouldn't say she's short, closer to average in height, but her personality usually makes her seem larger than life.

This isn't the case tonight.

When I saw her in the police station, sitting on the plastic chair, waiting for me, her brown hair a mess and her makeup smudged beneath her eyes, I wanted to find the fucker who attacked her and kill him.

I wanted to scold her for going down that alley. *Sadie,* of all people! I also wanted to crush her against me and carry her home. I didn't talk in the Uber drive on the way to her condo, afraid I'd lash out. She didn't talk either, just huddled in on herself in a sweater that's two sizes too big.

She walks to the kitchen and sets her purse on the counter as if it takes effort. A gasp leaves her.

I tense and race over. "What is it?"

"Detective Pickles. He didn't get his dinner. He must be starving."

She turns for the dwarf hamster in his cage. Succulents and hanging plants surround his enclosure, creating a verdant oasis.

"Stay." I touch her shoulder. "I'll feed him."

I met Detective Pickles the first time I came to Sadie's place. I was in town, staying at Daire's penthouse. A shelf had torn from the wall and almost crashed onto Detective Pickles's cage. Naturally, Sadie freaked out. Her boyfriend was busy working late and couldn't help, so I came over to offer my skills. As the spare to the heir, known for my carefree ways, Sadie was surprised I was handy and knew how to use tools.

"I grew up on a farm," I reminded her. "And I'm not afraid to get my hands dirty. Just don't tell anyone my secret. It might make me look useful." I winked and was sure I saw a spark in her beautiful hazel-green eyes.

I get the hamster food from the rubber container in the cabinet under Detective Pickles's cage and fill the bowl with pellets. He lies in a ball buried under some hay but scurries over when he hears the food.

I check his water bottle. Looks good.

"Is he okay?" Sadie asks, sounding tired.

"He's fine. Happy as ever."

"Thank you."

"Sure." I face her. "What do you need?" *I want to ask, why did you call me and not Dash?*

He lives in Atlanta. I was at the farm. When I got her call, I made sure the pilot and helicopter were ready to take me here at a moment's notice.

Daire bought the chopper so he could fly back to Everleigh if he was in Atlanta on business and she needed him. I thought it was over the top. Now, I'm thankful for it or else it would have taken me two hours to drive here.

"I need a shower."

"One shower coming up." I race to the bathroom, get her a towel, and turn on the water so it's hot for her.

When I return to the kitchen, Sadie's sweater is off. Her lace sleeve is torn, and the collar of her shirt is ripped. My teeth mash together with the force of a vise grip.

"He did this to you?" I approach her calmly.

She looks at her shirt, her brows drawn. "I guess. I don't remember it happening." She sighs. "I really liked this shirt."

"I'll buy you a new one," I blurt.

"That's okay. I don't like it anymore."

My jaw clenches harder. I'm going to find this man and kill him.

Sadie unbuttons the blouse, then slides it off and stuffs it into the trash can.

Her tanned skin catches my gaze, so much on display. Her nude, lace bra hugs her small pert breasts, the mounds swelling nicely from the tops of the cups. I've seen her in less, at the estate when we went swimming with Daire and Everleigh. What draws my gaze this time and sparks rage inside me are the bruises on her forearms from the bastard who grabbed her.

I don't remember walking to her, just that I'm in her space, towering over her and shaking.

"What is it?" she whispers, her hazel eyes widening with fear.

"Your arms..." I brush a finger under one of the bruises.

She looks at her purple skin. "Oh. I didn't know he left marks."

"Sadie, I'm..." I struggle to keep my voice calm. "I'm so sorry this happened to you."

11

She nods and inhales a deep breath. "It's my fault. I shouldn't have taken the alley. I—"

I put a finger to her lips. "You didn't do anything wrong. *He* did."

"But I know better. I nag everyone to be safe all the time, and I didn't even follow my own advice."

"It's over. You're safe now, and if the cops don't find the guy who did this to you, I will."

She lets out a small laugh.

I'm happy to see her smile, even if it doesn't reach her eyes, but why? "That's funny to you?"

"Kind of. What are you going to do that the police can't? I mean, you're not a detective."

"I have a PI. A good one." My gaze drops to her chest and breasts. I quickly force my eyes to hers.

"The PI Daire used to find out about Benedict?" The piece of crap who took advantage of Everleigh back when I graduated from college.

"He told you?" It's not like him to share that kind of information.

"Everleigh did."

Ah. Yes. That makes sense.

She runs her fingers through her messy hair and lets out a weary sigh. When she lowers her arm, her bra strap falls from her shoulder.

"You should shower. I'm sure the water is hot." Possibly cold. I need to get a grip. This scenario has my mind all over the place.

She nods, and without a word, shuffles to the hallway that leads to the bathroom.

Damn. She looks exhausted and weak. If she'd let me, I'd carry her to the shower, wash her body gently—and platonically—and tuck her into bed. Sadie would never allow it. Even if I promised to keep my eyes closed. She's the only woman who's ever refused my advances the first time we met.

She was visiting the estate with Everleigh. We all had dinner together, and I gave Sadie my usual charm—charm that has never failed me before. Throughout the night, she entertained me and flirted a little, but when I went in for a kiss, she turned her head away faster than I could blink. I was shocked. Still, I didn't quit. It wasn't until she explained that she knew exactly what she wanted, and I couldn't give it to her that I backed off. A commitment. She wanted a relationship with a man who wanted the same. She found it soon after too, with Dash, and we've been friends ever since.

Before her, I've never had a girl who was my friend and not a former lover. Sadie and I were destined to be in each other's lives after her best friend married my brother.

Anytime I do something with Daire and Everleigh, Sadie is a part of it.

I was the best man, and she was the maid of honor at their wedding. We were together for every event and dinner prior to the big day and every special event for them or for the farm after.

Many times, we were left alone together when Daire and Everleigh took off. A friendship grew from those moments, one separate from Daire and Everleigh.

We check in with each other regularly. And right now, I want to kill the man who hurt her and made her worst fear come true. Well, one of them. When it comes to Sadie and her murder-show loving, paranoid personality, she has many fears.

My phone vibrates with a text.

Daire: How's Sadie? Everleigh is about to call the helicopter back so she can fly there to check on her.

That's why I'm here. Daire didn't want Everleigh rushing to Atlanta. When we lost Sadie on the phone during the attack, Everleigh got so upset she vomited. Daire insisted she stay home while I came to sort things out. I was eager to help. Sadie had called me, after all. Not her best friend. *Me*.

I'd be lying if I said it didn't stir some new emotion in me I can't quite place.

Easton: She's fine. Well cared for. I won't leave her until you and Everleigh arrive tomorrow.

Daire: We have a change of plans. We want her to come here. Everleigh thinks being in the city won't help her get past this. She needs peace and security. We can offer her that here, plus it will keep Everleigh at the farm. She'll run herself ragged caring for Sadie. It's how she is. At least if Sadie is here, we can both help.

Easton: We?

Daire: Yes. You. You're back, living in the lake house. You can help.

Easton: What if she doesn't want to come?

Daire: Use your charm.

I laugh.

Easton: That doesn't work on Sadie.

Daire: Tell her Everleigh wants her here.

Easton: Okay.

The shower turns off.

I fill a glass with water and grab two Advil from the bottle on the counter near the box of tampons.

Should I bring her those, too? I don't want to overstep. She's not herself, clearly after her earlier strip tease—which reminds me, where the hell is Dash? What kind of asshat leaves his girlfriend alone after something like this? Now,

I'm wondering something else. Was I Sadie's first call or was Dash?

"Easton?" Sadie's tired voice sounds from the hallway. "Can you bring me the box on the counter, please?"

"On it," I call out and snatch the tampons.

Have I ever brought a girl feminine products before? Not that I can remember.

It should feel weird. It doesn't. Why is that?

Chapter 3

Sadie

"I'm so tired," I murmur, lowering my head onto the pillow.

"You had a busy night." Easton pulls the covers to my shoulders.

The weight of the soft sheets and blanket have a comforting effect.

"Since when do you tuck women into bed?" I tease groggily.

"Since now." He winks.

My eyes close, then spring back open with a jolt of fear. "Are you leaving?"

"I told you I'd stay," Easton says, his tone calm and soothing. "You have nothing to worry about. I'll be here all night."

I nod, exhausted again. "We talked about that, right?"

"Yep. After your shower."

"When you brought me tampons?"

"When I brought you tampons," he repeats with an amused grin.

"I don't have cramps."

His brows lower. "I didn't ask."

"You gave me Advil."

"For your bruises."

"Oh." I roll onto my side, my cheek pressed into my pillow, and close my eyes.

"Sweet dreams, Sadiecakes." Soft fingers brush my hair from my face.

"You should spoon me," I murmur.

"What?"

I drift to sleep.

* * *

I cross the busy street, leaving work later than I'd like. By later, I mean after sunset.

A man steps out of the darkness and grabs my necklace, ripping the chain.

"My whistle!" I yell, anger mixing with my fear. I throw punches trying to hit my attacker in the face. I should run. Why am I fighting? I'm not a fool.

I clutch my purse. It's gone.

The man holds up my wallet, his laugh a dark chuckle. "Now I know where you live."

"Help! Help!" I shout to the now deserted street. My heart pounds.

"Sadie," a gentle voice says. "Wake up. Wake up."

I follow the voice and open my eyes. I'm in bed in a dark room. My room, based on the glowing nightlight plugged into the wall.

I let my head fall back onto the pillow. It was a dream, just a dream.

"You okay?" a deep, sleepy voice asks.

Strong legs push against the back of my thighs. A hard chest warms my spine, and a large cucumber pokes between my legs.

My muscles tense, fear and disbelief rising inside me. Who is this person?

A big hand lands on my upper arm. "Sadiecakes?"

"Easton?" I glance over my shoulder at the silhouette spooning me. "What are you doing in my bed?"

"You invited me."

"I most certainly did not." I sit up and face him. "Why are you here?"

Did he need a place to crash? I don't remember him calling last night.

He sits up and runs his hand through his grown-out brown hair. "What do you remember?"

"Nothing. I remember nothing," I squeal through my tightening throat and try to calm down. Easton isn't dangerous. He's my friend. My super sexy playboy friend who I would never invite in my bed because I know better.

"Okay. Let me think." He runs his fingers through his hair again.

My gaze catches on his sculpted bare chest and flexing biceps. His disheveled hair puts him in a mythically hot category that only exists in the movies and in books.

"Stop doing that." I gesture to his hand in his hair. "Where are your clothes?"

"I don't have any. I came in a hurry. I didn't even think to pack."

"Why would you pack? Why are you even here? I'm so confused." I touch my temples and focus on slowing my erratic breathing. My muscles ache around my biceps. *Ow.* I lower my hands and touch my arms. "Ow!"

"Sadie, don't." Easton moves my hands to my lap. "They're bruised. You don't want to make them worse."

"Bruised? How...?" Memories trickle into my mind. The alley. The rain and thunder. The megalodon of a man who tried to kidnap me.

"Oh my God." It's a whisper. Ice slithers down my spine. I shiver. "It wasn't a dream."

"No." Easton's hand covers mine, his thumb soothing my skin with gentle strokes. "I put the Advil on your night-stand with a glass of water if you need more."

I glance at the nightstand. Sure enough, the bottle and water are near my lamp.

"I called you," I murmur at the memory.

"Yeah."

"And you came."

"Of course."

"I'm sorry. That was a lot to put on you." I lower my head and touch my forehead again. My arms ache, a reminder of the bruises and the attack. I get two Advil and swallow them with a gulp of water.

"Explain to me again why you're in my bed?"

He sighs, but it sounds like a laugh. "You asked me to spoon you."

"Why?"

He chuckles. "I don't know."

"And you eagerly jumped in?" It's so Easton to try to make a move after an event like that.

"No. I walked away, then you begged me to come back. You said you didn't want to be alone and, I quote, 'could use a good spooning.'"

I slump. It does sound like something I might say. And I've been lonely lately, going to bed alone while Dash works late or hangs out with the guys at their favorite sports bar.

"Most woman enjoy my spooning," Easton says. "I'm going to chalk your disappointment up to the circumstances."

"What time is it?" I grab my phone from the nightstand, vaguely noting that he plugged it into my charger and placed it where I like it. 6 a.m.

I set it down. Easton has his phone, checking the time, too. "Can we continue this conversation in three hours?" He reclines against the headboard. "You could use the extra rest and so could I."

I try not to gawk at his tanned chest and sexy abs. "Did you sleep in your boxers?"

"I don't wear boxers." He sets his phone on the table on his side of the bed.

"Briefs?"

His upper lip curls. "Do I look like a briefs guy?"

"Leopard print?"

He cracks up like it's the funniest thing he's ever heard. His glorious smile lights up the dim room, his flexing muscles making him look like a model—a naked model.

"Are you naked under there?" I gasp and point to the sheet covering his groin.

"It's the only way I sleep, baby." He tucks his hands behind his head, a pleased grin on his face.

I must have experienced more trauma than I realized because a small part of me wants to lift the covers and see what Easton has going on.

Ridiculous. Stupid. Behavior.

Easton would seize the moment and try to use it to his advantage. Also, do I want to know how amazing he looks naked? I've no doubt every inch of him is perfection. The closest I've seen of him to naked—before this—was in a bathing suit. Even his feet are attractive.

"What are you thinking, Sadiecakes?" His flirty tone draws my gaze to his whiskey eyes.

Was I staring at his groin that whole time?

His smirk says I was.

"I'm just processing this. You're naked and in my bed."

Easton and I hang, we joke, we text, we call, we complain, occasionally. We don't strip together—not that I'm naked—or lie in bed for a night, spooning.

"This is new territory for us." I tug at my t-shirt. "Hey? Did you put me in this?"

He tilts his head and stares at my collar. "It's not on backwards, is it?"

"No." I don't think. I check. On the correct way. I check my panties to see if those are on the right way and glower at what I find. "A thong? Really?"

"What?" He shrugs.

"It's black lace." I glower.

"Sexy as fuck, too. You've got a good underwear collection. I wasn't expecting it."

"What were you expecting? Granny panties?"

"What are granny panties?" He slides lower until his head is on the pillow.

I roll my eyes and have a seriously delayed realization. "You saw me naked. Like, completely naked."

"Sure did." He grins, his eyes closed as he snuggles under the covers.

"And...?" Why am I asking this? I don't care what Easton thinks. Besides, he has sex with lingerie-model-worthy woman on the reg.

He peeks one eye open. "You really want to know?"

"No. I don't, actually."

He closes his eyes. "So, are we sleeping for a few more hours or what?"

A yawn escapes me, and my body suddenly feels exhausted again. Is it the trauma from last night?

"I could sleep a little more. But no spooning, and keep that cucumber pointed in the other direction." I turn onto my side, my back to him.

"The biggest cucumber you've ever seen." He chuckles but flips onto his other side, following my orders.

"Trouble," he murmurs.

"What?"

"That's what I thought when I saw you naked."

"You thought I was trouble?" That doesn't even make sense, and why am I hot with anger? I don't care what he thinks.

"No. I thought *I* was in trouble because you're better than I imagined."

Shock hits me first, followed by a burst of excitement. "You've imagined me before?"

"Ask me again in three hours." His words are so slurred I wonder if he's sleep-talking.

Better than he imagined. That could mean a few things. He thought I'd be hideous, and I was better. He thought I'd be mediocre, and I was better. He thought I'd be sexy enough for someone like him, but I was better.

I doubt it was the last one. And it's fine. Easton is my friend. He's the guy who will never have a wedding, only attend them. The guy who'll never know love, only observe it in others. Who'll never fall for that one special girl who gives him meaning and a reason to wake up in the morning. He'll never know true companionship or loyalty. He'll be the guy who grows old alone, but with no shortage of women warming his bed at night. The single-or-plus-one-to-every-event guy, but never the to-have-and-to-hold-forever guy. Never the through-sickness-and-in-health guy, or until-death-does-us-part guy, and that's sad. Because he deserves so much more.

Chapter 4

Easton

I flip the eggs in the pan, then butter the toast. Almost everything in her pantry and fridge is organic. For someone who embraces a natural lifestyle, her addiction to murder and crime shows is way off in left field. There is nothing natural about murder.

Once, I asked her why she's so obsessed.

Shortly after her mom married her stepdad, Tim, he told her, "You live in a bubble world and could benefit from being more aware of your surroundings." He jokingly followed that with, "Watch a few crime shows on murder. It'll open your eyes to how easily people can become prey."

Sadie was nineteen. She took his words to heart and watched Dateline, loving it so much she binged years of episodes. Her addiction grew from there, and she says she's a better person because of it, more alert and aware.

She's completely paranoid, but it's endearing on her. Sadie cares in all ways. She means well. Her heart is always in the right place, and she's loyal. When Sadie lets you in, she lets you in for life, which is one of the reasons why I'm going to kill Dash.

Her piece-of-shit boyfriend should've been here. At the very least, he should have called. I promised Sadie I'd never cross the line between friendship and trying to get her in my bed; despite my teasing, it's only that. Harmless flirting. But Dash doesn't deserve her. He's out all the time with his friends. He puts himself before her and for some incomprehensible reason, she wants to marry him.

She told me Dash is the one she is going to spend her life with.

I questioned her decision, asked if she thought he felt the same, and bit my tongue—hard—when she said she wanted to have babies with him.

I met him one time over the summer. She waited on him hand and foot. The man sat on the couch watching TV while Sadie and I discussed Everleigh's birth announcement party. Sadie did most of the talking, all of the talking. I'd been roped into this when I offered to help if she needed it. I should have known she'd reel me in as a co-party planner.

I didn't even know people threw parties for birth announcements. But I did my part. I met up with her when I was in town, like she wanted. I agreed to have everything she ordered shipped to my lake house on the family property and delivered to the main estate for the party.

Dash didn't even care that I was here. My presence didn't threaten him one bit. I've seen the way other guys react when I'm around their girlfriends. The fact that Dash showed more interest in the game than the dude hovering over his woman—and I was hovering close, just to provoke him—spoke in volumes. I'd be lying if I said I didn't wonder if he were gay. But then he wasn't eyeing me, so I knew that wasn't the case. Regardless, something is up with him.

Sadie stumbles out of the hallway, rubbing her eyes. She

looks sexy in her white t-shirt, leggings, furry socks, and rumpled maple-colored locks.

"I thought I smelled eggs. Why did you let me sleep so late?"

"You needed it."

She faces the large window and stretches her arms high above her head, her back arching as her chest pushes forward. Sunlight spills over her, revealing her pert breasts and hardened nipples.

Should I tell her that her shirt is see through? If I do, she'll accuse me of choosing it on purpose. I didn't. I grabbed the first one in her drawer. Same with the thong. I didn't dig through her clothes; I was too busy holding her steady. She was so tired she couldn't stand without swaying.

The memory of her damp, naked skin against my side last night has me hard.

I've seen Sadie in a bikini. I've seen her in a tank top and daisy dukes at the farm. She has a nice body and a great ass. I never focus on her for too long and always avert my gaze, wanting to keep my promise. Friends. We'd only ever be friends. It's cool. I have more than enough friends with benefits. I can be platonic with Sadie. Only now that I've seen her naked, I know the perfection underneath the clothes. Hell, I felt it against my body and again when I dressed her last night. Not on purpose. I wasn't feeling her up. Dressing someone who's standing and wobbly is harder than I thought it'd be, even someone as dainty as Sadie.

I usually date women who are above average in height. They're sexy as hell, but I wouldn't call them dainty. It's easier to navigate things with women who are taller. I don't have to bend down or hoist them up to my level. But having Sadie in my arms to protect and care for last night drew out a different side of me. It didn't help knowing that

I could lift her and maneuver her however I want, and wherever I want, either. The things that I could do with her sexually...

My dick strains against the zipper of my jeans.

"Can I help?" She comes up behind me, standing way too close for comfort in my current condition.

"I got it. Why don't you sit over there." I point the spatula at the couch. "I'll bring you everything when it's done."

"Okay." She giggles and shuffles toward the adjoining family room.

"What's so funny?"

"You cooking eggs in my kitchen as if we just hooked up."

"If we'd just hooked up, I wouldn't be cooking you breakfast."

"Right." She nods and drops onto the couch. "You would be long gone by now."

I was going to say, I'd have her naked and on her back again. I don't typically stay for more after a night of sex, but I suspect I'd want more if I were to sleep with Sadie. More to fully explore everything she has to offer. More than she probably knows. Her boyfriend is so self-indulging, I doubt he knows or cares if she orgasms.

"Did Dash call you?" My jaw tightens. Undeserving prick. "Invite him over. I'd love to chat with him." And by chat, I mean kick his ass.

She stares out the bright window, obscured by the sheers blocking the view.

"Sadie? Did you hear me?" I add salt and pepper to the eggs before transferring some to a plate with the buttered toast.

"Yeah." She keeps her gaze on the window.

Something is definitely going on here. "Do you want honey or jelly on your toast?"

That gets her attention. She turns her head to me. "I've never had honey on my toast before."

"My mom loves it."

"Really? I can't imagine your mom eating anything like that. She's so proper."

"And honey isn't proper?" I tease and slather honey on the toast.

"It's more like I'd imagine her eating toast, if she did, with a fork and knife."

I laugh and bring the plate of food with a cup of coffee to her. "Do you want any juice?"

One corner of her mouth hikes up with amusement.

"What is that look for?" I push a small succulent plant and some books aside to make room for the food and coffee on the small table.

"Nothing." Her cheeks turn bright red.

"That is not a nothing blush. Tell me." I sit beside her on the couch.

She scoots to the edge of the cushion and picks up the fork near the plate. "Smells good."

"Sadie. Tell me."

"I just imagined you walking here with my apron on and nothing else. I don't know why." She giggles and shakes her head.

What the hell? She's picturing me naked now? *Oh, Sadie, you surprise me.*

With her cheeks still flaming, she scoops a bite of egg into her mouth.

I watch her lips close around the fork. Lips that have a whole new appeal to me, like her naked body.

"Mmm. You can actually cook."

28

"Eggs are hardly cooking. And you've seen me grill." At every backyard pool party at the estate, Daire and I grill steaks and chicken.

"Huh. I never noticed. I always thought it was Daire."

I sigh and fall back against the couch. "Always invisible when Daire is around."

Her eyes fill with compassion. She touches my knee with her small hand. "You're not invisible. On the contrary, you stand out."

"Not when Daire is around."

"Daire has a presence. A boss-type presence. You have a presence too. It's just more fun."

"Fun. That's even worse." I close my eyes.

"I thought you liked being the fun brother." She nudges my thigh.

I give her the stink-eye.

"Someone has to be in charge of entertainment." She eats more eggs.

"You think of me as the family entertainment?"

She purses her lips. "The sexy family entertainment."

"In case you haven't noticed, I've pulled my life together." I sit up. "I finished my degree in less than a year." To Daire's delight and surprise.

"You did." She points her fork at me. "That was impressive."

"And I've been working on a side project for the farm."

"You have?" She stops eating.

I nod.

"What is it?"

"Something new. Something we don't offer. Something profitable."

"Something Daire approves of?"

It's unsettling how well Sadie knows my family dynamics. "Daire doesn't know about it yet. It's not ready, but it will be soon."

She turns to me again, her face bright, her hazel-green eyes sparkling. "Easton. That's great. I'm so happy for you. You found your calling."

That word. She's been saying I need a calling and trying to get me to meditate so the universe can tell me what it is. "It's not a calling. It's a business venture."

"That you're passionate about?"

I nod.

"It's a call—"

I press my finger against her sensual lips and stare into those wide, knowing eyes. Trouble indeed.

Her lips part, and her tongue darts out to the corner of her mouth, grazing my finger.

My dick stiffens. I jerk my hand away. "What was that?"

"I had a piece of egg on my lip."

I shove from the couch and stalk to the kitchen.

"Easton. Why are you upset? I'm celebrating you. I'm so proud. And I did have a piece of egg on my lip. I swear. I wasn't trying to be gross and lick your finger."

Gross? I scoff. Only sweet little Sadiecakes would think I'd find her licking my finger gross. "I'm getting food, that's all." And putting some much-needed distance between us. Physically and mentally.

The women in my life know how I like sex. They know nothing about my personal life, my goals, or anything beneath the surface. Sadie knows me. At some point, I let down my guard, and she was able to breach my walls. I can't recall the exact moment when it happened, only that it did, and it's scary as fuck. She doesn't know all my secrets, though. Some things are better left unknown.

Chapter 5

Sadie

"You're upset." I walk to the counter that separates the living room from the kitchen. "I can tell by your expression and quick escape."

His posture stiffens, and he stands taller, like he's using his height to distance himself, too.

"You're mistaking hunger for upset." He scoops the rest of the eggs from the pan to a plate and refills a near-empty coffee cup.

I'm not mistaking anything. He's closing off, the way he does. When we talk, usually at night on the phone, or when he's been drinking, he opens up to me. I don't think he remembers everything he says, but I do. I love the parts of him he hides behind flirting and acting like he doesn't care about anything.

Easton cares. He's here for example. I think that's why I called him. Deep down, I knew he'd come. Everleigh would have come too, but she doesn't need to upset or over-exert herself right now.

I didn't call Dash because I wasn't sure he'd come. Even though he should still care enough to show up. We just broke up the other day. We've been together for almost a year, reconnected from high school when we dated for almost two years. I'm quite certain he was going to ask me to marry him on our vacation in two weeks to Napa. And I would have said yes, had I not realized—a bit late, I admit—that I want more than a man who puts his work and friends above his girlfriend/future wife.

Easton sips his coffee—I think to hide his frown.

Compelled to comfort him, I round the counter and give him a hug from behind. I bury my face in his long-sleeved shirt and inhale his masculine scent, my hands locked around his waist.

His entire body hardens like stone.

"It's okay to show feelings, especially to me. I like that side of you. And I never judge you. I wouldn't dare. You are who you are and are allowed to live life how you choose. You're the most fun person I know, but you're more than that. You're important. A dear friend. And whatever this business venture is, I'm sure it's brilliant, like you."

He doesn't relax, but he doesn't move away.

I take it as a win until he unhooks my hands from his waist and glares at me. "Where in the hell is Dash? He's your boyfriend. He should be here!" He slams a fist on the counter.

I've never seen Easton angry, and he's furious. Nostrils flaring. Whiskey eyes blazing.

I didn't want to get into this, but it's only fair I tell Easton the truth. He came when I called, which is more than I could say for my unreliable ex-future-husband.

I hug myself and stare at the wood floors. "We broke up."

"What! When?"

"Yesterday. No. The day before."

"He dumped you?" he asks with rage.

"I dumped him."

"Why?" His tone turns gentle.

Finally, I meet his gaze. A crease marks the skin between his warm eyes. "I..." How to explain this to someone like Easton. "I didn't feel like I was important enough. It probably sounds dumb to you, but I want what Everleigh has with Daire. I want my future husband to look at me like I'm the only woman in the room. I want to be the most important to him. More important than his work and friends. I'm not saying he can't have those things, and they can't be important. He should. It's healthy. I know that. But...but...I'm important, too."

"I get it, Sadie. I agree."

"You do?"

A soft smile tilts his lips. "You deserve better than Dash."

Doubt creeps into my mind. "What if I never find someone like that? What if I'm unrealistic, searching for a guy like—"

He raises his hand. "Don't say my brother."

"I was going to say like in my romance novels."

His brows hike up and he smirks. "What kind of romance novels are we talking about? Sweet? Steamy? Erotica?"

"How do you know those exist?"

"My book club." He shrugs.

"Shut up." I give him a playful shove. "You are not in a book club."

"Ah, but I am." He bites some egg and spits it onto the plate. "Cold."

"You're lying. What book club?"

"I dated a woman who owns a small bookstore. She

asked me to come to a meeting, thought it would be a treat for the book club members if I read a steamy chapter."

"Shut up." I shove him again. "You did?"

He nods, unabashed. "Women love porn just as much as men, only in written form. You girls are kinky."

I can't keep from blushing. He knows how dirty these books get. He knows I read them, and he's totally support-ive. When Dash saw my collection, he said, "Only cat ladies read romance novels." I hid them from that day on.

"I can't believe you read sex scenes to a book club."

He leans against the counter. "I'm an honorary member now."

"I bet. Do you still attend meetings?"

"If April, the owner, or the book club needs me for a special event and I'm in town, I do."

I shake my head. "You are unbelievable, and I mean that in the best way."

"Seriously, though." He inches closer to me. "Are you okay about the breakup? I imagine it was hard for you. I mean, last we spoke, you were set on marrying him."

"I know." I hug myself tighter and let my head fall forward, resting it against his chest, needing the connection. "What if I'm making a mistake?"

"You're not." He rubs my hair and back. "Dash wasn't right for you."

"You thought this before?" I say to his bare feet. They're so sexy.

"I did."

"You didn't say anything."

"It wasn't my business."

I lift my head and straighten. "I prefer my friends to be brutally honest with me, even if it hurts."

"Did Everleigh say anything about him?"

"She questioned me a lot. Asked if I was happy. If I was ready to get married. If I should date more or wait." I gasp. "Oh my gosh. She was trying to tell me he wasn't the one." I smack my forehead. "I can be so dumb."

Easton catches my wrist and lowers my hand. "You are not dumb. You figured it out and dumped him. Tying your ass to him in marriage would have been...not smart. But you didn't."

"You know what the messed-up thing is?"

He slides his hand down to my fingers and slowly releases, leaving tingles on my skin.

"I didn't cry. I *haven't* cried. Shouldn't I be sad? I mean, I am. Sort of. For the future I thought I was going to have with him. For the promise of forever with him. Someone to grow old with. To make babies with one day. To share all the wonderful things that come with having a family. All of that is gone. And I haven't even cried." A tear slips down my cheek. I wipe my eyes and realize they're flooded.

Easton wraps me in his arms and lets me cry into his warm chest. I can't believe I am. I can't believe the number of tears that are falling. Because of all I hoped for and lost, because I spent almost a year waiting to be all Dash saw. Because I wasn't enough to compete with his friends and job. Because maybe, just maybe, I'm not enough for anyone, least of all the great romance of my dreams. And that breaks my heart.

Chapter 6

Sadie

I remove Easton's shirt from the dryer and hold it out to him.

"I can't believe I left a small puddle on it. I can't believe I cried over Dash. I didn't expect that to happen."

Easton takes the shirt and pulls it on, concealing his perfect torso under the warm fabric. "That's what friends do. Right?" he asks in all seriousness.

I laugh. "You've never held someone who was crying before?"

He scratches the light stubble on his chin. "No. Guys don't cry, and girls don't cry around me. They yell sometimes and throw things, but no tears. You're my first."

A smile splits my lips. I shouldn't like that as much as I do. "I'm honored to be your first something. I'm sure the days of firsts for you are long gone."

"You're also my first female friend who I haven't had sex with."

"Two firsts. But then, our friendship was inevitable. Written in the stars." I gesture to the ceiling. He's heard me say this before and thinks it's silly. He thinks I'm silly. Maybe I am.

Grinning, he follows me out of the small laundry room and to the kitchen. "Why is it so important to you to have a fairy tale marriage? Most people aren't as lucky as Daire and Everleigh."

"I know." I feed Detective Pickles and give him a pet before moving on to watering the plants throughout the room. "My mom never had anyone when I was growing up, but she dreamed of the perfect man. She is a romantic through and through. We watched all the Disney movies. The original versions. We loved love and romance and the idea of happily ever after. My mom didn't get that with my dad. He was a one-night stand. She would have wanted more, but she didn't get the chance because he disappeared. No number. No nothing. She couldn't even reach him to let him know she was pregnant. It was hard on her. She wanted more for both of us. But we made the best of what we had, which wasn't much. Then Mom met Tim, her knight in shining armor. He loves her the way she always wanted. So, I guess that's why I'm always chasing the perfect relationship. The one that leads to marriage and a family."

I set the water can on the counter. "I know some people would say I'm ridiculous. That I need to love myself and that should be enough. I don't think it's wrong to want a fairytale, though. Taylor Swift makes a living off songs about the hope of forever with the perfect man."

"She also makes a living off heartbreak songs."

"True." I wipe a drip of water from the copper spout. "Maybe I'm going about it wrong. Maybe I'm trying to force something that should happen naturally."

"Were you forcing Dash into marriage?"

"Not that I'm aware of. He wanted it as much as I did. We talked about our future a lot."

Easton's phone dings with a text. He lifts a finger and reads the screen. "Shit," he says as if he forgot something.

"What?"

"Everleigh has been trying to reach you."

"Where is my phone?" Oh, yeah. My nightstand still. Geez, I'm a wreck today. I race to get it, but Easton stops me from entering the hallway.

"What are you doing?"

"I was supposed to ask you something. Convince you, really. Everleigh's texts will show what that is, I'm sure, so I want to prepare you."

Heat prickles my neck. "Prepare me for what?" I'm seconds from shoving him out of the way.

He scratches his neck. "I guess, I'll just say it. Everleigh wants me to bring you to the farm where you can relax for a while and feel safe."

"I can't."

"I'm supposed to convince you."

"Well, I can't. My parents won't be back for a week. They rely on me to make sure the office is open and closed properly. You can't trust realtors to remember to come back to the office if they're out showing properties."

Tim's agency sells homes, condos and such, and corporate real-estate. The agents come and go a lot. Someone needs to make sure the place gets locked up properly at night.

Another text dings on Easton's phone.

While he reads it, I sneak past him and read my many texts from Everleigh and my mom.

I reply to each with a *sorry and I didn't have my phone.* My mom is in a different time zone in Europe. I doubt she'll

38

get this. I didn't tell her what happened because I didn't want her to worry. She's finally living the life she'd always dreamed of. Far be it from me to ruin her romantic escape with the man of her dreams.

According to my texts, Everleigh contacted her to get her in on the plan to get me here. Mom was shocked that I hadn't called her and upset, rightly so. Everleigh apologized to me for telling her when I hadn't had the chance yet. I'm not mad. I could never be mad at Everleigh. It just complicates things.

I quickly explain in a long text to my mom that I'm fine. I'm with Easton, and I didn't want her to worry.

One of Mom's texts urged me to please go to the farm and that Vanessa would make sure the business was opened and closed properly. Vanessa is new and doesn't have many clients, so she has a lot of free time. She also loves to help. I guess I could trust her to do what I've been doing.

The last text Everleigh sent said she'd come here if I wasn't up for staying at the farm. Well, we can't have that. This seems like a big deal for nothing. Not nothing, but I'm fine. The police said they'd search for the guy but that it's unlikely they'll find him without more than I was able to tell them. I couldn't even leave a description of his face. He didn't steal from me, either so I'm not sure what charges they would press. Attempted kidnapping?

A memory tugs at my brain.

"That is a serious face." Easton stands near my bed, watching me.

I didn't even hear him come in. I blink at him, the memory haunting my thoughts.

"What is it?"

"It's probably nothing."

"It's never nothing with you," he teases.

"You're going to say I'm paranoid." I walk to the second bedroom and get my suitcase from the closet.

"You're coming?" He perks up. "That was much easier than I thought."

"I'm only coming for a short time. One night. Maybe two. I want to appease Everleigh. If I show her I'm fine, she'll stop worrying."

"If you say so." Easton carries the suitcase into my room. "Bed or floor? Don't tell me. I know. Floor."

"Yes! Suitcases carry germs. I don't want that on my bed."

He opens it for me and straightens, resting his hands on his hips. "Now, what has you paranoid?"

I scoff and dig in my underwear drawer. "Forget it. You're already teasing me."

"I'm not. I'm serious. It was a bad choice of words. What has you concerned?"

I pause, my back to him. "I can't be sure. My mind could be playing tricks on me after what happened, but I just remembered…"

"Yes?"

"I might have seen the man who attacked me before."

"What makes you think that?"

I glare over my shoulder. "I knew you wouldn't believe me, and right now, I don't trust my brain, so maybe I am paranoid."

"I believe you. I'm just trying to get information to help me understand." His tone is gentle.

I gather a few pairs of bikini briefs and toss them into the suitcase.

He frowns at my selection, then eyes me, his brows raised expectantly.

"I've been locking up the office, and a couple of nights

ago, when I closed the blinds to the front window, I remember a tall, shadowed man standing across the street. I remember thinking he's huge—like, Thor huge. He wasn't walking, just standing still, and facing the office. No one stands still around that part of town." It's the business district. "People race up and down the sidewalks on their phones often and in a hurry. Anyway, it was late, so I told myself I was being paranoid, like I get sometimes, and went about my business closing up. When I left, he was gone."

Another memory returns, and a chill slips down my spine.

"You just shivered. Are you cold?"

"No." I stare blankly at the suitcase. "I just remembered something else."

"What?" He steps to me, his hand at my elbow.

"Vanessa said she almost ran into a huge man when she was bringing back coffees the other day. She said he was like a brick wall, and she hadn't noticed him standing outside the agency because she was focused on carrying six cups of coffee and not spilling them, which she did a little when she dodged hitting him. She kept saying how rude he was for not even trying to move out of the way, especially given how much space he takes up. She has a thing with individual space."

"Hang on." Easton raises his hands. "This guy has been hanging around your office?"

"Maybe. It could be someone else."

"Or it could be him and he's stalking you."

I laugh, partly from disbelief and partly from fear. "Why would a stalker follow me? I'm not wealthy." I make decent money doing marketing for Tim's business, and I live in a nice condo, but only because Tim and Mom bought me the place for earning my degree in digital arts and a minor in art. "I'm not an heiress to a family fortune. I'm not a celebrity or of any value. I may be dainty but I'm tough. I fought that man and even punched him in the dick."

Easton bursts into laughter. "You...punched him...in the...dick?" He chokes out between his hysterics.

"Yeah. It helped stall him from the chase. My defense instructor always said to run and scream, but if you can immobilize your attacker somehow, too, do it. I figured he couldn't chase me if he was holding his dick and in pain, so I went for it."

Easton's face is bright red from laughing so hard. "Sadiecakes. There is no one in the world like you." He throws his arm around my shoulder. "My little badass fighter. I'm going to get you a boxer's belt."

My lips hike up on their own accord. "I guess it is kind of funny. Not at the time, though."

"Definitely not at the time. But the possible sighting of him has me concerned. Did you tell the police about that?"

"I just remembered now. How could I?"

"I think we should tell the police before we leave. They gave you a card, right?"

"Yes. I'll call them, but they'll think I'm being paranoid." I take pajamas and clothes from other drawers and add them to the suitcase. "Three days' worth should be more than enough."

"You'll need more than three days, because I don't want you back here until we know if that guy is stalking you. Everleigh won't be okay with it either."

"Then don't tell her."

"This is your safety, Sadie. I'm not fucking with that. You, of all people, shouldn't either. Where is the over-concerned, over-protective, adorably cute woman I met a year ago? She never would have been blasé about this."

I jut a hip. "I'm not blasé. My mind is twisted. I'm still in disbelief."

"Then I will be over paranoid for both of us. You're staying until we find out who this man is and if he's random or a stalker." He takes his phone from his pocket and types something.

"How long will that take? The police don't even think they can find the guy. They don't have a description."

"They don't have a personal PI, former CIA agent, either." He types on his phone.

"He's ex-CIA?" No wonder he was able to learn everything about what happened between Benedict and Everleigh when Daire hired him.

He nods and continues typing on his phone.

"What are you doing?" And why am I annoyed?

"I'm texting him so he can get started."

"Oh. Thanks." When Easton wants to get things done, he does it. I'm not sure he even knows this about himself, but he doesn't slack when given a task. It's why I rope him into so many projects with me. He's reliable that way.

I take a moment to admire his golden-brown hair and how it falls over his face, shielding his eyes as he texts, and the bulge of his biceps and the tanned skin covering his Adonis body.

If only he were reliable in other ways. But then, guys who look like Easton aren't meant to settle for one woman. *Daire did*, my brain argues.

I maneuver around Easton's big form, collecting more things, but he always seems to be in the way. "Wouldn't you be more comfortable doing that in the living room?"

"Is this your polite way of kicking me out?"

I shrug.

He walks to the door.

"Oh! And can you pack up food for Detective Pickles? He's coming, too."

"He is?" Easton looks like the idea is absurd.

"I can't leave him here alone." I give him my back and continue packing. "He can't feed himself."

"A hamster on a helicopter," he murmurs. "This should be interesting."

He leaves the room before I can explain we won't be traveling the way he thinks.

Chapter 7

Sadie

After a brief conversation with my groggy mom, where I reassured her five times that I'm okay and to stay in Greece, I finally finished packing. I have stuff for two weeks, with a little extra because I always pack extra, just in case.

Reva, my middle-aged neighbor and fellow plant lover, said she'd water my plants and sing to them to make sure they stay happy while I'm gone. I don't sing to my plants. I talk to them, though. They're great listeners.

Reva and I are on the landscaping committee for the condominium homeowner's association. One of the reasons I chose this place is for the lush courtyard. It's an oasis in the city. I also chose it for the gated entrance, security guard and cameras, and the underground parking. I can open my curtains and enjoy the trees and plants outside without worrying about being spied on by strangers. The thought makes me shiver, even more now after what happened. The more I think about it, the more I'm certain I've seen that man before.

Pushing the thoughts away, I recheck my room and

bathroom to ensure I haven't forgotten anything. Everything seems packed.

I close and stand my suitcase, ready to— "Oh no!"

Easton rushes into my room, faster than seems possible. "Are you okay?"

"Yeah. Are you? You're usually calmer." In fact, I've never seen him up and down like this. Playful? Yes. Flirty? Always. Unintentionally vulnerable? A few times.

"I'm usually calmer because I'm not protecting a friend. In fact, I've never protected a friend." His brows tighten. "This is another milestone for me. Adulting like an adult." He rests his fists at his waist in a Superman stance.

I grab a makeup sponge from the vanity and throw it at his head.

He catches it and throws it back at me.

The soft sponge bounces off my forehead. "Hey! I didn't hit you."

"Only because I caught it."

I rub the spot, even though it doesn't hurt, and scowl at him.

He smirks. "Want me to kiss it and make it better?" he teases.

I raise a stubborn chin and lower my hand. "Yes."

His jaw drops for a moment before that devilish grin of his returns. "Oh, Sadie. You should know not to invite my lips anywhere near you."

His deep voice and the wicked glint in his whiskey eyes sparks tingles in all the right places, particularly my lower region. That look is sinful on him, but with all his charm, he's never stirred tingles in me. I tell myself it's because his attention is laser-focused on my wellbeing. It's sending mixed signals to my body. This will pass. Soon, he'll turn his charm elsewhere.

"I don't have gas," I blurt, remembering why I gasped in panic a moment ago.

His thick brows rise. "Okay," he draws out slowly, his tone unsure. "Thank you for sharing."

Oh God! He thinks I'm talking about stomach issues. "I mean I don't have gas in my car. I never drive it in the city. It's for road trips only. The last time I took it, I drove it here on fumes because I was too tired to fill it up and just wanted to get home. That and city gas stations suck. I think the oil engine light was on, too." I nod, my pulse climbing. "It was. How are we going to drive to the farm if my car dies?" So much for remaining calm.

"There's my little paranoid friend. I wondered where you went." He rests his hands on my shoulders. "It's simple. We'll take the helicopter."

"Easton!" I march around him and gesture to Detective Pickles's cage when he follows me into the living room. "I can't take a hamster on a helicopter. I don't know how he'll react. What if he dies from fright? Hamsters do that. And I can't leave him here for two weeks. Reva likes plants, but she's afraid of hamsters. We have to drive. I do, anyway. If you want to fly, you can. But I can't. I can't!"

He raises his palms. "Okay. We'll drive, and I'll take the car to get checked before we leave."

My shoulders relax. "You will?" Dash never would have offered that. He wouldn't have been around to.

"Yeah." He shrugs and grabs the keys from the bowl on the foyer table. "It's not like it's a big deal. Are you okay to hang out here while I take care of it? Your complex is pretty safe, but if you're scared..."

"I'm fine. We'll be fine." I gesture to Detective Pickles again.

"Okay. Keep your phone with you, and text me if you need me."

He leaves.

The silence becomes incredibly noticeable, except for the light bobbing sound of the water bottle where Detective Pickles takes a drink.

"We're good, aren't we, little guy?" I say to him. "We're all good. Right?" I eye the plants on the wall shelves, the tables, and counter. Flowers are lovely, but I prefer succulents, heart-leaf philodendron, and string of pearls. "Be good for Reva while I'm gone. No dead leaves or root rot."

I laugh at myself, then flinch when a bang sounds on the far wall. My hand cups my throat. I force out a calming breath. Reva's shower curtain must have fallen again. Her bathroom shares a wall with the corner of my living room. I told her to get one that screws into the wall and have maintenance install it for her. Will is pretty handy, and he's been working here for over a decade, long before I moved in.

Naturally, I feared him at first. For one thing, I'd never lived on my own in a big city. My paranoia was at an all-time high for a good six months. For another, I've seen multiple murder and crime investigation shows where the victim dies at the hands of a security guard or maintenance worker. But after talking with Will and watching—spying on—him with other residents, it became obvious he's just a harmless older man who cares about this complex as much as I care about plants.

For the most part, my instincts are spot on, but they fail me on occasion. They failed me with Benedict when Everleigh and I met him and his friends in Savannah that one time. They failed me again with this possible stalker. How could I not put two and two together?

I'm sure I saw him. I think. Argh. I press my hands to

my head, my bruises barely hurting thanks to the Advil. Why can't I remember better? What's wrong with me?

My breathing grows loud and my heart pounds against my ribs. *Calm down. Calm down. It's okay. You're fine. Everything is fine. No one is stalking you. That's ridiculous. Absurd.*

My phone rings. I squeal. Seriously, I need to get control of my emotions. Without Easton here distracting me and keeping me company, I'm in bad shape.

I check to see who's calling. Everleigh.

"Hey!" I put on a perky voice.

"Hey," she says tenderly. "How are you?"

"Good. You? The baby?"

She giggles. "We're good. It's still weird to say that. *We're.* Because I'm two people right now."

"That is weird." I smile, having never considered that.

"Easton says you're almost ready to leave and you're driving instead of flying?"

"He called you?"

"Daire's been checking in on him constantly for updates."

"Oh." That must not be fun for Easton. No wonder he's on edge. He has Daire riding his ass about me for Everleigh, and he has me to deal with.

"Is he helping?"

"Easton? Yeah. He's been great. He's a good distraction. He's been taking care of everything, too. It's weird. Dash never really helped. I never expected him to. Could have been part of the problem. But Easton just gets things done."

"He didn't use to, according to Daire. But he is changing. I'm glad he's helping."

"We'll be at the farm by tonight," I say to ease her

worries. She always worries about everyone else before herself. "How are the renovations going?"

They're turning part of the estate into an inn for farm guests. After Everleigh and Daire's wedding in the barn there, she decided to turn it into an optional wedding venue. I loved the idea. Her wedding was so beautiful. Then she got the idea of adding a place for people to stay and either relax, learn about pecan farming, or to get married. Another brilliant idea. Daire cherishes everything she comes up with and makes it happen. Everleigh's biggest concern was offending Mrs. Livingston by turning her former estate— which she and Daire inherited from his parents—into an inn, but her mother-in-law loved the idea. I don't know how Everleigh handles herself so well around her mother-in-law. The woman makes me feel not worthy. She's always kind. It's a me problem.

"The bulk of the renovations are over," Everleigh says. "No more dumpsters or major construction. It's all interior work now and still scheduled for completion before the baby comes."

"That's important." I pull out a barstool and sit at the counter.

"It's weird how different the house is, basically two homes now divided in the middle but connected. What do we need all this space for, anyway? Even with the estate split, our side is huge."

"And guests can't access your side of the house, right?"

"No. There is an entrance hidden behind a bookshelf that we know about and have control of locking from our side. It's where the old butler's pantry used to be, if you remember."

"Maybe." That place is huge, and I was only there a handful of times. I didn't roam the house, either.

"We were going to redo the house anyway, as you know. Daire's mom encouraged us to make it our own, although I know she hadn't expected us to do this."

"It's who you are, Everleigh. You're a giver. You always have been. I'm *so* happy for you." I've told her that at least one thousand times in the last year.

"And I'm so happy you're coming to stay for a while."

"About that..." I rub the soft leaves of a nearby plant between my fingers.

"Oh no."

"Nothing bad. It's just I don't like the idea of crashing your house. I mean, you and Daire have only been married a year, and now you're pregnant, and you have so much going on. I'd feel like a third wheel in your home."

"And if you feel uncomfortable, you won't stay," she says, knowing me like a sister. "Fortunately, I thought about that and have a plan."

"I'm listening." Clueless to this plan but listening.

"How would you feel about staying in a loft overlooking a huge lake?"

"Where is this loft?"

"On the property."

"It's just a loft?" I tap my fingers on the counter.

"It's a house with a private loft on the third floor. It has a balcony, a beautiful lake view and...a charming owner who you already know and who you've said has been very helpful."

"It's Easton's house?" I ask, aghast.

"It is. But it's private, he's hardly there, and it's on the property. The estate property. It's safe and protected, and you wouldn't have to worry about anything but relaxing."

"Does Easton know about this?"

"Daire is talking to him right now."

The way these two orchestrate things is unreal. "What if he doesn't agree? I doubt he wants me in his house. Where will he bring his women?"

"Daire is working that out with him."

I stand and push in the stool. "I don't know. This seems intrusive. He can't be okay with this. He's never lived with a woman before."

"He'll be fine. Daire will convince him."

"He shouldn't have to be convinced. And I really wouldn't be comfortable staying if I know he's being forced to have me as a guest."

"Just let him show you the place and then you can decide. I can meet you. You have to leave the estate and drive to the back gate near Easton's house—it has its own entrance—but it doesn't take long."

"How big is their—your—property?"

"Massive."

"Is his house on the lake with the make-out dock?" We jokingly christened it after swapping stories about how she and Daire almost hooked up there and Easton made a move on me there when we first met.

"It's a bigger lake with a bigger dock. Well, you'll see. It's cool. I think you'll really like it, and the internet is strong so you can work. It's spotty at the house right now, with all the renovations that have been going on. But it should be fixed soon."

"You are really selling me on this."

"I am. I want you to stay."

"I'll check it out," I say to appease her, but I don't see Easton being cool with me staying in his personal space. I also don't think I want to know what Easton does in his free time with women.

"Is his house big?"

"Not like the estate, but it's a good size house. Maybe 4000 square feet, a little less."

"Good God. I knew he had a lake house on the property, but I'd always pictured a small cabin."

"I believe it was very cabin-like, but he had it redone while he was away finishing college. Daire checked on it for him. It's really beautiful, even if it is a bit masculine."

The front door flies open, and a giant man walks in.

I scream and duck behind the counter, my phone gripped in my hand. Everleigh's voice sounds from the speaker. "Sadie! Sadie, what's wrong?"

"Sadiecakes, it's me."

I rest my forehead against the lower cabinet door and catch my breath.

"Sadie! Sadie, are you all right?" Everleigh pleads.

Easton's big form rounds the counter. "Shit." He takes the phone from my hand. "Hello? Oh hey, Ev. I scared her by accident. I'll make sure she's okay. I will. Bye."

He squats down next to me and runs a palm over my hair. "I'm sorry. I turned the knob, thinking the door was locked, but it opened, and I kind of barreled in. I didn't mean to scare you."

I drop onto my backside and sit with my legs criss-crossed. "I forgot to lock the door?" I ask in disbelief.

He nods.

"I never do that. Never."

"I know. I think you're more shaken by the attack than you realize. People aren't typically grabbed on the street. You are the most cautious person I know. You warn everyone to be careful, fearing they'll be a victim somehow, and then it happened to you. It's scary."

He sits and mirrors my position, his knee touching one

part of my backside, his other near my knee. He slides me into the V of his crossed legs.

I let out a shuddering breath, comforted by his presence in a way I can't explain. Dash didn't even make me feel this safe.

"What's scarier than that," I say, "is he didn't take my purse, or my rings, or phone, or ask for money. He wanted me. Just me. Why?"

"I don't know." He brushes my hair behind my shoulder.

"Do you think he wanted to traffic me, or hurt me, or murder me?"

"I don't think we should think about those things. You're safe. You got away, and I have my PI looking into him. If there is something to be found, he'll find it."

I stare directly into his eyes. "And then what?"

"That's up to you. We can turn what we find over to the police, or we can use more private methods to deal with him."

I gasp and whisper, "You don't mean murder?"

He chuckles softly. "I mean roughing him up, getting information, and then anonymously dumping him off at the police station."

"Would you be the one roughing him up? I wouldn't want you to get hurt."

His eyes dance with amusement. "I wouldn't be the one, and I'm not worried about getting hurt."

"I am. I'd die if you got hurt because of me or for me."

"You'd die?" he asks, doubtfully.

"Yes. Inside, I would. I told you, you're important." I brush his bangs from his eyes.

Moments pass as we sit there on my kitchen floor, staring at each other. What is he thinking? Does he want to leave? Is this boring him already? Does he have a date tonight and she's on his mind?

My gaze drops to his lips. Like the rest of him, they're perfect. He and his brother won the gene pool lottery. I used to believe people as beautiful as him and Daire were descendants of the Nephilim. The offspring of humans and fallen angels from long ago, because how else can you explain such angular features? The symmetry. The chiseled perfection of his body. Even his whiskey eyes are scattered with thin black stripes, like spokes on a bike wheel. I've never seen eyes like his. You have to be really close to notice. Every woman he's ever kissed has been treated to the rarity.

"Sadie," he purrs. "Don't look at me like you want to kiss me unless you want to."

"And if I did, then what?" Dangerous questions lead to dangerous answers.

He hesitates, his gaze on mine as a tiny smirk appears at the corner of his lips, then he bends to my ear. "Typically, I'd slip my tongue in your mouth and tease you until you're breathing heavily. I'd drag you onto my lap so you could feel how hard I am for you, then I'd take you to the bedroom, lick every inch of your skin, spending extra time on your breasts and sweet pussy—because I know it would be sweet. I'd make you come in my mouth before spanking your ass, as promised, then I'd fuck you until you saw stars and forgot your name."

I'm drenched, panting, and in need of every single thing he just said. His words alone were better than sex ever was with Dash.

"But I wouldn't do that with you."

"You wouldn't?" I ask, dazed, horny as hell, and still fantasizing over what he described.

"I think, for the first time ever, I don't want to ruin a

friendship with sex. I also think you'd regret it when your mind is more clear."

"So, no spanking?"

"No spanking," he says with an endearing smile.

"I've never been spanked. I might like to try it."

His pupils dilate. "That's not making this any easier. Come on." He stands and hoists me up with him. "Let's get Detective Pickles and hit the road."

"Oh my gosh. How's the car?"

"All good. Filled up the tank, got the oil checked. We're good to roll, baby." He winks.

I hold up a finger. "One second." I race to my room and change my soaked panties to a dry pair. My period ended this morning. Is that why I'm suddenly horny? But then, Dash never elicited that much arousal from me after my period week. Hmm...

Easton thinks I'm trouble. He's such an incredible flirt, he makes you forget that all his talk and lustful exploits, which I'm even more sure now are Olympic-medal-worthy, are nothing more than a moment destined to end.

It's better *not* to know what you missed out on than to experience it and live with the memory, knowing you can never have it again.

Chapter 8

Easton

I text Daire that we're on the road and our ETA.

I can't wait to return to the farm, just to get him off my ass. When I was back in college, he didn't bother me. It was nice. I can't piss him off and tell him to ease up, though. I need him to be in a good mood when I present my idea for the farm. I also need him to like it and see the benefits.

Daire and I don't always agree on things. He still sees me as the goof-off who doesn't want to grow up. I fear he'll struggle to get past that with my idea and brush it off as foolish.

It's not foolish. It could be extremely profitable if done correctly. I've used the best people and resources to create it. Everleigh opened him to changes I never thought I'd see on the farm. I need his mind to stay open for my proposal. I need him to trust me. That will be my greatest challenge of all.

Sadie holds Detective Pickles in his travel cage on her lap while I maneuver through traffic and head for the highway.

"Do you always travel with Detective Pickles?" I've never asked before, never thought to. He's a hamster.

"Not when my mom's in town. She cares for him. He's with us now because I don't want him to feel abandoned."

I chuckle. "Why would he feel abandoned?"

"Because he almost was. I told you the story about how I got him."

"I don't think you did." In my mind, it was a pet store.

"Oh. Well..." She smiles sweetly at him. "My neighbor bought him for her teenage daughter to teach her some responsibility. Nina, the mom, ended up doing all the work instead and didn't want to keep him anymore. He's blind in one eye, so when she tried to return him to the store, they said she'd injured the hamster, and they couldn't take him back."

"The store wouldn't take him back?" I change lanes, trying to drive as gently as I can for the hamster's sake.

"Nina swears he wasn't blind when she bought him, but who knows the truth? Anyway, I heard the story from Reva. She said they were taking the hamster to the SPCA, so I offered to adopt him instead."

"Does the SPCA take hamsters?"

She shrugs. "I don't know. But it doesn't matter. He's mine now, and I love him." She lifts the lid and pets his head with her finger, where he lies in a ball in some hay.

The story warms my heart. Sadie the rescuer. "I'm glad you took him."

"So am I."

And now I love the little fur ball, too.

I shoot a quick glance at him and then at Sadie before focusing back on the road. An odd sense of comfort and peace comes over me. I've heard Daire talk about feeling this way when he looks at Everleigh and their unborn baby.

I've never experienced it before. Is it normal? Temporary? I don't hate it, but I'd be lying if I said it didn't scare me. I scratch my hot neck and slam on the horn when a truck tries to cut us off.

Sadie gasps and squeezes Detective Pickles's cage.

"Sorry. That driver just thought he'd get over without looking, I guess."

"It's okay."

"How'd you come up with the name, or did Nina's daughter name him?"

"She called him Hamster."

I laugh.

"I thought he deserved a real name, something unique."

"Which led you to Detective Pickles?"

"Not necessarily. I was struggling to come up with a good one. Names are important."

"My dad would agree. Livingston is an old family name that will forever be tied to the farm and pecans around the world."

She smiles at that. "I might have been watching Dateline and eating pickles at the time, and the name just came to me when this little cutie tried to eat my mini dill pickle."

I laugh again. "Did he like it?"

"No." She makes a face. "He bit a piece and then backed away, actually falling off my thigh. But we were on the couch, so he was okay."

I chuckle. "Only you would have a story like that."

She beams, not offended at all by my remark. I love that about her, how she doesn't get uptight or offended easily.

"Have you brought Detective Pickles to the farm?" She's stayed there a couple of times before the renovations, back when the house was huge.

"Once, when my mom and Tim were in Hawaii."

"Hawaii. That's a place I'd want to visit sometime."

"You've never been?" she asks, surprised.

"Not yet. We tend to stick to this side of the US. I've been all over the Caribbean on my dad's yacht."

I adjust the wheel a little lower in the Lexus. The older coupe pulls slightly to the right. The mechanic said it needs an alignment and the tires need rotated. I didn't have time for that, and I wasn't sure if he was trying to get more business and money from me. Now that I'm on the highway, I can tell it needs a lot of work. The oil was low, so she *had* noticed the light. The mechanic checked for a leak but said it's fine. I had him do what he could so we could get to the farm, but it'll need more repairs. Did Dash never check her car for her?

"The mechanic noticed some other things that need fixed on the car when I brought it in," I mention. "We can get it done at a place near the farm. I know the owner."

Her hazel-green eyes, so bright in the car, widen on me. "Oh no. What does it need?"

"Nothing major, but you'll notice it drives better once some work is done."

"Oh. Okay. Thank you." Her shoulders relax.

She checks the GPS.

"It's the fastest route."

"I was checking the time."

We have about an hour and a half left. "Do you need to stop for the bathroom?"

"Nope. I'm good." She taps her nails on Detective Pickles's cage.

"Something wrong?"

Her fingers halt, and she blows out a breath. "I was going to wait until we got closer to the farm to talk about this."

"Talk about what?" Whatever it is, she's obviously nervous.

She focuses on the hamster's cage. "Did Daire talk to you about where I'll be staying?"

Ahh. I see where this is going. I nod.

"And?"

"And...?"

She huffs, looking so cute with her cheeks puffed out and that crease between her perfectly shaped brows. "Did he say where I'd be sleeping?"

"He said a few things."

"Are you messing with me?" She's like a pretty teapot, ready to blow.

As much as I love to tease her, I have a new desire to ease her, too. "He said you wanted to kick me out of my house and sleep in my bed." So much for not teasing her.

She gapes. "He said that?"

I chuckle.

She gives my bicep a little shove. "You're not funny."

"Why don't you just say what you're not saying?"

She crosses her arms above the small cage on her lap and stares out the side window. "Never mind."

So stubborn. "Okay," I agree, curious to see how long she lasts before asking if she can stay at my house.

I'll admit when Daire asked me, my first response was no. I only moved into the house a few months ago after graduating this summer. The house was a gift for earning my business degree. I'd been promised it when I was a freshman in high school. Back then, the house was old and dated. No one had used it for years. I had my room in the estate and was either there, in Atlanta, or at college. When I took a gap year, to Daire and my father's disappointment, I stayed at the estate, Daire's penthouse, or with friends.

But after this last year of living with two people off-campus, I knew I'd want a place to myself. I also knew that place would need serious updating—another perk from my graduation gift. My parents are the most giving people on earth, in my opinion.

It's one of the reasons why I doubled up on classes so I could graduate on time—as if I'd never dropped-out—and make my parents proud. I did it to show Daire I could, too, and to prove to myself I was capable of more than I'd become—an unambitious freeloader with no goals other than to have a good time with friends and women.

It was easy once I got back into the swing of college. From there, I got new ideas and wanted more for myself. I had the house redone with the help of an architect and interior designer. I graduated with honors. And I moved back home to my newly renovated house and adult life. The adjustment was easy. I love the freedom of living alone, especially when it comes to dating. I can screw wherever I want, whenever I want. It's liberating and secluded.

But then I imagined Sadie alone at night having a nightmare and no one there to wake her up or hold her. Not that I want to share a bed with her and hold her. I mean, I do. Fuck yeah, I do. But I won't. I made a decision to respect her wishes long ago. I've been doing one hell of a job so far. I'm not about to screw it up. I'm adulting now. Sadie is another step toward my maturity. I can continue our platonic friendship while she lives with me. Some boundaries aren't meant to be crossed. Besides, Sadie deserves better than anything I can offer her. She deserves the dream she wants.

"Fine." Sadie huffs and turns her pink-cheeked face to me. "Daire was supposed to suggest I stay with you. *Sleep* with you. Not with you. Sleep in your house...with you there or not. You don't have to be there. But I'm not kicking you out. I don't have to stay there. I just don't know how comfortable I am being a third wheel—fourth if you count the bun in the oven—to Daire and Everleigh. They're still in their honeymoon phase, and the house is smaller now. I'd be on top of them basically. But I don't want to impose on you. I mean, you have a life and women to...date. I don't want to crowd you, either."

I can't hold my laughter in anymore. I lift one hand from the steering wheel to silence her, but she stopped talking the moment I started laughing. "It's fine, Sadie. You can stay with me. I talked to Daire, and it's all good."

She points those stunning eyes at me. "Are you sure?"

"Yeah, I'm sure."

She exhales a breath of relief. "Thank you."

From the corner of my eye, I see her nibble on her bottom lip.

"One more thing," she says, her focus on the hamster cage. "Could you warn me before you bring a woman home? I'd rather not see or hear any of that."

"Where would you go?" I ask, curious and turn the radio on low. Somehow, we managed to drive for an hour with no music. A first for me.

She nibbles more on her lip. "My room, I guess. It's a loft, right? On the third floor?"

"It is. It's also directly above my bedroom."

"Oh." She grips the cage with both hands.

"I don't sleep with girls in my bedroom, though. You'd be fine." I smirk, but it feels wrong. In fact, this whole conversation feels wrong. I've never had stage fright before, but I feel with Sadie in my house, I might.

"You don't sleep with women at your house?" She sounds confused.

"I do. Just not in my bedroom."

She gets quiet, thinking that over. That line forms between her brows again. "Definitely give me a warning before you do that. Please. I still have a few friends in Honeycomb. I could maybe stay with one of them for a night."

She really is too much. "I can refrain from sex for the two weeks that you're at my house."

"I appreciate that, but you shouldn't have to because of me."

"You could always watch or participate."

Her lip curls with disgust.

I laugh. "Bad joke."

She doesn't look reassured, with her shoulders hiked up near her ears again.

"I promise, it's fine. We'll have fun. I've gone without sex for two weeks before. I think."

"This is a bad idea. I'll just stay with—"

I touch her dainty wrist. "I want you to stay. It'll be a good thing for both of us."

"How will it be a good thing for you?"

"I get to practice the art of restraint. And bond with a woman on a platonic level. We'll roast marshmallows and watch murder."

Her face brightens. "For real?"

The hope in her eyes is too much to deny. "You can show me the good crime shows to watch. I may become addicted myself."

She rolls her eyes. "You won't. Your only addiction is to sex."

Which reminds me. "I have a request, too."

"I'm listening."

"Don't walk around in your towel or without a bra under your t-shirt when I'm around."

Her features scrunch with obvious confusion.

Because of last night, I'm sure. We slept together. I was nude. I changed her and saw her naked. We were very relaxed, but if I let my guard down, I might slip up and try to kiss her again. For some reason, I feel like if I did, she wouldn't turn away this time.

"Too much of a temptation for you?" she teases, clueless to how right she is.

"Yeah," I say in all seriousness.

We ride in silence for the rest of the way.

Chapter 9

Sadie

I message Everleigh that we're almost at the farm. We've been texting for the last hour, ever since Easton said what he said and didn't follow his comment with a joke.

Easton flirts. It's as natural to him as breathing. He loves to tease me, too. I love it just as much, even though I get a little frustrated at times. But when I teased him about being too much of a temptation and his reply was a serious, 'yeah,' I didn't know how to react. Silence followed his comment, and the look of turmoil on his face confused me even more. So badly, I wanted to know what he was thinking. I couldn't ask. What if it had nothing to do with me and I took his comment all wrong?

So I texted Everleigh for a distraction. She just finished meeting with the designer for the nursery. She'd wanted to decorate the room herself, but Daire encouraged her to hire someone who can bring her vision to life and help lighten her already busy schedule. I kept up the messages asking about the color scheme and style for the room. Eventually, Everleigh caught on and wanted to know if Easton had upset me. I told her things were fine, and I was just bored. I'm not sure she bought it.

Thick woods hug either side of the road, the leaves fluttering with varying shades of crimson, ginger, gold, and mint. Soon, the colorful trees are replaced by a rustic stone wall on one side. The structure surrounds the property of the estate. The entrance won't be far away.

"Everleigh wants us to stop by when we get here," I say quickly.

Everleigh said his lake house has a separate entrance. I'd hate to make him backtrack if it's farther down the road.

"Is that who you've been texting?" he asks, a bit annoyed.

"Yeah. Sorry, she asked if we'd stop by a moment ago."

"Is Daire there?"

"I think so. I don't know, actually. I can ask." Why is he so moody? Maybe driving for two hours makes him tired or cranky.

He hits the blinker and pulls up to the call box. He enters a code, and the gate opens. We drive through and follow the long road to the estate.

From here, the house looks the same, apart from a new entrance to the left side with its own portico and horseshoe driveway. The entrance to the inn, I assume. A few worker trucks and vans line the driveway on that side.

Easton parks under the large covered entrance parallel to the front doors.

"Thanks for driving," I tell him.

He nods then opens his door and gets out of the car.

I climb out, too, eager to stretch my legs and spine. Detective Pickles's waits for me on the seat. I get his cage and carry it up the steps.

Everleigh opens the front door before I ring the bell.

Her skin glows, her ebony hair shines, and her cobalt eyes soften with a warm smile. "You're here. And you brought Detective Pickles." She raises her arms to hug me.

I move the cage to the side and throw one arm around her shoulder.

Her belly, hidden beneath a long black jersey dress and a sweater, bumps my hip. She giggles. "Sorry. It gets in the way." She releases me. "I'm so happy you're here."

"Me, too." I hadn't realized how tense I was until now.

The estate, surrounded by moss-draped oak trees, a gentle breeze, and chirping birds, would put anyone at peace. The scent of nature infuses my senses. I breathe it in and feel myself relax more.

"You look thin," Everleigh says, taking in my leggings, cropped t-shirt, and long open sweater.

"I've been busy," I say, unaware that I'd lost weight. If she's pointing it out, it must be true. It used to be the opposite with us. Everleigh was constantly overworked and underweight as a result.

She's a much healthier version of who she was a year ago. But then, a happy marriage to a handsome, caring man will do that.

"You look incredible." I rub her small-for-five-months belly. "How's the little guy doing?"

"He's good. Active today, kicking and moving a lot."

"Aw. I can't imagine what that feels like."

"It's weird. Last night, Daire and I saw his hand push on my stomach. It was cool but freaky. Daire tried to high-five him, says his little man is cool already."

I giggle.

Everleigh glances behind me to Easton, who's lingering by the car

He pockets his phone and gives her an easy smile.

"Delivered safely, as promised." He nods at me and stops by my side.

Everleigh hugs him. "Thank you so much for doing all this. I owe you big time."

"You're welcome." He straightens when she lets go. "And I'll hold you to that favor."

"Whatever you need. I'll throw in another favor if you take Detective Pickles so I can show Sadie around."

"No problem." He grins, but it doesn't reach his eyes.

I give him the cage. "Thank you."

He holds my gaze for a moment, then focuses on the hamster. "Come on DP, it's male bonding time."

"DP?" I arch a brow.

"It's less of a mouthful."

Can't argue with that.

Everleigh takes my hand. "Let me give you a tour."

The entire side of this house has been transformed. The kitchen is complete and private for the cooks and servers she's hiring. We enter a room with several sitting areas comprised of plush couches and tables with built-in checkers and chess boards. Next, we see a reading room with bookshelves and cozy nooks, then head upstairs to see the multiple bedrooms. The second floor is not finished at all. Workers paint the walls and lay tile in the bathrooms.

"We're adding wallpaper to the bedrooms. The curtains and furniture will come in a few weeks. I saved the best part for last."

We head back downstairs and enter a room surrounded by windows that overlooks the side yard. "I give you, the dining hall."

The room is light and airy with topiaries and plates and teacups in weathered hutches. She'd sent me pictures of the English cottage theme she was going for.

"What do you think?"

"It's beautiful. Perfect." I walk to one of the many walls of windows. "And I love the view."

It's surrounded by a stone wall fence. Plants, flowers, and trees are in strategic areas, waiting to be planted in the ground. The entire area is private for the inn. A large chessboard on the grass and a brick patio for dining or sitting around an outdoor fireplace make up the rest of the yard.

"This is all new, right?" I gesture to it, never remembering seeing a space like this before. I think it was just a yard and trees.

"It is. I wanted a sanctuary retreat for the guests that doesn't encroach on our side of the house or the backyard. Do you think it's okay without a pool?"

I understand her concern. It gets hot in the summer.

"Daire didn't think it made sense to add a second pool to the property," she explains. "But he wants to keep the one out back private for us."

"It's shady with all the trees and a really beautiful retreat. I doubt the guests are coming here to swim."

"They have access to the lake at the farm, too. For canoeing or kayaking. We added a dock to accommodate the new activities."

"That's what people will come here for, the farm. Well, that and to get married." I clasp my hands together and give her a dreamy smile.

She frowns. "I know, which makes me think we need to add a jacuzzi, since we don't have a pool." She points to an area near the patio. "Over there."

"Would it be ready in time?" It's remarkable how big the space is, and it's only the side yard.

"I can make it happen."

I turn to her. "Are you making sure to rest and take care of yourself?"

"Daire wouldn't have it any other way. He massages my feet every evening when he gets back from the office at the farm."

I cover my heart and sigh. "You won the husband lottery."

She beams. "I did, didn't I?"

"Where do you think Easton went? I should rescue him from Detective Pickles."

"I'm sure he's fine. My guess is he's in the kitchen." She rubs her belly, then turns and heads in the direction we came. "Let's go find him."

I follow her through the inn to a hallway and the secret bookcase door she'd told me about earlier.

"I love secret doors," I gush as we pass through.

She closes it and pushes a button.

"What did that do?"

"Locked it."

"So cool."

This side of the house with its new design and renovations, I've seen. They did this first before starting work on the inn. I call it southern chic. Daire let Everleigh have full reign. She kept the study and billiard room modern for him, but the rest is so my best friend with its neutral colors, hydrangeas, comfortable furnishings, natural woven rugs, and light stone fireplaces.

The house on this side smells fresh, with a hint of floral. "I love what you chose for this house." I've told her this before. It's like stepping into a magazine. For how big the estate is, even with the separation for the inn, the décor makes it cozy.

"It takes my breath away," Everleigh says over her shoulder, leading the way to the kitchen. "I can't believe it's mine."

We pass under a large archway. Sure enough, Easton stands at the kitchen island eating a sandwich. Detective Pickles's cage is by his glass of tea.

Everleigh sends me a knowing smirk. "The Livingston boys are always hungry."

Is that why he was grouchy and got quiet in the car? He was hungry?

"I hope this wasn't Daire's sandwich?" He finishes the last bite.

"Nope. I made that for you." She takes the plate, rinses it in the sink, and puts it in the dishwasher.

"I made us quinoa salads with cranberries," she says to me. "Are you hungry?"

"A little. Are you?" I don't know how often pregnant women eat.

"The answer to that is yes," Easton says. "I've never seen her eat so much, but then, I barely saw her eat before."

"I'll get us some," she says.

"Thanks for watching him," I say to Easton and move Detective Pickles's cage to the side of the island with bar stools.

"He's a wild one, you should try to tame him." He gestures to the sleeping ball of fur, eating pellets from his small bowl.

I laugh and excuse myself to use the bathroom, happy Easton is joking again.

I take a moment to finger comb my hair and blot my face. I look like I was doing work outside instead of riding in a car. Once I'm done, I stop before entering the kitchen when I hear Easton say my name.

"I really appreciate you letting her stay with you," Everleigh says. "Sadie hates to be a third wheel. Hint, hint."

"Are you hinting that I'd make her a third wheel with a date?"

"I don't know what you do at your home."

He laughs. "I do exactly what you think I do. But don't worry. It'll be fine. It's only for two weeks."

"Could be longer," Everleigh adds, hopeful.

"She won't stay longer. No matter how much you want to keep her, she has a life in Atlanta."

"She doesn't like city life. She misses small town living."

"Really?" He sounds surprised.

Had I never mentioned that during our conversations?

"Really," Everleigh assures him. "She wanted to move back here when you first met her. She didn't because of Dash. He prefers the city."

Before Easton says anything about the breakup, I enter the kitchen. "I'm back."

Everleigh sits at the island on a stool, a bowl of quinoa salad in front of her and another by the stool one over, near my hamster.

I join her. "Looks good." Everything she cooks is delicious.

"I'm going to make some calls. Text me when you're ready to leave," Easton says and strolls from the room.

Everleigh watches him leave, then leans close. "Is there a weird tension between you two, or is it me?"

"I don't think he's happy I'm staying with him."

"He's fine." She bites her food.

I taste mine. Mmm. "Is that citrus?"

She smiles and nods.

"I'm telling you, you missed your calling as a chef." I

73

used to say as a baker too, but now that she has the café on the farm, she gets to wear that hat whenever she wants.

"Does Dash know you're staying with Easton?" she asks, nervously.

I bite more food, hesitating before unleashing this bomb. "Dash and I broke up."

She drops her fork in her bowl. It makes a loud clunk. "Sorry. I'm just shocked. You have your trip in two weeks. I thought you were getting engaged."

"We probably would have, but I ended it."

I explain how he's never around and that I want more for myself. I also express my doubts about my choice. "Am I making a mistake?"

She chews, thoughtfully—I suspect to find the right words. "I think you ended it for worthy reasons, and you should trust your decision. Dash isn't who he was in high school. He was all about you back then. Now, he has his job, which requires most of his time, and he divides the rest of his time between you and his friends."

"Mostly his friends these days."

"That's not fair to you." Everleigh lays her hand on my knee. "I always noticed it, but I thought you were happy with having a lot of alone time."

I slump. "I think I appreciated it at first. I'd been alone for six months, and if Dash had smothered me in the beginning, I'm not sure how I would have liked it. But when I wanted to be closer and do more, he wasn't on the same page. I mean, we're not even living together. It's been almost a year of dating, and he wanted to wait to live together until after our marriage, said it was tradition in his family." I let out a sad sigh. "I respected him for wanting to follow his traditions. He's always said he believes in that, and it's why he knew he wanted to marry me one day. He said I'd be the best wife. He wants kids, like I do. In those ways, we were on the same page. But now I'm wondering if me and our kids, should we have been blessed, would ever see him."

Everleigh tucks stands of my hair behind my ear. "Are you okay?"

"I'm confused about what to do now. I had a plan for my future, and now it's gone."

"Maybe it's time not to have a plan. Take things one day at a time, take a few risks even, and see where life leads you."

"Is that what you did with Daire?"

She has another bite and considers my comment. "I think I did. I didn't realize it at the time, but I did take risks with him. It wasn't my usual behavior, especially after what happened. But I did, and had I not, I wouldn't be here." She pats her belly.

"If only Daire had a twin," I tease.

"Don't say that around Easton." Everleigh glances behind me, even though I don't hear anyone else around. "He's super sensitive about being compared to Daire."

"I'm learning. I don't get it, though. Easton's pretty amazing in his own ways. He's an incredible friend. Loyal. Helpful. And he's turning his life around, maturing. I think we're going to see great things from him soon."

Everleigh grins, her blue eyes glinting. "You like him."

"Of course, I do. He's one of my closest friends." I shovel quinoa into my mouth.

"I think you might like him a little more than that." Her voice hints at concern.

"Not at all," I fire back. "That would be unwise and a waste of time."

She chews on her bottom lip.

"Stop it." I point my spoon at her mouth. "You're worrying for no reason again."

"I want you to be able to relax while you're here."

"I will. I am."

"Okay," she says, unconvinced. "I just think—"

"That we should eat our delicious food and talk about something else?" I smile and scoop a big bite into my mouth, moaning and rolling my eyes with delight.

She giggles and lets it go, as she should. There is nothing between me and Easton, and there never will be.

Chapter 10

Easton

I stand outside the kitchen, eavesdropping. I meant to grab my iced tea and go back to the library to finish my calls. Instead, I was stopped in my tracks by Sadie's voice and compliments about me to Everleigh.

Apart from my parents' optimism that I can do anything I set my mind to, no one has ever seen me the way Sadie does. She openly praises me to my face and now to Everleigh.

Her words stir feelings inside me. Feelings I can't explain. In one way, I love her compliments and genuine openness. In another way, I fear living up to the version of me she sees. There is no place for me to go but down. That's a lot of pressure.

I was mad at myself for asking her not to tempt me. Who says that to a woman who was just attacked and broke up with her longtime boyfriend? It was rude. I don't want to be rude to her. I never have before. All that talk about other women in my house had me tense. The way I relieve stress is with a hookup. Hookups are not an option right now.

Sadie would be the perfect hookup. She's already in my house.

On the drive here, my mind kept picturing her in various places. Spread across my kitchen island while I make her come with my mouth. On her knees, her perfect peach-shaped ass in the air, while I take her from behind on the fur rug in front of the fireplace. And worst of all, I pictured her in my bed—the place no woman has ever been.

My shared college apartment left me no other option. But this is my permanent residence. I don't plan to leave it, and I prefer my room to be my own personal space. No women allowed. Only I couldn't stop envisioning Sadie in my sheets. Her maple hair fanned out over my pillow. I was so distracted, I didn't realize we'd reached the estate until she said we needed to stop by to see Everleigh.

I walk away and return to the library that Daire now uses as his home office. He's at the farm, and it's good he is. He would have seen right through my moodiness and guessed my problem is with Sadie. He would have warned me not to mess with Everleigh's best friend and to seek pleasure elsewhere.

Problem is, I've had all the best women Oakville has to offer. Hell, I've had the best in the nearest small towns, except for Honeycomb. Sadie and Everleigh were the most attractive women in that town and neither lives there anymore.

Macon isn't that far of a drive. I could pick up a woman at a bar there—and take her where? Back to her house? To a hotel? It's not my style, but desperate times call for desperate actions. Maybe I'll need to travel to Atlanta and stay at Daire's penthouse.

I sigh and stare out the windows to the parklike backyard. A text comes through my phone.

Sadie: I'm ready if you are.

I use my new motto—No time like the present—to jumpstart me into this reckless adventure.

Easton: Meet you at the car.

I grab the book I've been waiting to get when Daire isn't around and tuck it under my arm. Ironically, the book Dad's owned for as long as I can remember will aid in my presentation. It has historical images of the farm from when my great-great-grandfather inherited the family business.

I don't see Sadie or Everleigh as I traipse through the house to the car. Maybe they're waiting for me outside. I exit through the front doors and take the steps down. The silence tips me off that the girls are not out here yet.

I open the passenger door and reach over the bag Sadie brought along with her suitcase to set the book on the other seat. Accidentally, I bump Sadie's bag to the floor. I catch it, but the zipper is open, and a few contents spill out.

I grab the first item, a bottle of apple-scented lotion. The second is a sketchbook. When I lift it, a polaroid of Sadie and Dash in a sports bar falls out. I snatch it and stare at the asshat who broke Sadie's heart, simply by being himself.

In the picture, they're at a table with other people—his friends, I assume. His arm is around Sadie, either dutifully or territorially, but he's not looking at her. He's laughing, his focus on the guys, while Sadie engages with the camera, appearing uncomfortable and sad. What did she ever see in his preppy ass? His hair looks plastic and unmovable, like a Ken doll.

I tuck the picture in the book and brush my bangs from my face. The wavy strands glide through my fingers. I keep it a bit longer on top because chicks love tugging it during sex. If Sadie touched Dash's plastered hair, she probably got a paper cut.

I grab the third item from the floor. Shit. It's her iPad. Quickly, I run a finger over the screen to make sure it's not cracked. It lights up with an image of a sexy, curvy woman in a bra and jeans sandwiched between two shirtless men, both of them caressing her. A full moon looms above, and dark woods fill in the background. In bold yellow font are the words, *Tempted by the Wolf Pack.*

It takes me a moment to realize I'm staring at a book cover. The author's name has my eyes widening. Sadie Sutton. Such a cute name. I thought so when I first learned it a year ago. It fits her, but this cover... is Sadie a closet erotica novelist?

A throat clears behind me.

I glance over my shoulder.

Sadie stands there with the hamster cage in her hands. "What are you doing?" Her gaze falls to the iPad. She gasps, and pink blooms across her cheeks. "Why do you have that?"

"I wasn't snooping. I swear. I accidentally bumped your bag, and it fell out."

Those cheeks turn beet red. "And you needed to turn it on to put it back?"

"I was making sure the screen wasn't cracked."

"Put it back," she screeches, the pitch so high it could crack glass.

One corner of my mouth tugs up. "Why are you embarrassed?"

"Are you kidding me?" She opens the passenger door and sets the cage on the seat.

I close the back door that's separating us. "You should own that you're an erotica author."

Her eyes widen. "I'm not an erotica author."

"But the name on the cover..." I gesture to the backseat.

"I put my name on all my pre-made covers until they sell. Then the author's name goes in its place. Lots of cover artists do it." She slaps her hands over her eyes. "I can't believe you saw it."

I can't believe she's so embarrassed. I need to make this better for her.

I peel her fingers from her face. "Sadiecakes, it's me you're talking to. Your philandering, sex god, honorary-romance-book-club-member bestie. I'm the last person to judge you. On the contrary, I'm impressed."

"You are?" she asks, surprised.

"That cover is sexy as hell. I'd buy it. In fact, I'm going to order it right now." I pull my phone from my pocket.

"You don't even know my website."

"You have a website?" I search her name and romance covers on the internet. "Found it."

She grabs my hand with the phone. "You can't buy it. It's under contract from a potential author. Once she makes the final payment, it's hers. Then you can buy the book when she publishes it."

"Maybe I will."

She makes a face of disbelief. "Why would you buy it?"

"Because you made it."

"Oh." Her posture relaxes, and her cheeks turn pink again.

"So, tell me, when did you start making sex book covers?"

"They're not sex book covers." She lowers her voice and glances around, but we're alone. "They're erotica and romance. The genres are very popular. It's something new I'm trying, a side gig."

"Since when?" I lean against the car, grinning down at her.

"Four months ago."

"What got you into it?"

"I don't read erotica. if that's what you're asking. I like romance novels, but I've never read the dark stuff." She glances around again.

"Too scared?" I tease, bending closer to her.

She crosses her arms. "If you must know, I'm more than happy with good old-fashioned steamy romance."

Little Miss Sadie has a secret I didn't know about. What else might she be hiding from me?

"Can we go now?"

"Only if we continue the conversation in the car."

"Fine." Her nervousness is almost palpable.

I get behind the wheel, drive to the entrance of the estate, and put the car in park. She's far enough away from the house to keep from thinking we might be overheard. Not that anyone was around us before.

"What are you doing?"

"Finishing our conversation." There's no way I'm going to let this drop without learning all I can about this hobby of hers. "So, you read steamy romance and make sex book covers."

She rolls her eyes, but the grin on her face says she's relaxed, which is what I wanted.

"Any other secrets you want to share with me? This is a safe space, Sadie. You can tell me anything."

Her grin turns sultry, and her hazel eyes take on a seductive gleam. "If we're sharing, I suppose I could tell you my deepest, darkest fantasy."

I was not expecting her to say that. My cock twitches.

Since when does Sadie have bedroom eyes? She always seemed like a Hallmark romance kind of girl.

"I'm listening and willing to help you bring this fantasy to life, should you wish it."

She closes the small distance between us and leans over the center console. Her warm breath brushes my ear.

Shivers break across my skin, possibly for the first time in my life from a woman, and my dick rises to half-mast.

"My fantasy is to swim naked in a lake at night, floating face-up under the stars for all of nature to see."

Full erection.

"Is anyone there watching in this fantasy?"

"Just the gator hidden beneath the surface, trying to bite my foot each time I kick and drag me to the depths of the lake, never to be seen again."

Instant deflation. I scowl.

She cracks up. "You totally bought my act."

Oh, I did more than buy into it. I was visualizing screwing her sweet naked body in the lake outside my house under the fucking stars like she wanted—or like I thought she wanted.

I straighten away from her, realizing I'd leaned closer, too. "You're cruel."

"*Aw*. What's wrong, Easton? You can dish it, but you can't take it?"

"I don't do that." I hit the gas and pull onto the road.

"You do, and it's so much worse because you're you." She gestures to my body. "Talk about cruel."

I almost blurt, "You can have this any time."

"When I was on my kitchen floor and you told me everything you'd do to me sexually, I almost came."

I tighten my grip to keep from jerking the wheel. "Fuck, Sadie. Do you want me to crash into a tree?"

"Sorry," she says to the hamster cage.

"Don't be sorry." I huff. "Just be less tempting. Please." It comes out as a harsh demand.

This is on me. I started it, enquiring more about her book covers. I didn't expect her to give me fuck-me eyes, breathe in my ear, and conjure images of herself naked, floating in a lake.

Every time I look at her, that's all I'll see now. And I'm going to see her every day and night. Things just got that much harder.

Before this, I thought I had Sadie figured out. She has secrets I never would have guessed, and damn, if that doesn't make her even more intriguing. To know she makes erotica covers and has a dirty side that wants to be spanked takes this arrangement to a knew fucked-up level.

At this point, I'm either going to have to move out of my house or screw Sadie from my mind until she's erased and all I see are random blondes.

Chapter 11

Sadie

Easton's house complements the natural surroundings without taking away from the beauty of the woods. Here, the red, orange, and yellow leaves are more vibrant. Must be because they're close to the lake—and what a massive lake it is.

I glimpsed it through the trees from the winding driveway.

Easton parks near the side entrance garage. The car faces the backyard, the blue lake glistening beyond colorful trees that shade the leaf-colored lawn. Backyard might be an understatement. It's like a giant nature preserve.

Easton takes the hamster cage from my lap. "Go. Run free, little rabbit. I'll take DP inside."

I turn my wide eyes to him. "Thank you." If I weren't itching to get out of the car and explore, I'd kiss him—on the cheek, of course.

I hop out, my jaw hanging. I didn't know what to expect. Something similar to the estate but more Easton. This is natural, untouched except for a few structures that blend in as well as the house. They're much smaller. A wood gazebo-like building on the far side. A fire pit made of stones and cut lumber for seats. A shed holds a kayak and a paddleboard. It's near a dock with a fishing boat. Nothing says luxury—the three-story modern farmhouse aside—even though the property is worth a fortune.

Leaves crunch under my boots as I inch down the sloped ground for a better look at the lake. The deep blue water curves and stretches to the left and right, trees shading the shore on either side.

So much nature. This is what I love the most about small towns, at least the one where I was born, although Honeycomb doesn't have any lakes this big. I don't remember it having this many trees, either. It probably does; I just forgot because I haven't been back in a while.

"What do you think?" Easton asks from somewhere behind me.

"I love it. I love it so much." I glance over my shoulder.

He stands several feet away, the house towering behind him. "I'm glad you like it." His chest puffs out with pride.

"This lake looks bigger than the one with the make-out dock."

He chuckles. "I like the sound of that. Where is this dock? I need to visit it."

"It's the one at the lake on your parents' property, where you took me when we first met and tried to kiss me," I remind him.

Daire took Everleigh there once. She said things got steamy between them, but Daire's snotty ex, Tennessee, interrupted them before anything could happen.

Easton's smile widens, his gleaming teeth visible from here. He looks in his element, rugged and sexy with his tousled hair. "Why do you call it that? We didn't make out that night. Unfortunately."

"Everleigh came up with it, and we didn't make out because I wasn't falling for your act."

"How do you know it was an act?"

I roll my eyes and return my gaze to the view. A stone path weaves through the trees to the lake where a thin long dock stretches a good distance into the blue depths. I point to what looks like a small island with an outhouse.

"What is that in the middle?"

"A floating dock with a small cabin."

"What is it for?"

Leaves crunch with his steps as he walks to stand by my side. "My grandmother always wanted a floating dock like the one at her childhood summer camp. My grandfather had this built for her. She loved to swim out there during the day and sunbathe. At night, she loved stargazing. She swore the stars were the best during the fall and winter, but it was too cold, so my grandfather had a cabin built for her. You can't tell from here, but it has a huge skylight."

I sigh and cup my heart. "That's so romantic."

His lips quirk with a crooked grin. "Yeah, I guess it was."

We stare at the floating dock both lost in our thoughts for a moment. A cold breeze cuts through my sweater, and I draw my arms close for warmth. "You said your grandma swam out there in the fall. Wasn't it too cold?"

"She swam out there during the summers. In the fall, she took either a canoe or a small motorboat."

"You couldn't get me to swim in that lake."

Easton smiles with amusement. "Why not?"

"Alligators? That floating dock is far away. You could get eaten. Your grandma could have been eaten."

He lets out a belly laugh and hooks his arm around my shoulders. "Sadie, I love the way your mind works."

"There *are* alligators in Georgia."

"Barely."

"But there are. It's better to be safe than sorry."

"Come on." He tightens his grip on my shoulder. "Let me show you the house."

I let him guide me up to the wooden deck that leads to the window-covered back of the house. "How far is this from the estate?"

We took the separate entrance Everleigh had mentioned to get here, but all I could see were trees.

"Too far to walk, but I have an off-road vehicle I can take through the woods to get there in about ten minutes. Otherwise, you have to drive to the main entrance."

I nod and glance around. "Do you get bears around here?"

"Never seen one. Or a serial killer in case that's your next question."

I snort.

"This place is secure," he says, his arm still around my shoulder. "Walled in like a fortress. Gated. Cameras. The works. You're safe from everything but me." He winks.

I roll my eyes and exhale a deep breath, letting the scents, sounds, and beauty of the nature around us seep in. "The off-road vehicle seems like it might be fun."

"Yeah?" He smiles, whiskey eyes glinting with surprise, and gives my shoulder a squeeze. "I'll take you on it sometime."

A grin pulls at my lips. I've been here ten or fifteen minutes and already I feel less stressed. Like I'm where I belong. I don't need to live in the city—that was Dash's priority. I can do marketing for my stepdad's business from anywhere. I'll be working while I'm here, and I'll be more productive because I won't be wondering if I'm being watched.

We enter through tall glass doors into a two-story great room that opens to the kitchen, dining area, and a bar, each with a view of the lake. The black, wood, and stone materials give it a sleek, masculine feel. Blankets, pillows, and rugs soften the space with what can only be a designer's touch. The coolest feature is the staircase. The steps appear to float up to the landing on the second floor, which has a modern railing overlooking the great room. The inside screams luxury.

"Does it meet your approval?" Easton watches me take it all in.

"It's very different from the main house." Traditional plantation style fits the estate's exterior, and there's Everleigh's relaxed, cozy décor on the inside. "Did Daire help design it?"

Easton frowns. "Daire? No."

That upset him? "It's just a question." I make my tone light and breezy.

"Why would you ask it?" He traipses to the large fridge and gets a beer.

"It reminds me of his penthouse in the city, that's all."

"That place is cold and lacks warmth. This has rustic stone, lots of wood, and views of nature." He gestures to the trees and lake with the beer bottle. "Want one?"

"No, thanks." I survey the room again and realize the accent colors are all navy, Easton's favorite. "You did this."

"My faith in you is restored." He disappears into the foyer and returns with something tucked under his arm.

"Detective Pickles!" I rush over and take his cage. "Thank you."

He grins and sips his beer before setting it on a nearby table. "Want to see your room?"

I nod excitedly and follow him up the stairs. We stop on the second floor. Easton points down a split hallway. "My room is at the end. The other two guest rooms are to the left. You're welcome to use either of them if you don't like the loft."

"I'm sure I'll like it."

We go up one more set of stairs to another landing and a set of open double doors. The bedroom has the same wood floors, but the color scheme is all cream, forcing your gaze to the balcony and incredible view. I gasp and walk toward it.

"Easton, why isn't this your room?"

I can't imagine his is nicer.

He shrugs. "I didn't even consider it. I just took the main bedroom."

For someone who lives carefree and disregards most rules, he follows certain ones without question. I imagine that's the spare to the heir coming out and his inherent take-what-he's-given mentality.

I set Detective Pickles's cage on the dresser on the way to the balcony. Easton opens the door and I step outside, breathing in the crisp, cool, pine scented air.

He joins me. "You like it?"

"I love it. This is how I would like to live. I wouldn't need a house this big. A cozy cottage with a lake view and a fireplace would keep me happy."

Easton's brows knit together as he stares at me. "Really?"

"You sound surprised." I grip the wooden railing and scan the tall trees. "Why do you think I have so many house plants? I love nature. But who needs indoor plants when you have all of this?" Not that his place couldn't use some succulents.

"Hmm." He scratches the light scruff on his chin.

"You're very blessed, Easton."

"Me? The spare to the heir?"

I give him a tender smile. "Most of the time we're so close to our own lives we can't see it the way others do."

How many people saw Dash as wrong for me? Why did it take me so long to figure it out for myself?

"I'm going to unpack, shower, and then maybe order food for dinner. Would that be okay?"

He rests his back against the railing, the picturesque fall view of trees and the lake behind him, making him look like a sexy model in a cologne ad. "You don't have to ask me if you can order anything. It's your house for the next two weeks. Do what you want."

I bite the inside of my mouth and stare at my boots. "I know this was forced on you. I don't want to impose more than is necessary."

He touches my chin and lifts my face, so I meet his gaze. "Let's get something straight. No one forces anything on me. I could have said no. I have before regarding other things, to my brother's great dismay. I'm okay with this."

Nothing in his expression says he's not.

"Okay. Thank you." I walk back into the bedroom.

Easton closes the door to the balcony, taking the chill from the room. The trees block most of the sun around here and it will set soon, making it even colder. I want to be settled in before then.

"I should get my suitcase."

"I brought it in for you. It's by the garage door."

"Oh! Thank you."

How sweet. Dash never would have done something like that unless I asked him to.

I tell Detective Pickles I'll be right back, then follow Easton down the stairs to the first floor.

My glutes will look great after climbing these for two weeks.

"What are your plans for tonight?" I ask, so he knows I don't expect him to stay home on my account.

He spreads his arms. "You're looking at it. I might work out a little after we eat."

"At the gym?" Oakville is bigger than Honeycomb, but it's still a small town. My guess is the only gym is downtown.

"The basement has a workout room."

"Oh. Nice."

"You can use it whenever you want."

Laughter bubbles from me. "I wouldn't know where to start. My gym equipment is a yoga mat, and I don't even stick to that." I glance around the foyer and stairs, searching for my suitcase.

Easton disappears down a hallway and re-emerges with my luggage. "Looking for this?"

"Yes. Thank you." I walk over to retrieve it.

He rolls the suitcase behind him. "I'm not making you carry this up all those stairs. My daddy taught me better than that."

Ooh. He's sexy when he talks like this. "I rein in a too-big smile and pray my cheeks aren't as red as they feel. "Thanks."

"No problem." He turns and climbs the stairs.

Instead of following him, I stand there staring at his broad shoulders and backside until he disappears from my view. Wasn't I supposed to be doing something—unpacking and stuff?

It's like I'm suddenly an idiot. If I follow after him now, I'll look even weirder. But I can't hang out here and do nothing.

I hear him rolling the suitcase on the wood-floor landing above me and call out to him, "Want some pizza?"

He stops and yells down. "Sure, but only if you get me something with meat on it. I know your pizza will look like a veggie patch."

I laugh, then shout, "What about murder?"

"What about it?" His voice sounds closer, like he's leaning over the second-floor railing and talking down to me.

I back up until I see he's doing just that. Our eyes connect. "There's a Dateline marathon tonight. Mind if I watch a few episodes while we eat? One is about a stripper," I add to entice him. "But I can always watch it in my room."

He cocks a brow. "Murder sounds good. Feel free to reenact any of the scenes where she dances. I'll take notes."

I shake my head and turn away to hide my flaming-hot blush. He's such a flirt.

His steps continue up the stairs, growing more distant.

I focus on the room before me, the flat screen above the sleek stone fireplace and the large sectional, imagining scenarios I shouldn't. Like me doing a striptease for Easton while he lounges on the couch, watching me. I've never stripped for anyone before. Now wouldn't be a good time to start, especially for someone like Easton.

I whip out my phone and order pizza like a good girl.

Chapter 12

Easton

I end my call with the executives from the bourbon company. I've been talking with them for three months now, and I'm ready to close the deal. The last part is getting Daire to agree to the partnership. *Pecan bourbon brought to you by Livingston Pecan Farm.* We've never branched into the liquor industry. I also have the CEO interested in collaborating on a Pecan liqueur.

This will be my baby. I'll run this division and become the worthy partner Dad and Daire have always wanted me to be. I'm excited about it, too. This will be a new profitable venture for the farm if Daire sees what I see.

I check the time. 11:00 a.m. I'm taking the helicopter to Atlanta to get a case of the bourbon. I've sampled it several times. It's delicious. Today, I get to see the bottle logo. I approved the prototype but haven't seen the finished product.

With my laptop, I head downstairs. Sadie hasn't emerged from her room. She was up late binging murder. I went down around 2:00 a.m. and found her passed out on the couch.

Her hair fell in maple waves behind her while she lay on her side, her face smooshed in a throw pillow. She wore an oversized sweater with one shoulder exposed and tiny boxers decorated with the words ID ME in red letters. Only Sadie would have ID network pajamas. Her furry socks covered her little feet, but her tanned legs were on full display and the way they were bent at the knees showed off her round butt cheeks. So much smooth skin to touch. I bit my knuckles to stifle a groan—actually bit my knuckles.

These two weeks might be the death of me.

Assuming she was curled up because she was cold, I covered her with a fur blanket. The action woke her. She sat up with her hair plastered to her face on one side. Those tired eyes and that bare shoulder made her look even more desirable. Her lips curved with the cutest sleepy grin. When she stood, she was wobbly. It brought back memories of me holding her and dressing her while she was naked. My dick rose to the occasion in my cotton pajama pants.

I ignored it, and thankfully, Sadie didn't notice my bulge. I asked if she wanted me to help her to her bedroom. She nodded and put one arm around my bare back. It was like leading a drunken patron from a bar. Before we reached the stairs, I asked her to forgive me and scooped her up into my arms. She weighed nothing. Other than letting out a small squeal, she didn't object. It was easier to get her up the two flights of stairs and faster if I carried her. I didn't expect her to rest her head and hand on my chest or for her to breathe in and tell me I smell amazing.

I also didn't expect her to rub my pec and tell me my body belongs on a romance book cover.

My skin burned so hot from where she touched me, I practically ran from her room once I got her in the bed. I went back to my room, masturbated to my last sex partner, a tall blonde—the opposite of Sadie—and went to bed, still feeling uptight. I know why. I didn't masturbate to Sadie. That's who my mind and body want. But that would make it even harder to leave her alone.

Tonight, I think I'll head out and screw a regular local girl. I'm not a fan of seconds because it gives women the wrong idea. They think I'm back for more of them and a meaningful relationship. Delaney isn't like that. She's bisexual, but she doesn't date men. She only has sex with them. I've slept with her a few times. If she's not in a relationship with a woman, she'll be good to go.

I text Sadie that I'm leaving and will be back later. Later could mean this afternoon or tonight.

In the garage, I pass my motorcycle. Dad's a BMW fan and got Daire and me each a BMW of our choice once we had our college degree. Daire chose an M8. I picked a BMW sports bike. I also have my car from high school graduation. The M4 is a sick fluorescent yellow that still makes me grin when I see it.

I get into the M4 and head for the helicopter pad Daire had built on some unused land at the farm.

* * *

I finish my meeting in Atlanta and get the cases of liquor to bring home. Sadie hasn't texted me all day. It's only been about three hours, but I'm worried. Why wouldn't she text me that she got my text? Or to have a good day? Or something?

Before I get in the helicopter, I text her.

Easton: Want me to bring any food home from the farm?

Why did I send that? That means I have to go home

instead of meeting Delaney. Not that she confirmed with me yet, but she replied and said she'd text me after work.

I guess I could leave again after going home. I could tell Sadie I'm meeting up with some friends. What if she wants to come, or worse, feels left out? She's been dealing with that from Dash for their whole relationship. I can't do that to her, but I don't want to admit I'm going to get laid, either.

She replies.

Sadie: No thanks. I ate with Everleigh.

So that's what she's been up to all day. I'm glad she wasn't home alone.

I climb into the helicopter, strap in, and let the pilot know I'm ready.

We make it to the farm in forty-five minutes. I figure if Sadie is with Everleigh, I can head home, shower, and figure out my plans from there.

It's a short drive to the lake house. Sadie's car is gone. She must still be at the estate with Everleigh unless they're hanging out at the farm. The helicopter pad isn't visible, hidden by trees and out of sight from visitors. It'd be a hike to walk from it to the country store and café. Daire and I drive or take a UTV.

I'm checking out the case of liquor in the trunk when Sadie's car appears around the bend.

She parks to the side, so she's not blocking the garage access.

Her eyes are bright, and her smile is cheery, like she had a good time with Everleigh. Her jeans are a relaxed fit, and her sweater shows off a bit of her flat stomach.

She whistles when she sees me. "Looking good Mr. Livingston. Looking real good."

She likes it when I'm dressed in a suit. Not that I'm wearing my jacket, and my sleeves are rolled up. She complimented me at Daire's wedding and at their engagement dinner. On both occasions, I went all out, as did everyone.

"Sexy." She circles me from behind. "Day wedding?"

I laugh. "Nope. Work."

"Where?" She glances around as if to point out there aren't any companies that can't be run in jeans around here.

"Atlanta."

Her brows tighten with question.

"I took the chopper."

"Oh. That was fast."

"That's why Daire got it."

She looks in the trunk. "Are you opening a bar?"

I laugh again. "It's something else." I touch the trunk to close it, but she removes a bottle of bourbon before I can.

"Pecan bourbon brought to you by Livingston Pecan Farm," she reads the label aloud. "You guys make bourbon?"

I sigh. "This has to stay between us until I present it to Daire."

"Wait. This is the secret project you've been working on?"

I nod and gesture for her to put the bourbon back in the case.

She doesn't. "You had this made?" If she didn't sound so impressed, I'd take the bottle from her.

"I collaborated with a bourbon company."

"I can't believe you were able to do this without Daire knowing." She inspects the label. "This is so exciting! Easton, I think this is perfect for the farm. It's very your family because you're big bourbon drinkers."

Sadie gets it. I smile. "I think so, but getting Daire to agree might not be so easy."

"He'd be a fool to pass on this."

My ego rises in the best way. "Thanks, Sadie. I appreciate that."

"It's true." She eyes the label again. "But..."

Here we go. "But...?"

"I don't think the label represents you the way it could."

I hadn't given it much thought. I'm not in love with the label. Sadie does marketing for her stepdad's successful real estate company. "What are your thoughts?"

"Really?" Her hazel eyes widen on me.

"Is that so hard to believe?"

She shrugs. "I don't know. I figured you have someone for this."

"I do, and they haven't impressed you."

She frowns. "I don't think it's bad. I'm not saying that at all. I just think it could be a little more you guys and the farm."

"Let's take it inside, and you can give me your thoughts."

"Can we try it, too?" She leads the way up the stairs and into the house.

"Sure."

I get two glasses from the bar. Sadie's iPad is on the kitchen island. Was she working on more book covers earlier? She sits at the counter, opens the tablet, and removes the pencil. Is she going to draw something for me?

Intrigued, I bring her a glass with a square ice cube and sit beside her.

She's sketching already. "Thank you." She holds up the drink. "To you and your brilliant ideas."

Does she know what she does to my ego when she says stuff like that? I smirk, my gaze locked on her sultry lips, and clink my glass with hers.

We both sip the drink. It's as good as I remember; a smooth pecan flavor that's not overly sweet.

"Wow." She blinks. "Wow. This is better than sex."

I almost spit out my next sip. I cough and swallow the liquid. "Sadie, my sweet, if that's true you've been missing out." As I assumed, Dash's bedroom play is as stiff as his hair. "It is good, though, isn't it?"

She sips more. "So smooth. I can taste the hint of pecan."

I smile, pleased and a bit amazed at how well she gets it.

Sadie gasps and draws on her iPad, impressing me with her artistic ability. She's fast using layers and creating what looks like a new label. The background is black. In white, three pecans rest on a small bed of leaves. She draws a rectangle like a sales tag or a Christmas present tag in black. On this, in white, is the barn from the farm and a pecan tree. She adds string and points to it. "This would be twine. It would wrap around the neck of the bottle and hold the tag to it, advertising the farm. The label"—she points to the one with the pecans—"represents the flavored bourbon and would go on the bottle."

"May I?" I gesture to the tablet.

She slides it over. "It's a rough sketch. I think the lines should be thinner, so it looks more like a sketch drawing. You know what I mean?"

"I do and I love it." I stare at her, bewildered. "How did you come up with this on the spot?"

She shrugs again. "The black is rugged and sexy, like you. The pecans are simple and easy to understand. With the black, it stands out against the brown liquor. But the farm needs to be advertised, too. So I came up with the tag to showcase Livingston farms and the twine because it reminds me of hay and a farm."

"Sadie, you're brilliant."

The smile she gives me lights up her entire face. "I've never been brilliant before."

Before her, I hadn't been called that, either. "Can I hire you to do this in detail and to do it how you described?"

She stiffens. "You want to hire me?"

"If you're available. No pressure. I don't want to give your idea to someone else to take the credit. You designed it. And I think it's perfect for the label."

"Well, then, of course I'll do it. I'd be honored." Her posture softens, and her tender smile sends warmth through my chest.

I hold her gaze for a moment.

She takes the drink—I think to break eye contact with me—and sips more bourbon.

"You know what this would be awesome poured over? Pecan ice cream and a warm brownie." She closes her eyes and moans.

My mind reels with ideas from her comment. Ice cream. Millie and Everleigh make pecan ice cream this time of year. At a company dinner party over the summer, Millie and Everleigh made bourbon pecan ice cream sundaes for dessert. They'd made the ice cream prior, but that's not the point. The point is Everleigh already made this. I can use it to sell the idea on Daire. I can probably get Everleigh to agree with me because she loves bourbon pecan ice cream sundaes. It's why she chose to serve them. Holy shit! Excitement vibrates through my body.

"You just grew taller on that stool. What's going on in your mind?"

"Everything. Everything I need to make this dream happen. And all because of you. You." I cup her cheeks.

101

"And that beautiful, brilliant imagination." I kiss her forehead. Then her nose. Then her lips.

I hadn't planned to kiss her on the mouth, but now that I'm here, my lips pressed against her plump ones, I can't move away. She hasn't shoved me off her yet. I should disengage. This isn't what she wants. Only, she's not retreating.

My hands still hold her cheeks. I'm about to separate myself from one of my favorite parts of her when her lips open a little and she kisses me back.

I test this further and mimic her movements.

She kisses me again with more pressure and sweeps her tongue over my lips.

Before I can stop myself, I tilt her head and kiss her at a sensual angle. Her mouth opens more, and she releases a shuddering breath.

It sends a rush of blood straight to my dick. I kiss her harder and sweep my tongue across her bottom lip, asking—begging—for permission.

She opens enough for me to plunge in, and I do. The sweet taste of bourbon on her tongue has me on fire. My grip on her cheeks tightens. I stand and devour her with a desire I haven't felt from a kiss before.

She cups my hands and gives me her all, meeting my licks and thrusts. It's hot, wet, and greedy. She spreads her legs for me to slip between her thighs. Her hands go up my back, caressing my taut muscles. I'm so hard, my dick is trying to poke a hole in my pants.

Her breath races, and little moans keep escaping her throat. I can't remember a kiss ever causing me to lose control. And that's what I'm doing. If I don't stop this now, I'm going to hoist her onto the counter and fuck her right here.

Stop. Don't stop. Move away. Move closer.

She sucks my tongue into her mouth. I almost come.

Fuck!

I wrench away from her, my breath racing like I ran five miles on the treadmill. I wipe my mouth.

"Shit. Sadie, I'm so sorry." I can't look at her.

I can't believe I fucked up so badly. I've been doing so well. A fucking angel, not making a move on her last night or when I was at her house on the kitchen floor. I've done the right thing—until this moment. I've screwed up everything. I don't even know how to ask for forgiveness. I'm an asshole. I took advantage of the moment and her trust. I'm a piece of shit.

"I'm so sorry." I walk off, get in my car, and drive to the nearest bar.

Chapter 13

Sadie

With the tip of my boot, I shove off the deck, sending me and the porch swing in motion. The rocking is soothing, like a baby in a cradle.

This back deck meets all my needs. A lake view through scattered red, green, and orange trees. The morning sun casting peach and gold across the sky and sparkling in the water. A crisp breeze, carrying the scents of pine, dried leaves, and all that is nature.

The swing is more of a daybed, covered in pillows. I found blankets in a chest nearby, the only items not weatherproof. It's cozy, perfect, except for the fact that I can't keep thinking about Easton and if he's ever had sex on this swing.

Knowing the truth could ruin this special outdoor escape for me because I want it to be virgin territory. And I want him to have sex with me on it. But that's crazy thinking, and I shouldn't go there.

I touch my mouth, recalling the moment he kissed me, the softness of his lips, the way he took control and swirled his tongue to a sensually choreographed dance. A dance that could lure any woman from her senses and into his bed. Not that he has to lure anyone. They come willingly.

I really wish he wouldn't have kissed me, though. Because now I know how good it feels to be in his arms and to be desired by him. I know how skilled he is and can't stop fantasizing about those kisses on other parts of my body. It would be a moment in heaven and nothing more.

Easton isn't capable of more. I'm not angry that he kissed me. It was an accident brought on by excitement. I'm smart enough to know the moment caught him off guard as much as his kiss took me by surprise.

My label idea and sketch for his bourbon was one of those stars-aligned occurrences that happened at the right time in the right way, and all was one with the universe.

That rarely occurs and has only happened once before. The night after I left here when I first met Easton. I'd thought about what I wanted on the entire drive back to Atlanta. I manifested, wished it, used it to distract me from other worse visualizations—like my tire blowing and forcing me to take a deserted exit, where a serial killer lives in a cabin in the woods and attacks me while I'm searching for a cell signal and help.

Instead, I kept those nightmares at bay by picturing my future, the man I'm meant to marry, the wedding, and even the house we'd live in back in Honeycomb or even Oakville, where Everleigh lives. She and I would have families and raise our babies together to be best friends, just like we are. I focused on making this happen so badly I stopped breathing and grew lightheaded from lack of oxygen. Not wise for a single woman driving through rural Georgia.

When I reached Atlanta, the traffic pulled me from my manifesting until I arrived home, safely parked in the garage to my complex. I'd just entered my condo, and only had time to text my mom thanks for feeding Detective Pickles and for watering my plants, when a text from my ex brightened my phone. His number was the same from high school.

Dash: Hey beautiful. It's been a minute. I'm living in Atlanta now. New to the city. I'd love to see you and catch up. Let me know when you're free.

He was my first of many things. My first serious relationship, first sexual experience, first homecoming and prom date, first boyfriend I imagined marrying, and my first real heartbreak. We separated because we went to different colleges in different states. It was the right thing to do, but that didn't make it easy. For him to contact me, after I'd visualized my little heart out for nearly two hours had to mean something. Right?

I texted him back, playing it cool, and agreed to meet him that Friday. We were sitting on my couch after joining his friends at a sports bar for drinks, darts, and pool. Dash was always the life of the party. It was as if no time had passed between us.

"I've thought about you over the years." He rested his hand behind me on the back of the couch.

"You have?"

"Yeah. You were my longest relationship. My best relationship."

"But you've had serious relationships since me?" I sipped the organic coffee I'd made us.

"I have, but none were for as long or as special." He scooted closer and covered my hand with his. "This might sound crazy, but I always knew we'd end up together."

"End up?" He didn't mean what I thought he meant.

"Yes. End up together. Married with a couple of kids down the road."

"Are you drunk?" I sat my coffee on the table and felt his forehead for a fever, because that made sense.

He laughed, his dimples appearing on both cheeks. His baby blues shone brightly on a face I knew so well, matured only a little and for the better. "Sadie. You must remember. We used to talk about getting married all the time."

"I remember." My cheeks heated at those and other intimate memories of us.

He brushed the backs of his fingers over my warmed cheeks. "Some things are meant to be. You and I make the best team. We always have."

I believed him, too. It was all I knew. But I have never, in all my life, out of all the guys I dated, including Dash, experienced a kiss as explosive as Easton's. It was cataclysmic in the best way. Bigger than stars aligning. A stellar collision that started at my lips and ended in my panties—and it was just a kiss.

I have to stop thinking about it.

I grab my phone and resume my search for a sexy shirtless male. Thirty minutes later of stock photo scrolling and I've yet to find a man who's even remotely sexy enough. On Pinterest, I've found plenty of celebrities and models, but those pictures aren't legally available to use on a romance cover.

Ugh. I drop my head on a pillow, close my eyes, and give the swing another push.

"No murder marathon today?" A deep, scratchy voice reaches my ears.

I flinch at the unexpected interruption but quickly relax when I open my eyes to find Easton standing at the back door several feet away.

"It's a bit early for murder," I tease, because it's never too early or late for a good Dateline episode. Lots of women feel this way. I've seen their social media posts about their love of real-life murder/crime shows and podcasts. It's totally normal.

He strolls over and stops at the swing, halting the motion of it with his leg.

I bend to see where the wood frame hit him. Just below his knee on his upper shin. "Didn't that hurt?"

He glances down, his wavy bangs falling over his eyes, and shrugs. When he looks up to meet my gaze, I notice his eyes are red.

"Did you sleep?"

He didn't come home—that I'm aware of.

"A little." He stares over my head at the trees on the side of the property and takes a deep breath. "Can we talk?"

"Yeah." I straighten and hang both my legs over the edge, giving him room to join me. Not that it would have made a difference had I remained in my sideways, one knee bent up on the cushion position. The swing is big enough for four.

He lowers onto the thick mattress and leans against the pillows along the back. His clothes are the same ones he wore last night, with an added corduroy jacket to escape the morning chill. He looks like he's been to a bar, but he doesn't reek of liquor or cigarette smoke.

"Where were you?" It slips out. I don't expect him to answer.

"A friend's house."

And by friend, I'm sure he means woman. Ugh. Before

he brings up our kiss, which I'm certain is what he wants to talk about, I take over, hoping to extinguish the topic before things get more awkward, or worse, he feels the need to explain how it was an accident and regrets it happening.

"It's okay. You don't have to feel bad about kissing me. It didn't mean anything. You were excited, and the moment got the better of you. Consider it erased from my mind. Like it never happened." I pat his knee. There I fixed it. "We can go back to how we were. No harm done." I pat his knee again, as if I need to touch him. I don't. I touched him before we kissed plenty. This means nothing.

Silence stretches between us, and Easton's features bunch as if he's thinking real hard. For a response to my awkward dismissal of last night?

My gaze catches on a bright red bird on a tree on the other side of the deck. I latch on to it as a distraction from the lingering silence.

"Look. A cardinal." I point and sit forward a little.

He blinks, looking even more confused by my sudden outburst. "What?"

"A cardinal. Did you see it?"

He follows my finger, but he still seems a bit dazed. "No."

I shrug and sit back. "You probably see them all the time."

"Sadie, I, uh..." He brushes his hair from his face, looking even more sexy and rugged with his thicker scruff and disheveled locks.

What lucky lady got to run her fingers through his hair last night?

His brows form a deep V, his torn expression making me curious as to what he's struggling to say. He opens his mouth and turns at the waist toward me. His hand bumps my phone, which lies between us. The screen brightens with a picture of a half-naked man, stretching in the sun.

"What is this?" He picks up the phone. "New screensaver?"

I could be wrong, but it seems like he's using the phone as a distraction from what he was about to say. Aren't we a pair?

"It's not a screen saver. I'm looking for a sexy man with brown hair and gray eyes."

"That's specific." He hands me the phone, his tone clipped.

"It's for a client. She wants a man who looks like her book character. The problem is this is the best I can find, and it's crap. These guys are not attractive. They're either too plain, too bulky, too skinny, or too feminine. It's impossible to find an attractive man in stock photos unless I cut off his head, and she wants his face, so that's not an option," I vent and sigh. "I shouldn't have taken the job."

"It's for a book cover?" He glances at the phone.

I nod and stare at the man on the bright screen. "Maybe if I use an app to tweak his face into something more chiseled..."

"They have an app for that?"

"Maybe." Hopefully. I sigh again. "If her budget was higher, I could buy a professionally photographed picture of a model. But she's strapped and a returning client, so I want to make this work for her. I just don't know if I can make his face better or his hair longer."

He chuckles. "That's a lot to change. I think you need to keep looking."

I lower my phone to the cushion and sigh for the third and final time. That's my limit. "If her book was about a sexy serial killer, any of these guys would do. But it's a rugged cowboy wolf shifter who's the most gorgeous man in his pack. He has to be mega-hot."

"Mega-hot, huh?" He crosses his arm and draws his lips in. "Let me think."

I turn to him. "Do you know someone? If you did, I would love you forever." That came out wrong. "I would be super grateful."

His features relax into a humorous expression, and he lowers his arms. "Sorry. I don't know anyone who fits that description."

I nudge his arm with my shoulder. "You got me all excited for nothing."

He smirks and opens his mouth but closes it before speaking a word.

Is he afraid to tease me now? "Don't do that." I sit up and face him.

"Do what?"

"Stop yourself from teasing me. I know that's what you were about to do. I love that part of you. It's fun. I don't want you to stop just because we kissed."

His gaze narrows on me like he's trying to read my thoughts. Easton isn't someone who's short on words. His lack of responses would be concerning if I hadn't just noticed something. This broody expression he has going on, combined with his scruff and corduroy tan jacket. Add jeans, no shirt, and a cowboy hat and we have a sexy wolf shifter.

"Don't move or change your expression." I grab my phone and snap a ton of pictures before I lose this vision.

"What are you doing?" he asks, concerned.

"I found my model."

"No." He shakes his head.

"Yes."

"No." He leans forward, like he's about to stand.

I press my hand to his thigh, stopping him from getting away. "Yes."

His wheel-spoke-brown eyes lock with mine in challenge.

"You owe me."

"How do you figure that?" A sexy grin tilts his lips, and I know—hope—he's returning to his teasing self.

That smirk is everything I need for this cover—sinful and wolfish.

"You owe me for the help I gave you with the bourbon label." He knows I'm right. "Fair is fair."

He leans close enough to kiss me.

I freeze in place.

"Nothing about us is fair." His breath brushes my lips.

I fight a shiver and repress the urge rushing my insides, telling me to kiss him.

He shifts away, freeing me from his spell, and stretches his arms high above his head. Even that looks sexy on him.

I openly gawk, my brain busy making mental notes of poses I want for him.

"Will you be ogling me like this the whole time you're doing the photo shoot?"

"Probably. It's so easy for you to look sexy. You move and it works. I don't know why I didn't think of this sooner. But I won't be taking the pictures. My neighbor is a photographer and owes me for feeding her cat last month. I'd need her soon, though. That could be a problem." I lift my phone to text her.

Easton lowers my hand before I can send her a message.

"I haven't agreed yet," he says with a grin.

"Will you do it for me, please?" I press my hands together, sandwiching my phone, and give him puppy eyes. "Will you be my model and pose for me half naked?"

"Which half?"

"The top half."

"Pity. My best feature is in my pants."

I giggle and cover my flaming face. Why does he make me blush so much? "I'll take your word for it."

His gaze drops to my lips, then he wipes his mouth and stands. "Tell me something... What do you want to do with this sex-book-cover side business?"

"Romance book covers." And hello, one-eighty. "What's this about?"

"It's a simple question." He crosses his arms and leans against the wood deck railing. "What do you want to do with it?"

I shrug. "I don't know."

"Yes, you do."

"No. I don't," I say, a bit annoyed.

"Do you like your job?"

"Yes."

"Is it your dream?"

"Of course not. You know my dream. I want to marry, raise a family, and live in a small town. It might not sound exciting to people like you, but to me, it sounds like home."

An endearing smile curves his lips. "I do know that. I was talking about your dream *job*?"

"Oh. Right." I think for a minute. "I guess my dream job would be to have a successful book cover business. I'd love to do more fantasy covers. They're so pretty and can be so intricate in design. I like making author and brand logos, too."

"And what's preventing you from making this dream come true?"

So much about him reminds me of Daire right now. I don't point that out. He'd take it the wrong way. "Clients, putting more time toward it, building my platform and social media presence for the business."

"Everything you do for your stepdad's company, then?"

"Yes."

"So you have the skills to do it."

Not a question, but I answer. "Yes."

"Can you put more time toward this dream?"

I frown at my bare ring finger, thinking of the engagement plans and vacation Dash and I were going on in less than two weeks. A vacation I need to either cancel, go on alone, or offer to my ex. I won't be planning a wedding now either or looking for a place for Dash and me to live and finally start our lives together as husband and wife.

The tears that form in my eyes aren't for the loss of Dash, but the disappointment he ended up being, the time I put toward us, and the promise for the dream future I'd hoped to finally achieve.

"I have a lot more time to put towards it now."

Easton lowers in front of me and cups my hand. "I think it would be good for you to focus on yourself for a while. Push yourself to try new things and pursue new dreams."

And here it is. Easton, in one of his rare moments, where he opens up and lets out his heart. "I like you best when you're like this."

"What's *this*?"

"All of you, and not just a piece of you. The piece you share the most but that hides the best parts of you."

Emotions stir in his eyes. Surprise, fear, admiration. He holds my gaze for a long moment, his warm hands cocooning my fingers. "I'll do it. I'll get naked and pose for you, but I have one condition."

"Okay," I draw out the word.

"No photographer. You have to take the pictures."

"But I'm not a professional. I don't know what I'm doing. I don't want to mess it up."

"It's me, baby." He winks. "How could you mess this up?"

I roll my eyes, the way I often do around him, and lean back, my hand slipping from his. Moments pass as I consider his requirement. Then, I blow out a noisy breath. "All right. But you have to do exactly what I tell you to do. You have to flirt with the camera. You have to give me bedroom eyes and help me however I need. These have to be porn worthy."

He stands, his thick brows arching high. "This is sounding better and better. Maybe I can get a few of you—"

"No."

"Just in your bra and panties. Not completely nude."

"No." I stand, my phone in hand.

"It's not like I haven't seen you naked."

I step close and peer up into his eyes. "That didn't count because I wasn't aware I was naked, and you were helping me as a friend, so you shouldn't have been looking."

"I only caught glimpses because I *wasn't* trying to look. That's what the pictures are for, so I can see what I missed."

A smear of red near the collar of his jacket catches my attention. It's not blood. He hasn't shaved and his skin is otherwise flawless. It could be ketchup, or worse, lipstick—a reminder that he could have been with another woman last night. I don't want to be jealous, but I am.

I step back and scoff. "What are pictures compared to the real thing?"

His brows bunch together. "Are you offering your naked body to me?"

"What? No. I'm referring to the women you sleep with regularly. Last night for example."

He pinches his brows and sighs. "You are a confusing woman, Sadie. The most confusing." A text sounds on his phone. He removes it from his pocket and reads the screen.

"It's from Steven," he says, as if I should know who that is.

"Who?"

"The PI looking into your attacker."

"Oh." I hug myself against a sudden chill in my bones.

I hadn't thought about that night since I got here. It was only a matter of time before it caught back up to me. I've been so occupied and distracted by Easton, Everleigh, the change of scenery, my day job, murder marathons, and working on my book cover designs, it had slipped my mind. For that, I'm thankful, especially to Easton for letting me crash his life.

And I have. I need to remember that. If it weren't for me, he would have had his sex partner in his house last night, I'm sure. Instead, he stayed out after kissing me. I don't want to be mad about that, but when I think of those lips on mine and then on another woman shortly after, a fire burns in my chest.

"Sadiecakes?" Easton touches my arm.

I blink and focus on him. His phone is down by his side. "Yeah?"

"Are you okay?"

"Yep. Just lost in thought for a second. What'd he say?"

"He's still looking into it and just wanted to keep me updated. It's a lot to find with little to go on."

"That's what the police said, too."

"He won't stop until he finds something. I promise."

I give him a grateful smile. "Thank you. I appreciate it

and for you having me as a house guest. It's been a good distraction."

He picks an orange leaf from my flannel jacket, the color blending in with the brown, tan, and burnt orange plaid. It must have fallen on me when I was on the swing.

"When do you want to do this photo shoot?"

"When are you free?"

"It's supposed to warm up a little tomorrow afternoon. It'd be easier for you to go topless."

I snort. "You mean it'd be easier for *you* to go topless."

"I don't have any issues with that."

"How do you feel about full frontal?"

"I'm game, if you are."

Of course he is. I laugh and walk toward the door to go inside. This man is too much. "Tomorrow. 1:00 p.m. I'll meet you by the dock."

"Where are you going?" he asks but doesn't follow me.

"To help Everleigh. I'll be back later."

In the reflection of the windows, I catch him watching me enter the house. His focus is on my ass, which happens to look phenomenal in these jeans.

When the door closes behind me, I glance over my shoulder to find him still staring at me. That gaze is dangerous, enticing even, like the Pied Piper, but instead of a magic pipe he lures women with his seductive eyes.

He said I was trouble at my condo. Truth is, I'm in trouble whenever he's around. Worried I'll do something reckless, worried I'll ruin what we have, worried I'll upset Everleigh for making a dumb mistake if I do let my guard down around Easton.

My phone chimes with a text on my way to my car. I snatch my purse from a hook near the front door. I could have asked Easton for a ride in the UTV, like he'd promised, but he seemed to want distance from me too—hence, his staying on the deck and not following me inside.

I get in my car, start the engine, and read the text. My heart drops to the seat.

Dash: I miss you. It's killing me. I miss knowing you are always there and having you by my side. Forgive me. I'll give you what you want. I'll even buy us a house in a small town outside of Atlanta. As small as we can find, so I can work in the city, but you can have your dream. My dream is to have you as my wife. I noticed you haven't canceled our upcoming vacation. Come on it with me and give me a second chance.

Shit. The phone drops from my shaking hand and falls between my thighs. Tears blur my vision. I can't figure out why. Shock? Happiness? Surprise?

Is he for real? Does he miss me or just having me by his side at bars and out with his friends, like he likes? Why does he only see *me* as his wife? He's barely around me anymore. Why did he have to send this when I was moving on? I made my choice to end it. I'd meant it. It wasn't a manipulative effort to get him back.

Ugh. I hit the steering wheel.

Can he change? Can he be what I need? Should I give him another chance? If I don't, will I look back and regret it?

I need help. I need Everleigh. I wipe my vision clear and drive to her house.

Chapter 14

Sadie

I'm not a professional photographer by any means, but Easton was right when he implied all his pictures are good because it's him.

He stands by the lake, a few green and orange trees to his left. The sunlight reflects off his sculpted back muscles. His bicep bulges from where his elbow is bent, his hand touching the rim of the cowboy hat he wears sometimes when he helps out at the farm. I'd love to get some pictures of his sweaty body doing that someday.

His profile is pure perfection. How can his nose and lips be so sensual? His long lashes curl up in a way that accentuates his seductive gaze. It's like he wants to have sex with the tree in the distance, the one I told him to focus on, and all I want to do is mount him like a wolf on a full moon. I've never behaved this way, but then, I've never done a half-nude photo shoot with an Adonis like Easton. I've never attracted a man like him. Everleigh's beauty attracted the mega-hot guys. Not that I dated dogs. The cute guys had an interest in me. I tend to draw the preppy ones, although I don't know why.

Easton is not preppy. He's rugged and sexy and more manly than any guy who's ever given me the time of day. I once asked Dash why he never got jealous when I hung out with Easton. He said he wasn't the jealous type and that he trusted me. It seemed like a mature answer brought on by confidence. Now, I wonder if he simply didn't care.

"Want that full frontal?" Easton teases and turns to me. His nipples are puckered into tight little balls. The sun is close to dipping behind the trees. Even though it had warmed up this afternoon, it's chillier now, and he's bare chested.

"Wait!" I rush toward him. "Sorry. Don't move." I stop a few feet away and take a picture of him with a blurred filter that showcases his chest in the last of the sun's rays.

"Got it. You can move." I race to snatch his jacket from a blanket I laid on the pine needles and leaf-covered ground. Other props are there, too. A blue button down. Leather bracelets, and a belt with a thick buckle that screams cowboy—both he had from a previous Halloween costume. A pair of sexy boots and black jeans in case the blue jeans he's wearing now don't work for my client.

I run the jacket to him, meeting him on his way to me. "Here, put this on before you get sick."

He laughs. "It's not winter, Sadiecakes."

"I know, but I'd hate for you to catch a cold because of me." I find his long-sleeved shirt and toss it to him before sitting on the blanket and perusing the pictures.

He drops beside me, his shirt in his hand. "How did they turn out?"

"They're amazing. I honestly don't know which one I'm going to use. Maybe the last one. You looked so freaking hot. But the one before that was panty-melting, too. Your body is like an erotica novel. I could make a lot of money off these."

"Really? How so?"

"Cover designers and authors pay big bucks for male models. And you, my friend, are the hottest male model I've ever seen. You didn't even try. You just moved and I got the perfect shot. It's like you were born for this."

He leans back on one hand, his jacket open, his abs on display. The grin on his face is as charming as it is sinful.

God help me.

"You're saying you can sell my pictures to be used for romance covers?"

"Yes. But not just covers, they'd use them in videos, and ads, and social media posts. You'd be famous."

"I don't care about that."

"You might when women start stalking you on social media, or worse, following you home."

"First of all, they already follow me home, and if it would draw attention to the farm, I don't see the harm in it."

"They'd draw attention to *you*. If women came to the farm, it'd be to see you or with the hope of seeing you."

"It's still business." He raises his knee and rests his wrist on it.

It's another picture perfect pose. I snap it.

He peers sideways at me, his expression saying I thought we were done.

"Sorry. I can't help it. I'm considering taking up your offer on nudes."

He arches a brow. "I suggest the hot tub or inside for those."

"Hot tub?"

He points to the gazebo slightly hidden behind a row of holly bushes in the near distance.

"Nice." I keep my gaze on it, picturing him reclined in the water. "That could work. Or I could get creative. No full frontal. That would be selling porn. But full-body with discretion would be enticing. I'd have to cover your manhood with a leaf or something." I snatch a red one from the blanket and lay it over his cock. "Perfect."

Amusement dances in his eyes. "I can't believe you kept this side of yourself hidden from me."

"I didn't hide it. I just didn't share it." Except with Everleigh. "You kept your bourbon business a secret."

"True." He removes the leaf and tosses it on the ground. "About this money you can make. Could you put it toward your cover design business?"

He didn't say sex book cover. Progress. "I suppose I could." I stretch out my legs and cross them at the ankles, my hiking boots rustling the dead leaves.

"Around how much could you make from a photo?"

His business mindset shows he's becoming more like Daire.

"Anywhere from eight hundred to sixteen hundred."

"Huh." He rubs his chin. "Could you use the pictures you took today?"

"Yeah, but, Easton, I don't want to exploit you or the farm. I'm not sure Daire would see it as good for the business."

"Valid point." He rubs the scruff on his chin. "You said authors like pictures of men with no heads. Crop mine out of the picture."

"They do that if the guys are ugly or not as attractive as their bodies. Your face is as perfect as your body. I'd pleasure myself to either." I slap my hand over my mouth, my cheeks ablaze. It's one thing to tease like this with Everleigh, but I've never spoken like this in front of Easton or any man.

A wicked grin stretches across Easton's gorgeous face. "Will this pleasuring be happening tonight?"

"I was teasing." I rise to my knees and turn toward the duffle bag on the blanket behind us. Easton used it to bring the props down here. I have to get on all fours to reach it. With one hand, I stuff the items inside.

"I've decided I'll need compensation for these pictures," Easton says. "Now that I know how much I'm worth."

Still on my hands and knees, I glare over my shoulder.

He's leaning back on his elbow, again looking like a God put on this planet to be drooled over. His eyes don't connect with mine, though. They're fixed on my ass.

"We had a deal." I push off my hands to sit on my heels. "An even exchange."

"That was before I knew you could sell pictures of me. Don't worry, this won't cost you money. But if you're game, it will cost you a piece of yourself."

Damn him. He knows how to present an offer with enough intrigue that I can't ignore it.

I rest my hands on my legging-covered thighs. "Fine. What's the compensation?"

"Depending on how many pictures you use now and in the future, I think one thousand is a fair agreement."

"One thousand what?" Sweat forms on my upper lip. What on earth could I give him of value if not money?

"Kisses."

"What?" I squint.

He sits up, putting his face dangerously close to mine. "I want my payment in kisses. From you. In case it's not clear."

Kisses? For some reason, my brain can't compute this request. He wouldn't suggest we kiss regularly. That goes against everything we've decided.

"But...we can't. We're...friends. It wouldn't be good for either of us."

"Oh, it'll be good. I can guarantee that."

"But we decided we're not going there."

"I changed my mind," he says, as if it's no big deal.

"You can't just change your mind."

"I can, and so can you."

My heart drums in my ears and flutters erupt inside me. "It's impossible. We'd have to be together for one thousand days." I'm only here for two weeks, less than that now.

"Not if we kiss more than once a day, and I'll give you bonus points for doing more."

"More?" My cooch twitches like it's excited at this idea. Traitor.

"Yes, more." He tilts his head like he's deciding which angle to come at to get his first kiss.

"I don't know..." Am I considering this? I close my eyes.

He uses his finger to uncurl my hands, which are in tight fists. I hadn't realized I balled them up. His strokes are soft and provocative against my palm. I feel the caress between my thighs.

"I've been thinking about your situation," he whispers near my ear, while stroking my fingers. "Now that you're trying new things, maybe you should try the single life on for size. Have you ever just dated without the need for more?"

I consider his questions, but it's hard to think now that his finger is caressing my wrist, just under the hem of my sweater. "I've dated, but the expectation that it will lead to something more was always there."

"This could be good for you."

I grasp for any reason not to do this because it's sounding like a really good idea. "At my condo, you said you wouldn't touch me and that you wanted to respect our friendship."

"I do. But I hadn't kissed you back then, and honestly..."

He moves close enough so that I can feel his breath on my ear. "I can't get that kiss out of my mind."

Him, too? My eyes spring open. I blink at the trees ahead while Easton brushes my hair behind my shoulder and runs his nose ever so gently along my neck.

Shivers break out over my skin. I need to process this new information and decide what to do before I give in to this without rational thought.

"How long do you want the kissing and messing around to go on for?"

"Do we have to put a time limit on it? Can't we just have fun?"

A cool breeze blows dried leaves across the blanket and onto my lap, distracting me enough to gain clarity. I lean away from his dangerous lips. "Fun that leads to nothing."

"That's the point," he says, as relaxed as ever. "The stress and pressure of dating for more are eliminated when you mess around for fun."

And like that, my clarity is muddled again. "I've never thought about it like that." I definitely put pressure on myself and the guys I date, because I'm always worried if it will last or work out or leave me heartbroken.

"Dash texted," I blurt, grasping at any reason not to agree with Easton's proposal. "He still wants to marry me."

"What?" He stiffens. "When did he text you?"

"Yesterday."

"Did you talk to him?"

"Not over the phone, just through texts." Brief texts where I told him I needed time to think.

He runs his hand through his rumpled locks. "How do you feel about it? I mean, do you want to go back to him?"

"Everleigh asked me the same thing."

"And?"

"Part of me wants the dream back. He says we can move to a small town outside of Atlanta. He wants us to go on the vacation we have planned and pick up where we left off. I asked him why he wants to marry me because I'm not sure I know. He said I'm marriage material and would make a great wife."

"He's not wrong." Easton frowns and plucks a brown leaf from my lap. "You're that kind of woman. Strong, fun, beautiful, sweet, and kind. If I were a marrying man, you'd have been mine long ago. I wouldn't have fucked around and risked losing you. I would have put a ring on it, ruined you for all other men"—he winks—"and worshiped you every day from then on."

My heart warms from all the compliments, and my mind sticks on certain parts, like when he said he'd 'ruin' me —with his sexual talents, no doubt—and 'worship' me. The way he declared them with such conviction has me hot and tingly all over.

Dash's response didn't have half the romantic sentiment or possessiveness that Easton's has. I should expect romance from the man I plan to marry, shouldn't I? The possessiveness Easton shows isn't something I've experienced with a man. I'd be lying if I said I didn't like it.

"What are you thinking about, Sadiecakes?" He brushes the top of my hand with the leaf.

"Why do you call me that?"

He shrugs. "It's a term of endearment, like sweetcakes. It fits you."

Dash never called me anything other than my name or babe.

"Do you use endearments for all your friends?"

"Only you." He touches my nose with the leaf.

"I was thinking I need a break from the life I've been

living." I answer his question finally. "And that maybe your plan makes sense. But how do we do this and not ruin our friendship?"

His eyes brighten, and it takes him a moment to respond. "That's easy. I've never lost a friendship over sex."

"Never?"

"Maybe once or twice, but only because those women wanted more. And that was a long time ago. I'm good at what I do. You'll find that out soon enough. And I've learned to be very clear about my intentions. I don't give false hope, and I choose women who understand that."

"But I'm not like the women you date. The women you have sex with—let's just call it what it is. I move slowly and only sleep with a guy after I'm certain it's not a one-night stand. I don't even know if I can have sex without complicating things."

He gives that a long thought, his gaze searching my face for an answer I'm not sure he'll find. "Then we'll keep things as they are until you know you can handle it."

That day may never come. I don't say that. Instead, I nod.

Chapter 15

Easton

I finish rolling up the sleeves of my business shirt. It's open at the collar, no tie, and I'm wearing dress pants. My appearance is to impress my brother without looking too over the top. I want him to take me seriously and to see I'm coming to him as a professional and not a carefree sibling with an outrageous idea.

When I enter the kitchen, Sadie stands at the island drinking coffee and reading on her phone. Her casual outfit shouldn't be sexy, but that off-the-shoulder cropped sweatshirt shows off her flat stomach. Those matching joggers make her strawberry-shaped ass beg to be grabbed or spanked. Her hair falls in messy waves around her pretty face. It's not as long as the other women I date, but it brushes her pert breasts right at her nipples in a way that draws the gaze.

I wipe my salivating mouth. "Morning."

She flinches—always so jumpy—and sets down her coffee. Her hazel-green eyes travel the length of my body, and she whistles. "Where are you going dressed to impress this lovely morning?"

"I have a meeting with Daire."

She gasps and cups her phone between her hands. "Are you ready? Do you need any help with anything?"

I love her enthusiasm. The fact that she's always willing to help makes her that much sweeter. "I'm good, and I'm ready. I'm excited actually."

"You should be. He's going to love the idea."

"Let's hope so."

"I'm prepared to hit him over the head with one of Everleigh's baking sheets if he doesn't get it. But I don't see how he couldn't. It's a no-brainer fit." She strolls to me, her gaze holding mine. She fixes my collar and cups my cheeks in her dainty hands.

I stop breathing as she draws me down to her level.

She plants a tender kiss on my cheek. "For luck. Not that you need it."

This flirty dance between us has me all out of sorts. I consider turning my head and claiming those sultry lips again, but then she lowers her hands and takes a step back.

"I'll be here when you get home."

That promise stirs warmth in my chest. No one has ever waited for me after something important, certainly not at my house. I like knowing someone will be here and how that someone is Sadie. No one else would do.

"Thanks." I straighten my spine, comforted in so many ways—ways that are strange and new. She's rooting for me. She wants me to succeed, not only for me but because she believes in what I'm doing and the idea I'm selling to Daire.

"Want any coffee before you go?" She turns toward the built-in coffee machine.

"I had some upstairs."

Her brows pucker, and she glances at the second-floor landing.

"I have an espresso maker in my room, in the office section. It's two separate spaces." She wouldn't know because she hasn't seen it. Few people have.

"That's convenient." She returns to the counter and her coffee.

"What do you have planned for today?" I ask, curious.

"Work. For my stepdad and my cover business."

This is why I grilled her about following her dream. She often refers to her day job as that or work for her stepdad. She never calls it *her* job. She doesn't hold passion for it. Her eyes don't light up the way they do when she talks about book covers. Sure, she's good at it. It's easy for her, but she deserves to do something creative. With her skills and talent, I'm certain she'll be a success.

"Want to go out later? To celebrate." I didn't plan to ask her that, but I would like to celebrate, if all goes according to plan, and I think she'd like to get out of the house and go beyond the farm and the estate.

She frowns. "I'd love to, but we have dinner with Everleigh and Daire tonight. Remember? She texted me during the photo shoot?"

"Maybe."

I don't remember. I was too distracted by Sadie. She kept touching me, posing me, undressing me, and dressing me in different outfits. She didn't realize how many times she touched my stomach or pecs, her hand lingering on my skin. She'd have apologized or been embarrassed. But she likes touching me. It's more than obvious to me. To her? Not so much.

"We can do something after dinner, though, if you want?"

The flirty smile on her face has my mind going to places

I doubt she's thinking. I wouldn't mind celebrating between her legs.

"What did you have in mind?"

"A bar? There's a sports bar in Honeycomb that's pretty popular." She wipes a drip of coffee from the counter.

"Would that be fun for you?" My guess is she's used to having to answer that way, never choosing something that interests her.

"This isn't about me. It's for you. I can have fun anywhere."

I believe that. But she shouldn't *have* to have fun for other people. "What would you choose if we were celebrating your new start with your business?"

She glances at the wall of windows to the backyard. "Maybe get a bottle of wine and explore that tiny house floating in the middle of the lake. By boat, of course."

No one would dare swim in this water during November.

"Now that sounds like a fun night." Would it end with her sharing some of her body with me?

"Really?"

Her shocked expression confuses me. I'd love nothing more than to have her alone with zero distractions.

"We'd have to turn off our phones," I say. "House rules. That place is for watching stars and enjoying nature."

She sips her coffee, her cheeks turning light pink. Could her mind be as dirty as mine? When she mentioned pleasuring herself to my pictures, I was shocked in the best way. I wouldn't have guessed she was the masturbating type. The secrets she keeps continue to surprise me.

"It's a date, then."

Her response pours through me like an Old Fashioned, smoky and sweet.

My phone vibrates in my pocket. I turn off the alarm I set for this exact reason. Sadie doesn't know how distracting she is to me.

"Time to go." I turn for the garage.

"You've got this," she calls out in her sweet voice.

I pump my fist in the air and exit the house, ready to prove myself but nervous as fuck. Daire can be harsher than my dad at times. I would have waited until the baby is born. I'm certain he'd say yes to anything on that day. But now is the time. The product is ready, and my connections are eager and on board. Now is the time. I just have to convince Daire of that.

* * *

I stand at the end of the conference table, one room down from Daire's office at the farm. It's on the second floor of the store and café, where Everleigh and our other baker Millie create and sell the sweetest desserts ever.

The presentation went flawlessly. Daire seemed interested at first, then a barrage of texts kept dinging his phone and distracting him. The last one was followed by him leaving the room for a moment and making a call.

"What do you think?" I gesture to the bottle of Bourbon and printed projections of sales and growth.

It's all in the presentation, but I want Daire to have something to sit on his desk, a tangible reminder of the product.

His phone dings again. I want to toss it from the room.

He reads the text and stands. "Today is not a good day for this."

"Seriously?" I knew this would happen.

"I need time to go over this and at present, we have a

situation with one of the pecan distributors. They're claiming we didn't ship the correct number of bags and— You don't need to hear this. But I need to deal with it. Let's revisit this later." He walks to the door.

I follow. "When? Later today? Tomorrow?"

He pauses, already out the open door on his way to his office. "With all we have going on right now, I think after the new year would be better."

No! "Daire." I'm on his heels. "This is ready now. Everything is ready now. It's the best time with the wedding venue and the inn. My investors could pull out of the deal if we wait until after the new year."

He stops behind his desk and meets my gaze. "I'm sorry. It seems like you put a great deal of work into this, but with the construction, the baby, and everything else, it's too much right now. I'm not saying never. Just wait a few months."

"I'm not asking you to do anything. I'll take care of it all; I already have. I just need your approval. Come on." I shuffle into the room when he sits in his big black chair. "Give me a chance to prove I'm not who I used to be. I'm smart, Daire. I can do this and bring in even more revenue for the farm. It'll be an expansion of what we already do."

He raises his hand, his focus half on his phone, half on me. "An expansion we don't need right now. The farm is more than lucrative for both of us. Keep doing what you're doing, and we'll revisit this in a few months."

I barely do anything. I help wherever I can. He has me go over spreadsheets and numbers sometimes, which is why I join the workers and get my hands dirty on occasion. But it's not enough for me to feel worthy. I guess that's what this comes down to. Worthiness, self-respect, and the respect from an older brother who chooses not to take me seriously.

"If I were anyone else other than your brother, you

wouldn't be this dismissive." I close the door and stomp down the stairs.

A few months, my ass. He'll say the same thing then. It'll be a merry-go-round of excuses that never lead to an approval. So much work went into this, and he treated it like I was a college dropout, taking the easy road through life.

If I'd have taken this anywhere else, to anyone else, they would have given me the respect and consideration I deserve. Hell, they would have bought it. Sadie is right. It's a brilliant idea. Daire should have thanked me and congratulated me for doing something worthy for once. He should have been proud.

Chapter 16

Sadie

Tonight's dinner isn't a festive occasion, but if Easton and I go out after to celebrate, I want to look like I'm celebrating him and his accomplishments.

I texted him hours ago, but he didn't reply. I wasn't sure if that was good or bad. He hasn't come home, either.

I check the time. We're supposed to be at Daire and Everleigh's in five minutes. I hate being late.

I call Easton.

He answers, then the call drops. Or he hung up. I'm about to call him again when he comes up from the basement wearing nothing but sweat shorts and sneakers. His sweaty skin glistens. Hot damn.

"How... When did you get home?" How did I miss seeing him? Was I in the shower? Doing my hair? I did spend extra time on myself.

"An hour ago." He chugs a bottle of Gatorade and walks to the fridge.

I follow him, my heels clicking on the wood floor. "I texted you."

He opens the fridge door and grabs a bottle of water, chugging that too. "I needed to release some steam."

Uh oh. At the island, across from him, I rest my hands on the cold stone counter. "I'm guessing Daire disappointed you."

He laughs, the sound dark and twisted. "You could say that."

"I'm sorry, Easton. I know how important this was for you."

He stares up at the ceiling, his neck and shoulder muscles flexing, as if reining in his anger. "He did what I thought he'd do. He didn't take me seriously. He didn't even try the fucking bourbon."

He swings around. When his gaze lands on me, his jaw drops a little. He walks around the island and drinks me in from head to toe. "Fuck me. Aren't you a sight."

Fuck him? With his tanned, glistening skin and six-pack abs, I'm thinking about it.

"Is this for the dinner?"

I almost lie and answer yes. "It's for you, actually, to—" I can't say the word celebrate now that we're not. I lower my head and shrug.

"Oh." He catches on. "Well, that's not happening. I should have known it wouldn't have worked out. Typical Daire, pushing me to be more and not seeing it when I am."

"Everleigh said he's been stressed lately, worried about everything. Maybe it has nothing to do with you. If he's overwhelmed and struggling to focus, it's, sadly family or close friends who get treated the worst because they know you won't abandon them. There's love there."

He sets the near empty water bottle on the counter and blows out a breath. "Do you always have to be so damn sweet?"

I open my mouth but close it when he stalks toward me with a predatory look, bare-chested and angry, although I don't think it's directed at me.

He touches the tie to my dress. The only thing holding it together. He tugs a little and watches my face for my reaction.

I want to stop him. I should. He's upset and not thinking. I also shouldn't be turned on by this, but God help me, because my panties are soaked. My breathing quickens when he pulls the tie, undoing the bow. The dress falls open, revealing my chocolate-colored bra and panties.

Again, he watches my face for my reaction. Will I stop him? Close my dress?

I do neither. I've never been so turned on before in my life, and he hasn't even touched me.

"Easton?" It's a desperate whisper.

"Turn around and face the island."

I hesitate for a second, then turn, giving him my back.

"Take off your dress." His voice sounds husky and on edge. "Sadie, show me that perfect ass."

I shiver and lower the dress, placing it on the counter. I'm wearing a thong.

He hisses out a curse and moves so close I can feel his body brushing mine, like a whisper. He sweeps my hair over my shoulder and runs his nose along my neck. I tilt my head, giving him better access, and grip the counter because I'm shaking.

"Sadiecakes, you smell good enough to eat," he breathes across my skin.

I sigh or moan. Who knows and who cares? Whatever this game is, I like it. I'm missing dinner. I haven't texted to say I'd be late. I might miss the dinner completely, which isn't me. And for the first time ever, I don't care.

In my ear, he says, "I didn't expect you to strip or stand here on display for me. I've half a mind to bend you over this counter, spank your sweet ass, and fuck you until we both see stars. To know you dressed up for me and wore this underneath..." He hisses, and then his warmth is gone, my skin suddenly chilled.

I wait for him to make his next move. I also don't trust myself not to collapse from desire and hormone overload. The anticipation is as much as a turn on as standing here almost naked for him.

Seconds tick by. He doesn't do or say anything.

The lusty fog starts to clear in my head. "Easton?" I glance over my shoulder. The room is empty.

What the hell? Where'd he go? I scan the massive space. He's nowhere.

My phone dings with two texts. I scramble to put my dress back on and grab my phone from the counter.

Easton: Had to get away before I did something you'll regret. I'm still waiting for you to tell me you can handle things. I told Everleigh I'm not making it to dinner. Have a nice time.

Everleigh: Easton isn't coming. Are you making it?

I glance upstairs still riding a wave of desire and frustrated as hell. As much as I want Easton to take me without me making up my mind, I appreciate him holding back. I imagine it was equally hard for him. I've never felt so desired before in my life. I could feel his need for me. And I liked it. I've never had a commanding lover. I never thought I'd want to, but Easton makes it different, appealing instead of scary. He'd never do anything I don't want. I trust him. So why am I not running upstairs to continue what he started?

My phone dings again.

Everleigh: Are you coming? If not, it's okay. You can tell me.

Argh. I'm being a shitty friend. I said I'd go to the dinner and I'm going. Maybe when I get back, Easton and I can talk or do more. I feel high and crazy and not like myself, but I also feel more alive than ever.

I reply to Everleigh that I'm heading over. I also text Easton that I'll be back later. On the way out, I stop in the garage and grab a bottle of the pecan bourbon, a plan in mind.

* * *

"That was amazing," I tell Everleigh.

"Thanks, but I can't take credit for any of it tonight. Not that I could make Veal Oscar and sweet lobster. That's all Olga. I couldn't decide between beef or seafood. She came up with this. My mind has been fuzzy lately, and I'm more tired than usual." She rubs her belly. "This little peanut is making me lazy and craving surf and turf."

Daire leans over, strokes her hair, and kisses her cheek. "It's hard work creating a human. Don't be so tough on yourself. It's perfectly fine to take it easy. Your body will thank you."

She kisses his chin, then his lips. I used to think he and Easton looked so much alike, but Daire is much more clean-cut.

No one has mentioned Easton yet. I want to bring up the topic of the bourbon I brought, but I don't want to look too obvious. If only Everleigh could try it or if I could have spoken to her before the dinner, when Daire wasn't around, I could have told her my plan. She would have thought it was worth a try.

"What's for dessert?" I say, "besides this wonderful Bourbon." I sip mine.

Everleigh's brows pull tight with a confused look. Is she on to me?

Daire leans back in his chair and swirls the liquid in his glass. "I was so hungry I haven't had a chance to appreciate it."

"He skipped lunch," Everleigh explains. "I hate when he does that, especially when Millie could have brought him up something."

"It was a busier than usual day." Daire sips the brown liquid. "This is really delicious." He sips more. "I don't think I've had anything like it." He eyes me. "You brought this?"

"I did. It's a new brand."

"New brand?" Daire eyes the bottle. "Can I see that?"

I pass it to him.

He reads the label and sits back with a laugh. "Did Easton send you with this?"

"No. He doesn't know I brought it. It was my decision. I really like it, and I wanted you to try it when you were able to enjoy it. Please don't tell him I brought you a bottle. He wouldn't be happy that I did."

He tastes more. "This is really good. I'm not sure about the label."

"That's just a prototype." I get my phone and show him the final label I sent Easton. "This is the label he approved."

"Wow. That's much more fitting. I like it a lot."

"It's perfect," Everleigh chimes in.

I smile at the table, trying to hide my excitement, and set down my phone.

"I need to try this bourbon." Everleigh reaches for Daire's glass. "A sip won't hurt the baby."

She takes the tiniest sip. "Oh, I like this much better than that Pappy stuff."

Daire laughs. "Pappy Van Winkle is the best."

"This is sweeter and not as spicy." She gives him back his glass. "Remember on Peaky Blinders how Tommy explained Gin is the drink ladies prefer or something like that? He must not have offered women pecan bourbon."

I nod. "I remember everything Cillian Murphy said in that show."

Everleigh nods.

We didn't watch it together, but after she and Daire binged it, she told me to watch it. Dash watched two episodes with me, but the rest I watched alone.

Daire drinks more bourbon. "I don't get what the fuss is about Cillian Murphy."

"It's his eyes," I say.

"And his accent," Everleigh adds.

"Irish?" Daire asks, seeming truly surprised.

She nods.

"And he's dangerous," I add.

Everleigh nods at that, too.

"You should not be interested in dangerous people," Daire says to me. "Has Easton spoken to Steven lately?"

"That's the PI, right?"

"Yeah."

"He hasn't found anything yet," I say.

"He will. Give him some time. Until then, I think staying here is good for you."

"I second that." Everleigh raises her hand and yawns.

"It seems like so long ago, even though it hasn't been a week."

"That's because you're here away from it all and you

can relax. If you were alone in that condo, you'd be buzzing with nerves. I know you, Sadie."

She's not wrong. "Do you think he'll know something by the end of next week?" I ask Daire.

"It's hard to say. Once he gets a lead, it's easier to find something and the process moves faster. This is a tough one, though, because there's barely a description."

"I know." I frown at the table.

"Don't worry. Steven doesn't quit. And in the meantime, you can stay for as long as you'd like. If Easton gets grumpy about having a house guest, we have room here."

"He's not grumpy at all." Tonight's sexy grumpfest seduction session aside. "He's been helpful in a lot of ways. He put a lot of work into this bourbon," I dare to say. "I've never seen him this passionate about anything, except maybe sex."

Everleigh almost spits out the water she's drinking.

Cecily, Olga's assistant, removes our dinner plates. "How was everything?"

"Delicious. Easton would have loved it." That man has a thing for meat. Maybe it's his inner wolf.

Everleigh narrows her eyes on me. "I wish he would have made it."

"That's my fault," Daire says. "I was a dick today. I didn't handle things well with him. He's not here because of me."

Everleigh covers his hand with hers. "You can always apologize. He'll understand."

"Did you hear his idea about offering a bottle of this with certain Inn packages or to guests here for a wedding or romantic getaway?"

"I don't remember that part."

"I love that idea," Everleigh hiccups. "Excuse me. It's the baby."

I laugh.

She tries to lean forward, but her belly only allows her to go so far. "I was planning on doing gift baskets with Champagne, but adding a bottle of our own Pecan Bourbon sounds appealing, too."

Daire sighs. "I really messed things up today."

"You can make it right." Everleigh squeezes his hand.

I wish Easton were here to see and hear this.

"I'll text him to meet me tomorrow and make it up to him."

My heart soars like a balloon taking flight. This is what I wanted for him. It's what he deserves. He wouldn't like it if I helped make this for him, though. He wants it to be because of his hard work, as it should be.

"Promise you won't tell him I brought the bourbon or told you anything. This is his deal. I don't want him to think I interfered."

Daire and Everleigh exchange a look then Daire says, "I won't tell him anything. I appreciate what you did, but you shouldn't have had to. I should have given him the time and attention he deserved. This is on me, and I'll fix it."

I sit taller, certain Easton will blow him away. The product he developed already has.

Cecily returns and serves us dessert. "Mrs. Everleigh's favorite. Cinnamon pecan ice cream over a warm blondie.

"Ooh!" Everleigh gasps after a first bite. "We could add an adult dessert to the menu at the inn and the café. This with a shot of pecan bourbon."

"Yes!" I raise my fist in the air. "I love that idea!"

"Well, shit. You two have this all worked out." Daire

eyes his wife and me. "I should bring you both to the meeting."

"Nope," Everleigh says. "It needs to be you and Easton. I know nothing."

"I know nothing, either." I splash some bourbon over my dessert, then take a bite. The cold ice cream with the warm blondie is heaven on my tongue. "Oh, man." I moan and imagine Easton licking bourbon or ice cream or the whole damn dessert from my skin. I moan again.

"Should we leave you alone?" Everleigh teases.

Daire's cheeks carry a red tint, his grin filled with wonder and amusement.

If I told them what I was really imagining, I'd probably get a lecture. We're grown adults, but Easton is a flirt, and I haven't said I could handle anything for a reason. I'm scared. What if I like this single life and give up on my dream to marry the right guy? What if I become a harlot? Or worse, what if I eventually regret it and grow to hate Easton? I can't imagine not having him in my life. So much to think about. He would say I'm over thinking. Maybe I am.

On my way out, Everleigh walks me to the door. "Before you go, can I ask you something?"

"Sure?" I adjust the dinner and dessert to-go bag that Cecily gave me. The thing is insulated.

"Are you aware that you've developed feelings for Easton?"

"As a friend? Yes. We've gotten close."

"And you don't think it's more than that?"

"Not at all." I laugh off her question. "I mean, he's sexy, and I'm not blind, but we're just friends." Who may start having sex soon. Oh God, am I that obvious?

She touches my arm. "You've been through a lot lately.

The breakup. The attack. Living here for a while. It's a lot. Your life is very controlled. You're a creature of habit. You make a schedule and stick to it. You alter it when necessary, but eventually you go back to being you. I love who you are."

"Do you think Dash loved—loves—who I am. How I am?" I'd rather stay home and watch Dateline than go to the sports bar.

"I think he's realizing what he lost. I also think you're very intuitive, but you tend to ignore that side. You second-guess your choices, always looking for the right answer. Sometimes there isn't one. Trust your gut to guide you."

Like she did with Daire. "It's good advice."

"But don't trust Easton's gut. It's connected to his penis, and while he's showing maturity and seriousness toward the business now, I don't think his attitude toward women has changed."

"I know it hasn't. You don't have to worry about me. He knows my boundaries and respects them."

"Good." She kisses my cheek, one hand on her belly. "See you soon. 'Night."

"Good night."

The roads seem darker on the way back to Easton's house. I don't see the moon. Rain drizzles on the windshield. I groan. Easton cleared out a spot in the garage for me. I haven't used it yet, not wanting to invade more of his life. Tonight, I will.

I pull into the garage. Easton's motorcycle is gone, but his car is here. I don't know if he moved the bike for me and stored it elsewhere or if he's out on it. That doesn't sound enjoyable in the chilly rain.

Inside, I take off my shoes and hang up my coat. The lights are off, and it's quiet. Is he gone? Maybe that's a good thing. The bourbon has me slightly buzzed and feeling free. If he came on to me, I would attack.

On my way upstairs, I stop on the second floor. His bedroom door is closed. I listen but don't hear anything.

"Easton?" I whisper. What am I doing? "Easton?"

After a few seconds, I go upstairs, strip myself, then fantasize about him taking me on the kitchen counter until I orgasm. I've never done that before. I've thought about it, but I usually watch murder and fall asleep instead. As good as the release is, it isn't enough to satisfy this new craving. I want Easton. I want him more each time we're together, and I fear nothing will make it go away.

Chapter 17

Sadie

I close my laptop, having finished my work for the day, which included checking in with Vanessa, making sure commission deposits are ready for Friday, and posting some stuff on social media. Very light work for a Wednesday. Who am I kidding? This is how most of the days go, which is why I started my side gig in the first place. Boredom mixed with the desire to be more creative than I'm able to be at the real-estate firm.

I text Reva to see how my plants are. When I get the reply that all is well, I clean Detective Pickles's cage, give him fresh water, and let him run on the floor, trapped between my legs and some pillows.

He tests the perimeter the whole time, like a prisoner trying to escape.

"You're not in jail, DP," I say, adopting Easton's nickname for him.

DP doesn't get it. I pet him and hold his little furry body until he pushes his nose through the cracks of my fingers, again trying to escape. "Back to the cage for you, little guy."

Instead of getting in his wheel and running as I assumed he would, he buries himself in a pile of hay in the corner.

I laugh and grab my phone on my way downstairs. I don't know if Easton is home, if he was home last night, or if he went out.

I leave my room and stop to read a text outside my door.

Everleigh: Millie made too many pecan muffins. Want to come to the farm to get some for you and Easton? If not, they'll go to waste.

Sadie: I can get them.

It would get me out of the house and give me something else to think about other than Easton. Was he with another woman last night?

Everleigh: I would meet you, but I'm waiting for the interior designer for the Inn.

Sadie: Don't worry. I wanted a reason to leave the house. Thanks!

Everleigh: I'll tell Millie to pack them up.

I tiptoe down the stairs, even though it's ten a.m. and I could be alone for all I know. After last night and my fantasy session, I don't know if I can handle seeing Easton.

I reach the bottom floor and head for my purse and jacket.

"Where are you going?" Easton says from the bottom of the stairs.

I tense and shriek, my heart in my throat. *So he is home. Breathe, Sadie.* Playing it cool, I turn. "You're awake?"

"I've been awake for a while." He walks toward me, dressed the same as yesterday but in different colors. It's sinful how good he looks like this. "Daire wants to meet," he continues. "He apologized for how he behaved and asked if I could present it to him again today."

I act surprised. "Really? That's amazing. You deserve this."

He smirks, and for a second, I worry I'm busted. "You're always so positive, Sadie. And hopeful. I appreciate that."

"I don't know if this would work for you," I say, casually, "but when I was there last night, Everleigh and I talked about adding gift baskets to the rooms for special events."

His eyes cast to the side, the wheels in his head turning. "You think the bourbon would be a good addition."

I let out a relieved breath. "You've thought of this already." Of course, he did.

"I hadn't. But I know how your mind works, and I could see where you were going. It's a great idea."

"Everleigh will love it."

He closes the small distance between us. "You know what they call a sexy best friend who inspires you?"

"A muse?"

He nods, his gaze on my lips.

Electricity sparks between us. My fingers itch to touch him. "You can kiss me, if you want."

His Adam's apple bobs with a deep swallow. "That would be a bad idea."

"Oh." I tense. What did I get wrong? Too early? No longer interested? "Okay." I back up.

He grabs my hips and draws me close. "I need to be focused on my presentation and not your lips or your body or what I want to do to it. I'll take a raincheck on this kiss for later, though. If it's still available. I hope it is."

He does still want me. Good. I don't want to ruin this for him, either. "Later then." I slip from his arms and grab my keys.

He growls.

I shoot him a questioning look. "Did you just growl?"

"I love a chase. It brings out the beast in me." He gives me a wolfish grin.

Good Lord.

"Well, you can chase me all you want later." I scoot farther away, making an impulsive decision to give a fling with Easton a chance.

I'm tired of resisting. I want to give in. My instincts want me to give in. It will help me decide if I should marry Dash or if there's more to sex and life than the image I've created. I can't know if I don't try.

He tilts his head, his eyes flaring with desire. "Taunting me isn't helping me focus on the task at hand, Sadie. In fact, it's doing the opposite." He glances at the bulge in his pants.

From my comment? "I had no idea you were this easily worked up."

"I'm not usually."

Phew. Is it hot in here?

"Is this you agreeing to my payment plan of kisses?"

"It's not a payment plan because I haven't decided if I'm selling your photos. I may use the one and keep the rest for myself."

With three long strides, he's in front of me. "I got naked for you in the cold."

"I created a beautiful bourbon label for you. *And* I got naked for you last night."

"Not naked enough. And it was in the warmth of the house."

"I was nipping, if that helps?"

He wipes his mouth. "No, Sadie. That doesn't help." His gaze rakes over my heated cheeks and down my body.

"Let's stay focused." I back away.

He follows. "I told you I like a chase, even a slow one."

He pins me against the front door, his body like a towering wall, blocking out the rest of the world.

"Easton." I press a hand to his chest to keep him at bay. "Your presentation."

"I'll make this quick then." He cups my chin and lifts my face. His lips come down to claim mine. This kiss is fire and ice. Hot enough to burn my insides and cold enough to freeze me in place.

It takes me a minute to catch my breath and give in to him. Neither stops Easton from invading my mouth. Tasting like mint and him, his tongue does exquisite things with mine until I'm moaning.

He growls again and hoists me up, pinning me to the door. On instinct, I wrap my legs around his waist and match his vigor. This kiss is sex—hot, steamy sex. His hard erection rubs against my clit in the best way. I cling to him, taking all he'll give and losing myself to the feel of his sculpted body, his flexing muscles, the friction of him between my legs, the way he tastes and touches me. His hands lower to my butt, and he caresses my cheeks.

"I love this ass. When I have you naked, I'm going to bite it."

That, combined with his perfect cock, and sensual kisses, almost shatters me. "Easton, oh God," I cry out and tighten my hold on him. "Don't stop."

He growls again, sucks my bottom lip into his mouth, and puts me down so quickly, my knees almost give out.

I lean against the door for support as I struggle to catch my breath. What just happened?

Easton runs a hand through his disheveled hair, his lips red and swollen, his cock engorged in his pants.

"I said don't stop," I clarify, thinking he misheard me.

"I know." He pants. "I'm walking away, or else I'll bury myself in you and never leave this house."

"Right. *Right.*" Clarity hits me. I tug down my shirt, unaware it had been lifted above my bra. "You have a presentation to do. Go. You need to go."

I can't be the reason he loses this opportunity, or the reason Daire thinks of him as careless, like he used to.

"Shit." I pat down my wild hair. "I'm so sorry."

Easton approaches me.

I stay still, not wanting to provoke that wolf that lives within him. The irony.

"I'm not sorry." He grabs my chin in a firm hold and kisses me hard. "When I get back, be prepared to run."

Chapter 18

Sadie

He wants to chase me. He wants to catch me, and he wants to do what with me? Kiss more. Make out? Have sex?

What do I want? All of it. But this has to move slowly. If we hop into bed, it will ruin the fun, right? The anticipation will be gone and then he won't want me anymore. I don't want that. But Easton isn't the kind of man who takes a small bite and saves the rest for later. He dives in. I don't want to disappoint him or cheat myself out of this player lifestyle I'm embarking on, but I don't want to hit the gas full speed. That can lead to a crash and burn.

Ugh.

I need to stop stressing. The problem is that when I stress, I unwind by watching murder. Normally, I'd put on my comfy clothes, get a glass of wine, and binge some ID. I can't do that now. I have to plan what to do when Easton returns. He'll want to celebrate with me. I want that, too. I also want to tempt him as much as he tempts me. I want to be sexy and adventurous. This is my chance to be whatever

I want. Easton would never judge me sexually. Hell, he'll probably teach me a few things.

But I'm not going to run around this house. Knowing my luck, I'd slip and fall and pull a hamstring. We can't mess around if I'm hurt. If he likes the chase, he might like a little hide and seek. Maybe a trail of breadcrumbs or instructions. Yes. I like this game. Excitement buzzes through me. I figure I have about an hour or two, if things go well, until he gets home.

I peruse the cabinets for something to use for the trail leading to me. A box of pecan crunch cereal triggers my memory. Dang it. I forgot I'm supposed to get muffins from Millie. I shoot Easton a quick text.

Sadie: Millie saved muffins for us at the café. I told Everleigh I'd get them, but I'm a bit preoccupied planning something titillating for when you get back. Could you get them from her before you come home, please?

Easton: Interesting choice of words. I'm tempted to cancel my meeting with Daire.

He won't. He's teasing. To be safe, I text him.

Sadie: Never mind. I'll get them.

Easton: Not a chance. Keep doing what you're doing. I'll get the muffins.

* * *

Two hours later, I'm shaved in all areas and in a bathing suit in the hot tub in the backyard. After trying to find a creative place to hide inside and coming up with nothing, I considered the bed swing. It was a little too chilly for a sexy nighty, which led me to the structure. A large patio heater stands near the hot tub, along with a towel cabinet and a coat rack for robes. I made sure the heater worked before choosing this spot.

A hot tub isn't an original hiding space, but it's sexy, warm, and in nature. I have a feeling it's one of Easton's favorite places. He seems to like the outdoors as much as I do.

I get my glass of wine, which is set on a nearby table high enough to reach. It's a Riesling that I happen to love. I don't know why Easton has it. Does he like it? Was it a gift, or did he buy it for other women when they're over?

Two glasses later.

I text him to see when he's coming back.

No reply.

What if I'm ready too early? What if he doesn't come back for hours? I'll be a prune.

I wait. And wait. And wait.

I finish the third glass of wine. My body sinks lower in the water, my posture more relaxed. Even if he doesn't make it to join me, I still got to enjoy the bubbling hot water and the lake view. I hold up my glass.

"To Easton. Sorry you couldn't join us."

"Us?" He appears to my right.

His hair is tousled, like he's been running his fingers through it. He lifts up a small collection of sticky notes. "Found your arrows."

I laugh, and it's totally buzzed sounding. I set the wine-glass on the table.

He eyes it. "I see you started without me."

"You took longer than I thought."

"I did." He focuses on the water as if trying to see my body beneath the bubbles.

I swim to his side and put my arms on the edge. "How did it go?"

His gaze lingers on my lips. "It went as I'd hoped. Better, actually. Daire was attentive, and he loved everything. He's agreed to move forward."

"That's wonderful." I beam up at him, certain it's not my sexiest grin. "I knew if he just listened, he'd be impressed. You did an excellent job."

"You did, too."

I tense. He doesn't know what I said at dinner. Daire and Everleigh promised they wouldn't tell. "How?"

"The label, to start with." He puts his hands on the edge on either side of my elbows and leans closer. "But it's more than that. You supported me from the moment you learned about it. You loved the bourbon, all my ideas, and you have unwavering faith in me. You get me, Sadie. I can't say that about a lot of people."

"You're easy to get." I roll my eyes at myself. "You know what I mean."

"I'm not easy to get. That's the thing, Sadie. I'm easy to fuck. But this"—he taps his temple—"stays locked away."

"And this." I tap his heart, leaving a wet mark on his shirt. "Whoops."

"It's coming off, anyway."

"It is?" My heart gallops. I lick my lips.

Easton runs his thumb across the bottom one.

I bite it and grin, our eyes locked.

His pupils dilate, and the energy between us crackles with anticipation.

"I'm going to need that back so I can undress."

Slowly, I release my teeth from his skin but keep my lips locked around his thumb.

When he removes it all the way, my mouth makes a popping sound.

He lets out a small growl. It reminds me he likes the chase.

I push back to the far side of the large jacuzzi.

His wolfish smirk appears. He rips his shirt off, buttons flying, and takes his shoes and pants off within seconds.

In his underwear, his gorgeously toned and tanned body on display, he climbs in with me. I send the small blow-up ball that's been circling the water with me in his direction and shoot to the corner farthest from him.

He growls and watches me, as if planning his attack.

To my surprise, he ducks under the water. Bubbles obscure him from my view. A moment later, big hands skim up my legs, then down, stopping at my ankles. A light tug. He wouldn't pull me under, would he? My hair is in a messy bun atop my head and dry, except for the back part near my neck.

I tense and squirm away as much as I can.

Slowly, he surfaces, exposing his wet hair, then his face, and his shoulders.

He spits water from his mouth.

"I peed in here," I say and then laugh.

His eyes widen to saucers.

"Kidding."

He grips my hips and pulls me to him. "That deserves a spanking."

I crack up, heated from his touch and stare. "You can't spank me in the water. It won't work."

"You think so, huh?" He drags me to the step and positions me over his shoulder like a sack of potatoes, my ass out of the water and in the air.

My bikini isn't a thong, but all the movements sent the material up my crack like one.

"Easton?" I squeal.

The slap hits my wet cheek, catching me by surprise. The sting is slight.

"Do you know how much I love this part of your body?" He spanks the other cheek.

I squeal again, but not from pain. The rush that he's touching my ass, spanking it, and loving it, has me all kinds of turned on. Having never been spanked, I have no idea what to expect. Gentle slaps? Rough ones? Pain? Awkwardness? This is none of those, only arousal.

He smacks the opposite cheek. I feel the sting, but it's nothing I can't handle.

"Did you hear me, Sadiecakes? This ass is mine now." He spanks the other cheek.

If my bikini bottoms weren't already wet, they'd be embarrassingly soaked. I'm even panting.

He rubs the cheek he smacked. "I love the red, watching it form and then vanish. Fuck. Sadie, your ass is perfect."

I moan and try to shift, wanting...I don't even know what I want.

He holds me to him. "You like this?" He kisses my cheek, then nips my flesh.

I moan again and drop my head over the edge. "Easton, please?"

"You want me to touch you more?"

"Yes," I breathe. Goosebumps cover my skin, but I don't feel cold. I'm so hot I could combust.

"I imagined doing this." He slaps my other cheek and then rubs it, his large hand making big circles. He squeezes. "One day I'm going to fuck you with this ass so far in the air, you won't walk straight for days."

Oh God. I moan and bite my bottom lip to keep from drooling. Never in my life have I been this turned on. I can't think. Too little oxygen?

I try to move down his body.

"Not yet, sweetcakes."

He runs his fingers over my core. I clench, needing more of him. The lower half of my body burns with a desire I didn't know existed within me. Someone could be watching us right now, and I wouldn't care. I wouldn't change anything. Let them watch. As long as he doesn't stop.

When his fingers slide under my bathing suit, I part my legs to make room for him. He lets me, and then his finger runs over my entrance.

He hisses a curse. "I smell your arousal. You're soaked for me, aren't you? You like when I spank your sweet ass."

I nod and wiggle, wanting his fingers inside me.

"Say it?"

I can't speak through my desire. I wiggle more.

He spanks me again. All I feel is arousal. Nothing else. No pain. Nothing but an extreme need to be screwed in a way I never thought possible. "Easton, touch me."

He spanks my other cheek and then licks it and squeezes it again. "Say it, Sadie, and I'll give you what you want. Tell me you're soaked, only for me."

"Yes," I breathe, lightheaded. "I'm soaked...for you... only you."

"Good girl." He slips his finger inside me. "Sopping." He pumps in and out a few times and inserts a second finger.

I hang over the edge of the hot tub, my torso over his shoulder, writhing and trying to screw his fingers. "More. Please, more."

He lets out another growl and inserts a third finger, stretching me to the point of light pain. It's incredible.

I groan as he works his fingers in and out at a brutal pace. I am nothing but a vessel for him to please and I want my release. I want it so badly, but I also don't want this new sexual experience to end. I have no idea who this desperate, uninhibited person is, but now that she's here I can't imagine ever settling for less.

"Are you going to orgasm for me, Sadie?" He pumps faster, harder, deeper.

I explode, clenching his fingers as if to drag them inside me. My eyes roll to the back of my head. I'm certain I'm screaming or chanting Easton's name.

"That tight pussy likes me inside it," Easton says, sounding vindicated. "You surprise me, sweetcakes. In the best ways."

My head falls limply forward as I gradually return to the present.

Easton slides me down his body to straddle his lap. I make slow blinks, catching my breath.

"How do you feel?" He sweeps strands of my tangled hair from my face, the majority of it still in the bun somehow.

"I feel...drained but amazing."

"It's the rush. The spanking, the heightened senses, the awareness, and anticipation... It's intoxicating. *You're* intoxicating." He touches my chin. "Look at me."

Unaware I was staring at his neck, I lift my gaze to meet his.

"I didn't know if you would like that. But you did. I think it's safe to say you loved it."

I laugh, reality hitting me suddenly. "I can't believe we did that. In the open. We didn't even kiss."

"I plan to fix that right now." He grips my chin and tilts his head before pressing his mouth to mine.

His lips are soft and inviting, luring me to give him whatever he wants. I feel like he owns a secret part of me now, a part that likes to be spanked. I couldn't imagine sharing that with anyone else. Easton has a way of making me feel comfortable and desired.

He licks the seam of my lips.

I open at once for him.

His warm tongue slips inside and twirls naturally with mine. Our first kiss was incredible, delicious. Our third is sweeter because we know each other in that way now. I love the taste of him and how he holds my cheeks when he kisses me. In a possessive yet gentle way. I rock my core against his hard erection. His cock is thick and big. I want to see it, but I also don't know if we should have sex. We could and I'm sure it'd be amazing, but what would be left after that?

Would he have gotten his fill? That's the Easton I know. Not necessarily one and done. He has a few regulars, but no one has ever held his interest for long.

He runs his hands down my body and grabs my ass, pulling me against his cock and adding more friction.

I moan in his mouth, and desire floods me again. His touch is magic.

His lips leave my mouth for the skin below my ear. "I want you naked. Take your top off for me."

He holds me still on his lap, keeping me secured to him.

I untie the strings around my back and neck and let the fabric fall away. My nipples float just above the surface and are hard.

He stares at them and licks his lips before bending to take one in his mouth.

I let my head fall back and moan as he kisses, sucks, and nips my nipple. He does the same to the other, using his hands to cup the bottom of each, pushing them closer and higher while he feasts.

Sensations bombard me, each carrying a direct current to my core.

Wanting to pleasure him the way he is me, I reach into his briefs and grip his thick cock. The size and width take me by surprise. If I weren't so lost to my lust, I might be scared. He's so fat, my fingers and thumb don't even touch.

"Tighter," he says, and I obey, working him up and down, hoping I'm not hurting him. He doesn't seem to be in pain. He seems enraptured.

He kisses me again and sucks my bottom lip into his mouth. I pump my hand faster, wishing I was able to use my mouth. Next time.

My hair comes undone and gets caught in our kisses. Easton brushes the strands back, then tangles his fingers at the nape of my neck. He tugs my head back and kisses me with more force. His hand finds my breast, and he pinches my nipple. I moan and pant, craving his fingers inside me again.

I take his hand that's pinching my nipple and move it between my legs.

"You want me to finger fuck you again?" he murmurs across my lips and without hesitation, he slips two fingers inside me. "So swollen for me."

His dirty talk is so hot. Dash barely spoke. When he did, it was to say he was about to come. Easton takes my breath away in so many ways.

I ride his fingers while pumping him hard and fast. Is this how long he'd last while screwing me? Could I take it?

We could be having sex right now, but neither of us has made a move to do it.

When his thumb rubs my clit, I erupt into pieces, screaming his name.

"The feel of you...fuck," he groans and gives a final thrust, releasing in my hand.

He thrusts in my fist a few more times before relaxing. I collapse against his shoulder, wishing I could stay like this for days.

Birds chirp around us, the wind whistles through the trees. The chill in the air and the scent of nature make this a moment I'll never forget. My first tryst with Easton that ended in two orgasms for me, one for him, and no sex.

"How do you feel now?" He strokes my back, the bubbles churning around us.

"Wiped, surprised, satisfied. How about you?"

"Mmm." He nuzzles my neck. "Same."

Finding the strength, I sit up and meet his content gaze. "What now?"

He locks his hands behind my back, his expression thoughtful. "We eat?"

I laugh. "That's a given, but—"

"Not what you meant."

I wipe a droplet from his stubbly cheek.

"How about you don't over-analyze this. Let it be what it is. Enjoy it. Think of what's to come."

"What's to come?" Fear creeps into me with the question. Not for what's next but for when this ends. How do I handle the ending? I've never done this. Do we pretend we never had sex? Will I wish we still were?

"You're already doing it." He takes my chin again and holds my gaze. "More orgasms are to come. That's all you need to know. For now, your only concern should be what we're going to do in the next fifteen minutes. I'll even tell you. We're going to dry off, run into the house, and eat. Lady's choice." He kisses my lips and sets me on the bench beside the step.

He gets out of the hot tub, wraps himself in the extra robe on the hook, and holds the other out for me.

"Thank you." I emerge in a swarm of shivers, my body trying to adjust to the cold and the orgasmic adrenaline rush I had moments ago.

We race into the house with Easton watching to make sure I don't slip. Inside, the warmth isn't enough to stop my shivers. Easton takes a furry blanket from the couch and wraps me up.

He pulls his phone from the pocket of his pants that he carried from the hot tub and hands it to me. "Open Uber Eats. Order whatever you want."

"I don't need you to buy me dinner. This wasn't a date." I sound bitter. It's not my intention.

"I know," he says without a care and walks to the kitchen. "But we're starving, and I don't have anything to cook unless you went grocery shopping."

"It's on my to-do list." The casualness between us, like nothing sexual happened moments ago, feels weird. I don't think I like it. But then it could be because it's new to me and uncomfortable. *Focus on the now.*

"Want some coffee?"

"Coffee sounds good." I could sleep with all the energy I just used. "Cocoa sounds better, but I haven't bought any yet." Something else to add to the list. I look at the restaurants. "Which place is good?" I have no idea.

"There aren't many, as you can see. They're all pretty good. Depends on what you want. Barbecue? Burgers? Mexican?"

"There's a Mexican restaurant around here?" That's new. I scroll further down. A place I liked in Honeycomb comes up. They have the best soups and use produce from a local farm.

"Want soup?" I walk to the kitchen, wishing I had socks. I need to shower, too.

"Soup?" He glances over his shoulder, his profile and messy, damp hair romance-cover worthy.

"It's a restaurant near Honeycomb. I used to love it."

"Do they have meat?"

"They have chili." I scan the menu. "Oh wait. They have subs now."

"I'll have whatever has the most meat."

"One meat lovers sub coming up," I add it to the cart along with my cheddar and broccoli soup. "Done. It'll be here in 35 to 45 minutes."

Easton hands me a cup of coffee. "Did you add the cream?"

He nods.

"And one sweetener?" I took some from Everleigh's house when we got into town, assuming he wouldn't have any.

He nods and smirks. "I know how you take your coffee. And now I know how you take your orgasms."

I blush under his intense stare. "And how's that?"

"With a good spanking."

Chapter 19

Easton

I follow the trail through the woods that hugs the lake and push myself to go faster. Sweat coats my skin, even in the chilly morning temperature.

After sleeping like shit, wondering why Sadie disappeared into her room last night without a peep, I decided to punish myself with a run.

I understand messing around with a man who isn't her boyfriend, or a potential boyfriend, would leave Sadie in unchartered territory. I understand she wouldn't know how to act or proceed. Her nature is to question and put meaning to everything. I had no idea she would ghost me after the hottest make-out session I've ever had—and the hottest I'm certain she's experienced.

I hadn't planned to spank her. I was going to join her in the hot tub and see what she'd do. Then she swam away, encouraging the chase, and I went rogue. When I brought up the spanking and she challenged the topic, curiosity got the best of me. How would she react? If she didn't like it, I was prepared to stop. Once that small yet plump ass was in my face, I admit I almost lost my cool. I spanked her lightly, and she didn't reject the act. She moaned. So I spanked her again, and it became clear she liked it.

When I touched her sweet heat and found how wet she was, I had to remind myself not to push her further. This was her first time being spanked. I didn't want to scare her, but damn, if my brain didn't visualize multiple ways to take her in that hot tub. She was so turned on, she might have let me.

It was all I could do to keep from burying myself in her tight walls—so tight I barely fit three fingers inside her. She liked being stretched. Her reactions were dead giveaways. She'll need that if I'm to fit inside her. I might not be the heir to the Livingston throne, but I'm heir to a huge dick. She couldn't even fit her dainty hand around the girth of it. Fucking her would be a sweet kind of torture for both of us.

I didn't have a plan for how to end the night. That's a lie. I wanted to do more with her and see how far she was willing to go. To my disappointment, she didn't feel the same. She escaped to her room and that was the end of it. I'd waited to see if she'd re-emerge after her shower. Hell, I hoped she'd ask me to join her.

I spent the night envisioning doomed scenarios. She regrets what we did. She's upset. She hates me. She hates herself. She's gone.

That last thought haunted me until I got so desperate I checked on her early this morning. She hadn't locked her bedroom door. I opened it enough to peer into the room and found her asleep on her side in the bed. Her maple hair fell over the pillow behind her. I wanted to bury my nose in it and inhale her sweet scent. I wanted to climb in that bed and cuddle her naked body. From what I could see above the covers that came up to the middle of her back, she was nude.

Blood rushes my dick at the memory. Not now. How many times has this happened because of thoughts of her? More than it has for any other woman. Maybe because I've never fantasized about other women. I've never had one share my space and life. I've never been denied something that I've grown to want so badly. Will it fade in time? Will I tire of her like I did the others? I don't want to do that to Sadie. Not that I've ever tossed a woman aside. I'm honest from the beginning and end things on good terms. Sometimes I go back for seconds, if I know the woman won't assume it means something more. Two friends of mine share the same sex ideals as me. We take what we need, when we need if we're available for each other. It's mutual.

Sadie and I don't have that agreement. This is new territory for both of us. If last night was it for her and our encounters are over, I'll be dejected, but I'll accept her choice. I'll have to move out, as well. Living with her after knowing her intimately will be too much to take. She can stay for as long as she wants, but I'll be at Daire's penthouse, far away from her temptation.

The house comes into view in the near distance. Is she awake? Has she looked for me?

I haven't gotten a text from her, so my guess is she's still asleep or avoiding me.

The idea crawls over my skin like thousands of ants. I don't like it. I've never needed a woman to acknowledge or accept me.

I check the time. I've been running for an hour. Doesn't feel like it. I slow as I approach the incline of the property. My gaze catches on the gazebo enclosing the hot tub. She gave in to me. I didn't expect it, no matter how much I pushed and wanted her. Even when I got home after my extended presentation with Daire, I assumed she'd change her mind. Instead, she left a trail of notes that led right to her in the last place I expected.

I adjust my throbbing dick. The damn thing wants Sadie more than I do.

The house is quiet when I enter. No sign of Sadie. I get a sports drink from the fridge and head for my room to shower.

I pleasure myself to visions of Sadie's ass in the air while I take her from behind. When I return downstairs, nothing suggests Sadie emerged from her room. Fuck. I stab fingers through my hair and focus on the second-floor landing and the stairs that lead to the third floor.

Worry consumes me. I text her.

Easton: How are you?

Seconds pass.

I drum fingers on the counter.

My phone chimes. Anticipation roars through me. I almost drop the phone when I lift it to read the screen. It's just Daire. My shoulders slump.

Daire: I'm on the way to the farm now if you want to start early.

I have a conference call scheduled with the bourbon CEO and his CFO to go over the details of the deal with Daire. He's moving faster than I thought he would. It's all good, better than good. It's what I wanted out of this. My brother's taking me and the product as seriously as I'm taking it.

I reply.

Easton: Of course. I'll head over.

If I weren't in casual business attire for the Zoom meeting, I would take the UTV. I haven't even taken Sadie out on it yet. I need to do that if she'll let me. If she stays.

The fear of her leaving sits heavy in my stomach. I roll down the windows as I leave the garage and jerk to a stop when a text from her appears on the dashboard screen.

I touch it. The automated car voice reads it aloud.

"Sorry. I slept in. I was up late last night working."

I hit reply and say, "Working?"

Her reply plays in the car. "I sent my author a preliminary cover yesterday, and she loved it. She loved you and wants more."

"More pictures?" I'm tempted to rush back into the house and have this conversation in person, but I already told Daire I'm on my way. If I want him to take me as a serious business partner, I need to treat him with the same respect.

"More covers? I'll be busy all day. Wait. Are you here?"

Is she looking for me in the house? The desire to be there for her hits me like a windstorm. My skin grows sticky, like when I was a young teen trying to impress a girl.

Sadie does things to me and my body that I've never experienced before. I haven't been this unsure since my high school years. Even then, I was cocky, confident, and carefree. "The three Cs," my mom chastised me once and told me to be better.

She never asked Daire to be better. He was what she wanted in a son. Even when he caused trouble, and he did—not as much as I did, but he wasn't a saint—she was lenient with him.

She kept on me about this behavior and the way I went through women until this last year. But then she isn't around to get on me like she was when she lived at the estate. Mom and Dad are at their condo in Palm Beach more than they're here.

They started building a house on the property up the

street from the farm. Dad had offered it to Daire when he gave him the business and estate. They offered the land to me after he passed on it, but I decided to redo the lake house instead, loving the property and privacy.

With the Inn, the manor would be too crowded for our parents to stay with Daire and Everleigh, but their house won't be finished for another six months. I'd planned to let them stay at my place when the baby is born. Sadie will be gone by then. An emptiness settles in my chest at the thought.

I'm being ridiculous. We'll still talk and be friends. We won't be doing what we're doing now. We may never do anything again, and that leaves me with an emptiness I can't explain.

This situation is confusing me because it's with Sadie. A close friend. A tempting, close friend who also likes sex the way I do.

I stomp the breaks. I'm at the farm already? What's worse is I have no recollection of driving here and almost passed the entrance. I need to get my head in the right place. I can't screw up this meeting. I push Sadie to the recess of my mind and focus on work.

I don't leave the farm until dinner time. The sun has set, and I haven't received a single text from Sadie. We talked a lot before the attack, but having her live with me puts her front and center in my mind. I look forward to hearing from her and seeing her every day. It's new for me. All of this is. I imagine that's what she's feeling after yesterday's hot tub encounter.

Stephen texted me twice. He says he might have found

something and will contact me tomorrow after running another lead.

I decide not to share the news with Sadie in case it turns out to be nothing.

I'm at the house and inside faster than usual. I've never raced to get home for anything, let alone anyone. But I'm anxious to see how she is and if she wants to continue our exploration of each other's bodies. I know I do.

The kitchen and house look untouched. In general, Sadie is neat and tidy, but a glass on the counter or disrupted pillows on the couch usually alert me she's been around.

"Sadie?" I call out.

"Up here." Her sweet voice floats down from the third floor.

I take the stairs two at a time. Her doors are open and she's on the floor with her laptop open and her iPad beside her. A color printer plugs into the wall and pictures of book covers litter most of the floor. Each of them includes a picture of me.

"I'm afraid to enter." I stay near the doorway.

She sits surrounded by the clutter, her hair in a messy bun. She wears joggers and a cropped long-sleeved t-shirt. Her little feet are bare and a pencil sticks from the messy bun on top of her head. Tendrils fall around her face, show-casing her amazing eyes that look greener today. She looks gorgeous when she's in disarray.

"Sorry for the mess. I've been working all day."

"I can see that."

"I didn't know she has the series completed. Now she wants to launch all three books a few weeks apart and start advertising them." She sounds panicked.

"Have you eaten today?"

"I had Gatorade." She points, her gaze on her laptop. Three bottles sit a few feet from her.

"Just Gatorade?" Concern sends a surge of anger through me. "Come eat some food. I'll get you whatever you want."

"I don't have time. I need to make sure these are perfect."

The printer buzzes as it begins to ink a cover on paper.

"Where did you get that?" Did she go into my office?

"Everleigh. I got it from her this morning."

"Why didn't you use mine? I have one downstairs in my room. You should have texted."

"I didn't know, and I wouldn't go into your room if I did. It's private."

I love that she respects my space. That's so important to me. My family invaded my privacy, looking for whatever I was into, constantly during my teen years. My mom had the maids go through my stuff. The school searched my locker more than other students it seemed after finding pot in my possession once. Daire even spied on me a few times at the request of my dad. He didn't always tell on me. In fact, plenty of times he had my back. Still, I always found a way to get in trouble. It's why I covet my privacy like I do.

A few of the women I brought here for sex tried to explore the house against my wishes, when I was in the bathroom or showering before I gave them a ride home. I never hooked up with those women again.

"You could have texted and asked me. I would have let you use it. I trust you." I don't think I've said that to any woman before. Maybe because I haven't trusted anyone until her.

"I didn't want to bother you." She removes the picture of another book cover and sighs. "The color isn't right. I

173

think it's the printer, but I need to be sure before sending the proofs to her. I hate when a cover doesn't match the digital image."

She hasn't looked at me since her initial glance at my arrival.

"Sadie. Take a break and come back to it. I'll help you."

She balls up the paper and tosses it in a pile. She's making herself crazy.

Having been down this rabbit hole before and knowing how frustrating it can be, I make my tone gentle. "Sadiecakes. Baby. Let me get you something to eat. Please."

The *please* catches her attention. She stares at me, and the reason why her eyes are so green registers. They're bloodshot and the red veins make the green stand out.

"We don't have any food. I haven't bought groceries yet," she says, stressed.

"I brought food home from the farm," I mention, thankful I thought to bring us dinner before leaving. "Millie made us ham and three cheese croissant sandwiches with pecan butter."

It's my favorite butter. Nothing overpowering, but it adds something to the croissant that makes the sandwich next level.

"She made them for us?" Her brows pull together from where she sits on her heels, her knees bent. That can't be comfortable.

"I had her make them for us." I chuckle. "I had a feeling you'd be hungry."

"You did?" She turns toward me.

I shrug.

She takes in my clothes. "Did you have another meeting?"

"With Daire and the bourbon company."

"How'd it go?" She stands and stretches.

I love that she asks. Even with her busy day, she still cares enough to show interest.

"It went really well. We were busy, but that's expected. It's good, in fact, because we're moving forward and at a quick pace."

A tired but genuine smile forms on her lips. "Sounds like Daire knows a good thing when it's presented to him."

"Who'd have thought?" I shrug. "Not me. I expected the worst. I don't know what changed his mind. I'm not about to question him about it, though. I'll take what I can get."

"Not what you can get. What you worked for. What you deserve." The glow of pride in her eyes matches her tone.

Warmth spreads through my chest. I've half a mind to toss her over my shoulder and show her how much I appreciate her consistent praise.

I hold out my hand. "Come take a break."

She glances at the papers on the floor, at her laptop, and tucks stray strands of her hair behind her ears. "I guess I could eat quickly."

"When is this due?"

"I said Wednesday, but I'd rather have it ready by Monday."

It's Friday. "You have the whole weekend." I hoped to have her time and attention the entire weekend, but I'll settle for the evenings if she'll grant them to me.

"I stress when I'm on a deadline. It's not my best quality." She maneuvers toward me, careful not to step on any of the printed papers with her bare feet. She could have stacked them together but seems to want to keep them where they lay. "I haven't even showered today," she says when she's almost to me.

I take her hand and help her up the last few steps. "You showered last night. Right?"

She left me to shower.

She nods. "I did. But I feel like I need another."

"I can help you with that, too," I throw out to see her reaction. Will she blush? Accept my invitation? Blow me off? When have I ever been this unsure? Never.

Her cheeks turn pink, and she averts her gaze. This timid side of her turns me on. I've never been into timid women. Too much work. I like them eager. In the hot tub, after I spanked her, she was more than eager to get her fill. I would love to get her to that point again. The shyness she shows sometimes, like now, is more of a challenge than a turn off. It's like the chase I love so much. It makes me burn hotter for her. She has no idea how much she affects me. If she did, she'd probably run.

Chapter 20

Easton

We sit at the kitchen island with our croissant sandwiches and chilled apple cider. Millie makes it fresh this time of year.

Sadie finishes her sandwich without saying a word and chugs half her glass of cider. "That was so good. I was starving."

I grin from where I sit next to her, happy to have been able to help and care for her, even if it's just by providing food.

She wipes her mouth with her napkin, missing a crumb.

I point. "You've got a piece of food right here."

She licks the corner of her mouth.

My dick twitches at the sight. I stare at her lips, even after the crumb is gone and her tongue is hidden behind that sultry pout.

She averts her gaze. "What are you doing this weekend?"

You, if I'm lucky. "I was thinking about heading to the Four Seasons."

Her expression drops. "The hotel?"

"The floating dock and cabin."

She glances out the windows at the lake, the structure barely visible in the distance. Twilight paints the yard, casting the fall colors in a magical glow. "Why do you call it that?"

"My grandma named it after nature and all the seasons she enjoyed from her favorite spot."

An easy smile spreads across Sadie's face. "She sounds like she knew how to enjoy life."

I rest my elbow on the counter, angling toward her. "My parents used to say I was a lot like her."

"It sounds like it."

"Want to come with me?" I hold her green gaze. The red veins are still there, but she appears more alert now that she's eaten.

"To the Four Seasons?" Her eyes widen with both excitement and fear.

"Yeah. I'll have Millie make us a picnic, and if we bring blankets, we can stay until sunset and watch the stars."

She glances out the windows again at the lake and chews on her bottom lip. "Is the structure safe?"

"It's well-built if that's what you're asking. Think about it as a tiny houseboat. And in case you're worried about alligators, I believe they hibernate for the winter."

She shoots me a look. "That's not true."

I chuckle. "What happened to the girl who wanted to take a bottle of wine to the floating dock and cabin for the night?"

"She's here." Sadie scowls. "She's just nervous."

I chuckle again. "I promise nothing will get you. We'll take the speedboat and leave if you get uncomfortable."

She picks at her fingernail. "I might be okay with that."

I brush a loose strand from her face.

Her lips part with an uneven breath, and she goes still, her gaze locked with mine.

"I want to kiss you so badly."

"You do?"

"I've been thinking about it all day." I lean a bit closer.

"You have? I thought..."

I know what she thought. That I got some and I'm done. "Yesterday was just the start of us having fun. There's so much more I want to do with you and to you."

She visibly swallows, but her lips part again with her shallower breaths. She likes it when I talk to her like this. I cup the back of her neck and pull her to me for a kiss. My lips meet hers with gentle pressure. I take it slow and slip my tongue inside her sweet mouth for a taste. It's like kissing a sugary spiced apple.

I sink my fingers into her hair, the strands like silk. I hope she isn't mad if I mess up her bun. She places one hand on my chest and the other on my cheek. The touch of her dainty hand in that affectionate way triggers emotions deep inside me.

Sex has always been about release and the physical act. I don't catch feelings. I never have, but Sadie stirs them inside me. She's secured a place in my life, imprinted herself on me without even trying. I have no idea what to do with these emotions or how long they'll last, so every time they appear, I ignore them. But when she touches me like this, so fondly, my guard comes down and they seep back in.

Little breathy sounds escape her as I work my tongue at different angles, pleasing her in different ways. She leans closer, erasing the small distance I've kept between us. I stand and pull her hair. Her bun comes loose as I tug her head back, then I claim her lips with a possessive kiss, no longer being gentle. She might not know it, but she likes it a bit rough.

I've never been much of a kisser. It's not necessary to fuck. But when it comes to Sadie, I can't get enough. I could kiss her all day, every day. She's that addictive.

She slides her fingers up my arm to my flexing biceps. She wants to stand, I can tell, but I'm not ready to let her. I give her all she needs and more, until she's moaning in my mouth, lapping at my tongue, and gripping me tighter with both hands. I love when she moans and loses herself to me.

Changing tactics, her hand goes to the button of my pants.

"Uh-uh." I chastise her. "Tonight is about you."

"Me? How?" She looks confused. I bet Dash made it all about him all the time. Wasn't it like that in everything they did?

I smirk down at her and grip the hem of her shirt. "Do you trust me?"

She nods and licks her lips.

I remove her shirt and her bra, tossing them on the floor. Her nipples pucker tightly against the slight chill in the air. I'll fix that soon enough.

She reaches for my shirt.

I shake my head and grab her hips, hoisting her onto the counter before I feast on her breasts. I suck her nipple into my mouth.

She lets out a throaty moan that's sexy as hell. "Easton."

I love when she calls my name. She cups the back of my head when I take the other nipple in my mouth, teasing it with my tongue and giving it a good hard suck.

She bucks. "Oh God."

"Not God, Sadie. Me." I grab her chin and make her

look at me. "I'm the one pleasing you. I want my name on your lips. Only my name."

She nods, looking so sweet and sexy on the counter, her pert tits bare and mine for the tasting.

I ease her down to lie on her back, shove the stool away with my foot, and kiss her flat tummy. My tongue dips into her belly button while I use my fingers to pinch her nipples.

She squirms beneath me, her hand in my hair.

I grip the elastic waist to her joggers. "Lift for me, baby."

She does, and I slide the pants off easily, taking her panties with them. If I can, I'll keep her dressed like this daily for easy access.

I kiss her landing strip and part her legs, hooking her knees over my shoulders. Our eyes lock, and the sight of her has me almost coming in my pants.

"I want to hear my name when you orgasm, Sadie."

She nods and inches lower, eager for me to claim her sweet heat. I blow on her clit, then lick it. She moans and shifts her hips even lower.

I kiss her sensitive bud then lick her slit. She tastes like heaven on my tongue. A frenzy builds in me, driving my actions. When she touches my hair, I suck her clit into my mouth.

She arches her back. "Oh God."

"Not God, Sadie," I whisper over her moist mound. "If you want more, you have to say my name."

"Easton. Please, Easton," she begs.

Having her naked on my kitchen counter might be the most erotic thing I've seen. I've had women bent over the surface, face down. I like to see all of Sadie, though. Her body, her small but plump tits, those luscious lips, and the expression of ecstasy she makes when she comes.

Talk about picture perfect.

I lick her sex again and watch as her eyes close. My girl. I keep my gaze on her as I fuck her with my tongue and pinch her nipples at the same time. She squirms, her lips forming a sensual O as she pants. I'd love to have my dick in that mouth. Tomorrow maybe.

I remove my hand, part her slippery folds, and suck on her clit again.

"I need to feel you," she breathes and meets my gaze, her eyes glossy, her lids heavy with desire.

"You want this?" I push two fingers into her moist heat.

"Yes." Her head falls onto the counter.

I pump my fingers and lick her clit, holding her pelvis still as I enjoy her delicious sex.

"Fuck, Sadie," I hiss. "You taste like warm dessert on a winter's day."

I add a third finger, pumping fast and deep, paying attention to when she moans louder, and squirms more. Her hand finds my hair again, and she grinds against my face. I can barely move my fingers. I want nothing more than to shove my dick so deep inside her, she'll feel me for days. I resist and feast instead.

In a swift move, I clutch her ass with one hand, lift her off the counter to my mouth, and use the other to fuck her senseless. She gives into my control, her muscles soft, her body mine for the taking, however I please. I suck her clit and pump my fingers in and out so hard my biceps start to burn. She loves it, begs, pants, calls my name multiple times. She stops breathing for a moment, and her body stiffens, her tight walls clamping on my fingers while she cries out in ecstasy.

I wait until she's finished orgasming, then lick up every drop of her, needing more, fearing I'll always need more.

Her body hangs limp in my arms and sweat dampens

her skin. Gently, I lower her ass to the counter. She's going to feel what I did to her. I'm sure. Hell, I felt the punishment in my arm, and the last thing I am is weak.

"Stay there," I say, doubtful that she'll move anyway.

I race to the couch, grab the furry blanket, and take in her naked body sprawled across the counter as I return. Her skin looks tanned next to the white stone, her figure perfect.

Mine. For now.

"Come here." I wrap her in the blanket and pull her into my arms, cradling her. "You said you needed a shower, right?"

She nods and rests her head on my shoulder. "Easton?" she murmurs.

"Yes?"

"Thank you."

"Thank you?" No one has ever thanked me before.

"Yes. Thank you. For what you did for me. The food, the caring, the other part." Her cheeks turn pink. "I really like what you do to me."

So many needs bombard me at once. The need to care for her in all ways, to protect her, to please her more. The need to be inside her, to make her forget all other men, the need to make her crave only me. It's insane thinking. Illogical. I can't make her want only me when I don't only want her.

For now, I do. More than I've ever wanted anyone. But I've never been a man with staying power. I'd never want to promise a woman—Sadie, especially—more than I know I can give. It wouldn't be fair. But maybe this isn't fair to her, either. Getting her to try a lifestyle that has worked for me but might not work for her. So far, she has no complaints. She thanked me, for shit's sake.

With my foot, I push open my bedroom door and do the

same to the en suite bathroom. Sadie hasn't looked around. Her eyes haven't left my profile. I can feel them on me. I sit her on a stool near the tub.

She glances around, her eyes widening on the large tub and floor-to-ceiling window framing the view. The woods and lake are barely visible in the evening light. "Where are we?"

"My bathroom."

"The one in your bedroom? Your private room. The room no one goes in?"

I nod and turn on the faucet. Water pours from the ceiling into the tub.

She takes in the black and white theme, accented with wood and soapstone. "Why'd you bring me here?" Her eyes are on me now.

I shrug and stand, peering down at her in that furry blanket. "I guess I wanted to see you in my tub."

She takes in the floor-to-ceiling window again. "It's beautiful."

"Thanks," I say, looking at the space with pride. "I had a hand in the design choices."

"You did a great job." She studies the landscape, the trees and lake. "Can people see me?"

I follow her gaze out the window. "What people?"

"Anyone hiding in the woods, maybe. A pervert?"

"A serial killer?" I tease.

A worried look crosses her face.

I laugh. "No one is out there. No one can see you. Besides, if there was someone, they already got a show when we were in the kitchen."

Her entire face turns red. "I was the only one naked. You didn't show them anything in your clothes."

"Good thing there is no one out there, then."

"You don't know that for sure."

"I do. The property is gated, surrounded by a wall, and monitored. Need I remind you. I even have cameras recording the back yard. Two deer set off the sensor this morning." I remove my phone from my pocket and pull up the feed. "Want to see?"

She eyes the video. "Aw. I wish I could have seen them in real life."

"You could have out your balcony."

"I would have had to be paying attention."

"Can't help you with that." I smirk and hold up bubble bath and bath salts. "Want either of these?" Everleigh gave them to me as a gift after I showed her and Daire the finished bathroom. I've never used them.

"I like them both." She glances up from her spot on the stool, her eyes suggestive. The blanket falls and exposes her shoulders. Her sexy, messy hair adds to the sixties Playboy model vibe she has going on right now.

My dick, still semi-hard from eating her delectable pussy, goes fully erect.

I set the bubble bath and salts next to a clean towel by the tub. "Take all the time you need." I touch her cheek, then force myself from the room before I do something she's not ready for yet.

I need to take things slowly when it comes to Sadie. I don't want to. But she needs me to restrain myself.

I like drawing this out, too, worried that if I fuck her, I'll lose interest quickly. I have her for one more week. I don't want to scare her off or send her running because things get awkward. They could if I push her too far, too fast.

Things between us are going better than I could have dreamed. She's so much more than I imagined. But no one has ever stopped the panic from rising when the hint of serious commitment comes from a woman. The suggestion alone makes my palms sweaty.

In the past, a few women dared to bring it up, believing they could convince me to try a relationship and that I'd like it. Each time, my body breaks into a full-on sweat. My heart races, and my chest tightens like my lungs are collapsing.

I feel trapped with a strong desire to escape into fresh air and nature. And I do. I leave so quickly for freedom and open space I have to send a text explaining my rapid departure.

When I was little, I hid in an old trunk my father had in the attic. The lock got stuck when I closed the lid, and I was trapped. I spent hours banging on the wood, screaming for help, crying when that didn't work, and finally praying. It felt like I was in there for days.

Daire thought I'd quit the game, which I did sometimes, and went outside to play. It wasn't until my mother questioned why I wasn't at dinner that Daire explained we'd played hide-n-seek earlier and he hadn't seen me since. The entire family, the cooks, and the housekeepers searched the estate for me. Six hours later, my dad found me in that chest.

I was catatonic by then, frozen by fear and anxiety. To this day, I hate enclosed spaces. As I grew older, that fear of being trapped spread to relationships. Even friends that get too needy or close scare me off. It's why Sadie is an anomaly in my life.

Our friendship happened slowly over time and through events that put us together. She was easy to talk to, funny with her paranoia, and cute as fuck. She was also off-limits once she rejected me, and my brother and his wife decided I needed to treat Everleigh's bestie with total respect.

Sadie friend-zoned me, and I did the same, by force, but

it worked. We were able to grow close without the fear of more. We didn't see each other often at first, but we texted and then evolved to phone calls. I felt I could tell her anything, and it was easy to be me. Not the useless version everyone assumed or expected from me, just me. Even with that, I held a lot of myself back. She's seeing it all now. She's even seeing my room. I don't know what it means or if it means anything at all. This could be another evolution of our friendship. We've never spent this much time together in person consistently.

I imagine when she leaves, things between us will go back to the way they were. At the thought, a cold sweat breaks across my forehead. That's never happened before.

I change out of my business attire and into workout clothes. I could use a good run outside, but I don't want Sadie to think I abandoned her, tiring of her already. She's so paranoid, waiting for me to end this. Honestly, I don't know how she's doing it and not becoming needy, like other women have, or clingy, or trying to trap me into a relationship.

Is it because I don't meet her needs? Sexually, I do. That's more than obvious. I don't know what her relationship criteria is, other than marriage and a family one day, but I must fulfill some of her other criteria. Attractive, genuine, supportive.

If I'm honest with myself, it stings that she hasn't tried to push a relationship on me or even hint about one. Like I'm not worth her time or effort.

But in a way, it makes sense. My own family has never expected more from me. As the spare I have nothing to gain by proving my worth. I exist as a backup.

I scratch my head and take the stairs to the basement.

I still can't believe Daire asked to see my presentation

again and agreed to move forward with it for the farm. I was convinced it'd be much harder to gain his serious attention. Graduating college early didn't do much for me when it came to recognition from him.

He patted my shoulder and said, "See what happens when you change your focus?" Yet at the farm, he didn't give me any new responsibilities.

Dad rewarded me with the sports bike and encouraged me to go have fun. Mom kissed my cheek and told me, "Leave the hard stuff for your brother. You were born to enjoy life."

I know Daire didn't have it easy, always striving to fit the mold my parents created for him after birth. He had a position to fill, and he did it without complaint. He didn't argue or question their expectations, he simply became who they wanted him to be. If your parents never expect more from you, you grow up to believe there's no point in trying.

I'm not my brother. I never will be. It doesn't mean I can't bring great things to the table and do it my way. Yes. I like to have fun, and I love women. I struggle to commit. I assumed Daire would use that against accepting my bourbon business venture. I can't quite wrap my head around his sudden change of heart. I could ask him, I guess.

I turn on the lights in the basement. The ceilings are higher than normal, and it's completely finished. I haven't bought furniture for the movie room yet. The other two rooms could serve as guest rooms in the future. As of now, they're either empty or used for storage. The part in the basement I use the most is the gym, which includes multiple machines and a sauna. I turn on the flat screen, find my favorite nature trail on YouTube, and run on the treadmill until I'm drenched with sweat and clear in the head.

Chapter 21

Sadie

"**H**ere." Easton hands me the pictures of the covers I made.

He's been fetching them from his printer for me. The colors are much better from this one than the one Everleigh let me borrow.

After my bath, which I thoroughly enjoyed, in his private en suite last night, I searched the house for him and assumed he left me.

As much as it hurt that he didn't even say goodbye, I tried not to let it bother me. This is my problem, not his. Unfortunately, I can't help but feel he owes me more because I'm not just a woman he picked up at a bar.

I don't know. Maybe I'm not cut out for the single sex life. I'm a one-man kind of girl. Yes. I'm with only one man right now, but I don't have him, not really. We're experimenting. I can admit it's the best sexual experiment of my life. I don't know why he hasn't had actual sex with me yet. At first, I thought it might be his big size. I'm going to feel that if he can even fit it in. Dash wasn't large, a bit below average, from what I've experienced. Part of me thinks

Easton is dragging it out so he doesn't get bored too quickly, or worse, he fears he won't like sex with me. How awkward would that be?

I'd be humiliated. I most certainly wouldn't be able to talk to him or see his face for months, if not longer.

"Are those the ones?" he asks from behind me, probably tired of the many I've dismissed or tweaked since we started this morning.

I give them another once over. "I can be happy with these."

What I'm not happy about is the hot jealousy in my stomach at the thought of other women—lots of women—ogling these covers with pictures of him.

"Three book covers means you owe me. We never agreed on a payment plan."

I set the printed pictures on the dresser and turn to him. "I think we're even now. If I remember correctly, we agreed to a payment in kisses and additional payment for *more* than kisses. We've done more. I also recall you telling me this is a way of life for me to try out. That would void the payment plan, wouldn't it?" I rest my hand on my jutted hip.

He strolls to me. "Someone is in a sassy mood today."

I've been more uptight than usual, that's for sure. Time away from Atlanta and what happened has definitely helped ease me back into myself. "Have you heard anything from the PI? I forgot his name."

"Steven." Easton puts his hands on my hips, as if to hold me in place. "He's still looking into it."

I sigh and focus on his dark blue shirt. "He's not going to find anything. There isn't enough to go on, and I don't feel threatened anymore. Maybe you should tell him to stop wasting his time. I doubt he's cheap, and I can't imagine it will lead to anything helpful at this point."

His grip tightens on my hips. "He's not wasting his time. He will find something, and you don't feel threatened anymore because you're here and you know you're safe. That could change when you get back to Atlanta."

"Maybe. But my mom and Tim will be back by the end of the week. I won't be alone, and I won't have to go into the office. I can work remotely. I miss my plants and DP misses his home." I glance at the hamster cage on the dresser. He runs every night, but it's like white noise to me and doesn't disrupt my slumber.

"He seems happy to me," Easton says. "If he's lonely, you can bring him downstairs during the day. He might like the view out the windows."

"I hadn't thought about that."

"You could put him on the porch for a little while, too. I can turn on the heater out there to keep him warm."

I can't stop a smile from forming. "That's really sweet. He might like that. I would like it, too."

"Speaking of heat. There's a fire pit in The Four Seasons. We can bring marshmallows and make s'mores while we're out there."

"A fire pit? Isn't that dangerous? What if the dock catches on fire?" From what I can see, the entire structure is made of wood.

He chuckles, and his hands slide to my waist. "It's small, portable, and on a metal plate. Nothing will catch fire. Even if it did—and it won't—the boat will be there for a quick, easy escape. But it won't. I promise."

I step away from him and stare out the balcony doors to the lake and the barely visible floating structure. "That's a long way to swim, and the water is freezing."

"Sadie." He chuckles again and stands behind me, placing his hands back on my hips. "Nothing bad will happen. You won't need to swim anywhere. I'm basically giving you your fantasy—to swim naked in a lake under the stars. It's a clear sky tonight. Too cold for nudity or swimming, but you'll be on the water, floating, warm and safe."

His visual and the fact that he remembered my teasing fantasy, has me melting toward him. I lean back.

His chin comes down on the top of my head.

It's such an intimate way to stand, as if we're a couple. I know him as well as I would a boyfriend. Better, even. I now know him sexually too, even if we haven't actually had sex.

It's getting confusing. I'll need space from him by the end of next week, lots of space to clear my head and set me on the right path. I'm not ready to date other people. What I'm doing with Easton is different. I trust him. I'm not ready to open myself up in any way to someone new. I still have to deal with Dash. He keeps texting me about getting back together, and I keep replying I need more time.

Easton's phone rings.

He moves away from me and answers the call.

"Daire? What do you need?" He gets quiet. "You're sure?" His tone carries an edge. I glance over my shoulder.

He's walking out of the room. "Uh-huh. No. I'll come there. I want to see them." He ends the call, his shoulders tense, his jaw tight.

"Is everything okay?"

He runs his hand through his thick grown-out hair, the golden-brown strands falling in disarray. Has anyone ever been as sexy as he is? No one I've ever known.

I walk toward him and place my hand on his cheek. "What's wrong?"

He stares at me for a long hard moment, a battle warring in his eyes.

"Easton?" I close the small distance between us.

He wraps me in his arms and pulls me close, holding me so tight I almost can't breathe. "I can't let you leave me."

"What?" What is he talking about?

"You have to stay here with me until it's safe. I don't want you out of my sight. You have to stay, okay?"

I pull back enough to tilt my head and look into his strained eyes. "I don't know what you're talking about."

"I don't want to tell you this, but Daire says you need to know."

"Daire? What does Daire have to do with this?" Fear trickles through me.

"A package came for you at the farm. To the store. Few people know you're here... I don't understand it."

I tense. "What kind of package?"

He pauses. "Pictures of you outside your work and your condo."

"H-how? Why?" My brain struggles to make sense.

"Daire says it looks like you were being followed and photographed."

"Holy shit." It's a grave whisper. My body turns cold. "I *was* being followed. I *did* see that man. Oh my God. Oh my God!" I repeat in a squeal. My heart hammers, and my body shakes. "I'm being stalked. Me! Why? I-I'm no one. I'm careful. The alley was a mistake, but I never do that. You know I never do that." Tears pool in my eyes and stream down my face. "I can't believe this."

Easton cups my head, pressing my cheek to his chest, and holds me tightly against him, his warmth and strength offering some comfort. A horrid thought occurs to me. I pull away from him again, as much as he'll let me, and meet his gaze.

"I can't stay here. You're not safe. None of you are because of me."

"This is the best place for you. With me, within the protection of the estate. Daire and I are going to hire security. The fact that no one got to you shows how safe we are. Only a few people know where you are, and he somehow discovered it. But you're still safer here than alone at your condo. The farm has cameras all over. I have cameras. The estate has them. We're gated. Now we'll have security guards. It's not like I'm defenseless, either. My dad trained me and Daire to handle guns long ago. I keep some in a safe in my office. I want to know where you are at all times until Steven works this out. The good news is, now he has something tangible for his research. This may be the key to finding out who's behind this."

My phone rings from where it rests on the dresser. I jump and force myself to calm down. At least listening to Easton talk got me to stop crying.

"I should get that. It might be my mom or Everleigh."

I pull away.

He stays close behind as I get my phone.

When I see it's Dash, I almost answer just to share this with him. Old habits. But then I haven't explained the attack to him. At first, I didn't tell him because I wasn't ready to have a lengthy conversation or to talk to him at all. It would have led to other topics, like our sudden breakup.

Easton sees his name. "You're not going to answer that, are you?"

"I think he should know. He cares about me still." He wants to marry me even.

"Sadie?" He moves to stand in front of me. "The fewer people who know, the better. He could inadvertently tip someone else off. He might be the reason the photos arrived here. The person watching you is most likely watching everyone you know or have been close with. We need to keep this between us."

The phone stops ringing. "Dash knows I'm at the farm, but who would he tell besides his bar-hopping buddies? And like they'd care..."

"It doesn't matter if they don't care. This is how it works. Think of your crime shows. Stalkers are creative and thorough. If he connected you to the farm, he has certainly connected you to Dash."

I gasp. "My mom! What if he's connected me to her?" The tears form again. I'd never forgive myself if she ended up as collateral damage. "This is too much. Stuff like this doesn't happen to people like me." I sniffle and wipe my cheeks dry from the onslaught of fresh tears.

"Oh, baby." Eason cradles me to him again, his steady heartbeat comforting me.

I focus on it and try to calm down. "I have to call my mom. I have to warn her so she can be prepared when she gets back. We don't know how long this will go on for."

"Okay."

"I want to call her alone." Some things you don't want an audience for.

"I'll be downstairs." He kisses the top of my head and releases me slowly. He catches my gaze. "You're safe here. Okay?"

I nod. "Okay." I don't know if I'll ever feel safe again.

I watch him leave and then call my mom. Once I've explained everything and cried with her, Tim gets on the phone and assures me he'll keep my mom safe when they get back to Atlanta this weekend. He also advises me to stay at the farm and not return to Atlanta. He'd rather I be around friends and security than alone or in a new place.

"I want to leave the state. I have a vacation planned, but it's not for six days," I remind Tim.

"The stalker could know about the trip," he says. "Stay put. Please."

I shiver. "I don't like this at all."

My mom gets back on the phone. "Sadie, sweetie, stay where you are. Don't worry about work. We'll make sure it's taken care of. Focus on yourself and getting through this as best you can. I'm a phone call away whenever you want to talk, and we'll be back in America on Sunday. I'll come to the farm if you want."

"Okay." I curl in a ball on the bed. I wouldn't ask her to drive here after traveling back from Europe. I gasp. "Is this going to ruin the rest of your vacation?"

"No sweetie. It's a trip. You're my daughter. You mean more. I love you."

"I love you, too."

"Call me if you need anything. I'll answer."

"Okay."

"Bye."

Exhaustion seeps into my bones. I didn't sleep well, over-analyzing why Easton left me to bathe alone in his tub.

This morning when I was making coffee, he joined me and explained he was working out in the basement last night—the one place I didn't check—and lost track of time.

I still felt like he was avoiding me, but he seemed genuine and offered to help me today with the book covers. It was his idea to use his printer. We worked together all morning and into the afternoon. If he had something better to do, he missed it, but he didn't seem to care. He wanted to help me, and I was thankful.

I also found the courage to go on our picnic date and really wanted to go.

Footsteps sound on the wooden stairs.

I lift my head from the pillow. Easton peers around the open double doors. "Did you talk to your mom?"

"Yeah. She said to stay here."

"I just talked to Tim."

"You did?" I sit up. "I just ended the call with my mom a minute ago."

He walks over and sits beside me on the bed. "I think he called me when you were still talking to her. I heard her voice in the background."

"How did he know to call you?"

"I texted him when you first got here. I wanted him to know you were with me and I would look out for you."

"Wow. I had no idea." Or that he was so considerate. To text my stepdad...

I hug him, my cheek pressed against his shoulder.

He chuckles and works his arm out so he can wrap it around me. I rest my cheek on his firm pec. "Thanks for caring about me the way you do."

"That's what besties are for," he teases.

I giggle. "I've never had a bestie like you."

"Me neither."

"Does Everleigh know? I don't want her to worry."

"Daire is going to tell her when he gets back to the estate. I'm sure she'll call after he does."

"I'm sure, too." I sigh. "I hate that I'm putting you all through this. It isn't fair."

"You didn't ask for it to happen. And if you leave now, Everleigh will be even more worried."

"True." I don't want that.

"I guess we can't go on our picnic." I move from his embrace and sit up.

"We can't let this ruin our fun. That's what stalkers

want. To make you uncomfortable. I think we should go and have so much fun we don't even think about him." He takes me by the chin and tips my head, so I meet his eyes. "You will be safe. No one can get you there or here or when you're with me. Understand?"

I don't answer.

"Yes, Easton." He mimics my voice. "I understand. Thank you for your protection and for being so hot. It turns me on."

I laugh, despite my grim mood.

"I'll make you forget," he whispers, his gaze dark and seductive.

That, I believe.

Chapter 22

Sadie

I stand in the back of the country farm store in the café section, waiting for Millie to return from the kitchen.

"Here you go." She hands me a medium-sized picnic basket with handles.

"Thank you." The basket isn't too heavy, but I can tell it's filled. "You spoil him, you know?"

"I know," she says with a sad smile. "He deserves it."

The sadness makes me curious. But first I need to make sure Easton is still upstairs with Daire. He went up to his office to get the pictures. I don't see him so they must still be talking.

Quickly, I turn to Millie, who's wiping off the counter. "You sounded sad when you said Easton 'deserves it.'"

She stops cleaning and gives me a sympathetic grin. "He's always been a bit of a loner, surrounded by many but always alone in here." She touches her heart. "He's different with you. It makes me happy to see that. I'm glad he has you."

If I think about it, she's right. Easton has many friends—both women and men—he has many bed partners, but even with all that, he's private. He shares his carefree and flirty side, but nothing else. He's slowly opened up to me over the year, but after living with him, I'm seeing so much more. He's generous and protective. He's thoughtful and honest. Such admirable qualities, and I can tell he doesn't consider himself to have them. He wants to impress Daire so badly with his business idea, but I think it's more. I think he wants his brother's approval, his parents even, because he's never had it. And that's sad.

"I'm glad I have him, too," I say. "He's special."

She tilts her head, her grin tender. "He is."

"Thanks again." I raise the basket and carry it to a table in the café so I can text him.

I find a missed text.

Everleigh: Just checking to make sure you're still okay.

She's always concerned for everyone else.

Sadie: I hope you're not stressing over this. I told you, I'm handling it well. Easton is distracting me with a picnic. I just got the basket of goodies from Millie. Please don't worry about this.

Everleigh: What did the police say? You didn't tell me.

Oh crap. I forgot to let her know. We talked before I came here, but I hadn't called the detective assigned to the case yet to give him the news.

Sadie: Nothing much. They want the pictures for evidence and to check for prints. Easton's having the PI take them to Atlanta after he looks at them and then Steven will stay in touch and get the results, probably faster than I could.

Everleigh: Thank God for Steven. He'll find something. He did regarding my situation, and that seemed impossible.

I remember when she and Daire told me the story. Easton was there, too. He was a big help in uncovering everything with Benedict. That day seems so long ago.

Everleigh: Have fun on your picnic. I'm glad Easton is distracting you.

She wouldn't be if she knew in what way he likes to distract me, and that I'm into it.

I text Easton. He's almost done and says he'll meet me on the back porch by the café.

We parked the UTV out there. When he suggested we take it to the farm, I got nervous. Once again, he assured me I'm safe and that it'd be fun.

I had no idea how much I'd like it or how hard I'd laugh. He drove a bit wild for me. We'll have to take it easy on the way home because of the food basket. I'd hate for any of it to spill. As soon as I step onto the porch my phone rings.

It's Dash again. The last time he called he left a message about the vacation this Sunday and wanted to know if I've decided to go with him. I can't keep avoiding him. He's called me more this last week than he has in the last six months. I don't get it. I kind of like it, but why did it take me breaking things off for him to realize what he lost? Maybe that was it. I had to end it for him to come to his senses.

Ugh.

I answer. "Hello?"

"Babe. I've been calling."

"I know. Sorry."

"Did you get my messages?"

"Yeah." I face the rows of pecan trees and squint against the late afternoon sun. The warmth of it feels good with the chill in the air. Today wasn't as cold as it's been. For that reason, Easton didn't want to wait to go on our picnic. Tomorrow the temperature will dip again.

"Have you decided anything?" he asks. "I miss you. When are you coming back to Atlanta? I'd rather have this conversation in person."

"Everleigh needs me so I'm staying longer," I lie.

He sighs with obvious disappointment. "Longer as in during our planned vacation?"

I've been avoiding making this decision. Time to fix that. "Yes. I'm sorry."

"Me too." He sighs again. "You can't always run to Everleigh's side when she needs you. I need you, too. You know what I had planned for you on this trip—for us. Are you willing to give it up for a friend?"

I scoff. "That's rich coming from you. You're always with your friends. You always put them first. Everleigh is my best friend. We have always been there for each other, no matter what. I won't change that for anyone and if you truly loved me, you'd understand and accept it."

My heart races. I can't believe I said that. I've never talked to him like that before.

Silence stretches.

"Hello?"

"I'm here," he says. "I'm just shocked."

Part of me wants to apologize. I don't let myself. "I tried to explain this to you before. You never wanted to hear it. It's not bad that I want more from the man I plan to marry."

"Look. I don't want to argue. I want to see you. Doing this over the phone is hard. If I could see you, I know we could work this out. What if I come to the farm?"

"No!" I blurt. "I mean, there's a lot going on with the renovations on the Inn and Everleigh being pregnant. There's barely any room for me." I'm lying through my teeth. Why am I not telling him I've been staying with Easton?

"I don't have to stay at the farm. I could pick you up and we could go to Honeycomb and that restaurant you love. The one with the soup."

The door behind me creaks open. I turn and lock eyes with Easton.

The sun shines in his beautiful face, showcasing his whiskey-colored irises.

I can't talk to Dash around Easton.

"Listen, I have to go."

"Sadie, wait! Please! We can't keep going back and forth like this."

"I know." I give Easton my back and take the steps down from the porch for some privacy. I hate how uncomfortable I feel, like I'm betraying him by talking to my ex.

"You know my wishes. They haven't changed. I want to marry you. The ball's in your court. Please come see me soon."

I end the call and paste a smile on my face when I turn to Easton. "Ready?"

He comes down the stairs and takes the basket from my hand. "Are you?" His gaze holds mine. He's letting me decide what to tell him.

I zip my jacket. "I'm ready for more adventures." I don't see a package or envelope. "What happened to the pictures?"

"We didn't want to risk contaminating them. Daire has them sealed for Steven. I snapped copies for you on my phone."

"Oh. Smart." And I'm supposed to be the crime show expert.

Easton takes it easy on the drive back.

The scent of burning leaves fills the air, the crisp breeze biting at my cheeks. "Are you sure we won't be too cold? The sun is setting."

"I have fur blankets, and I packed some bourbon to keep us warm." He grins, looking like a sexy rancher in his blue jean shirt, his tan, fitted pants, and his corduroy jacket. A leather band encircles his wrist near his watch. The bracelet is incredibly sexy on him.

"Is it your pecan bourbon? Or should I say, the farm's new pecan bourbon?"

"You know it, sweetcakes." He winks.

"There's no one else I'd rather be huddled up for my safety with," I confess.

He groans and shakes his head, his expression equal parts thoughtful and confused. "What are you doing to me, Sadiecakes."

"Being sweet?" I tease.

"You're always sweet." He keeps one hand on the steering wheel and uses the other to hook my waist and slides me closer to him on the bench seat.

I giggle and snuggle against his warmth.

Chapter 23

Sadie

I sit reclined on the dock and watch the pink and purple fade from the sky. "There goes the last of it."

"That's my cue." Easton takes the basket of left-over food and drinks to the boat.

Our picnic was amazing. The small fire pit offered the perfect amount of warmth, as did the blankets Easton brought. And the food was delicious. Millie outdid herself.

I can still taste the marshmallow and chocolate from the s'mores we made. Prior to that, we dined on a charcuterie board and butternut squash soup with warm biscuits.

I take another sip of bourbon—which happens to pair nicely with s'mores—from a paper coffee cup.

"We're fancy." I hold up my cup to Easton when he returns from packing up the boat.

The goal is to see the stars, but if I get too cold, he wants to be able to jump in the boat and go.

He toasts his bourbon-filled coffee cup to mine. "We are the epitome of fancy. Gilded age, look out."

I laugh. "You don't watch that show."

"I'm surprised you do." He heard me talking about it with Everleigh.

"Why?" I sip more bourbon, loving the sweet and smoky flavor and the heat that travels through my body.

"It doesn't have murder." He glances at the tiny cabin-like structure. "Want to move inside to watch the stars? It's warmer."

So far, I've been fine, but now that the sun is down, it's probably a good idea.

"Sure." I help him carry the mound of furry blankets inside and lay two on the floor. The entire ceiling is made of glass, similar to what they use on boats. Easton explained it all on the lake ride out here.

Once we're inside the shelter, Easton turns on a small lantern in the corner. It casts a low glow. We remove our jackets and pull a big blanket over us as we lie down, taking in the view.

"Are you warm enough?" Easton asks.

I nod. "You're very attentive."

"You say it like it's a bad thing."

"No. It's nice. It's just you're not even my boyfriend and you care for me—my needs—more than it seems Dash ever did."

"It sounds like Dash didn't know a good thing when he had it."

I laugh, but it lacks gusto. "He..." I stop myself. Before, I'd talk about Dash to Easton, but now I'm not sure it's fair. Of course, that implies Easton would care in a boyfriend way and that is not what he's about. Still, it doesn't feel right.

"Say it." He takes my hand under the blanket and laces our fingers. "It's still us."

"Yeah, but we have sex now."

"Technically, we haven't."

I bump his side with our clasped hands. "You know what I mean."

"Say the word when you want me to fix that. I'm all in."

I keep my gaze on the darkening sky, the stars not yet shining. The raft is motionless, the lake calm. "What happens after we do?" I dare to ask.

I feel his gaze on my profile. "We rest, or we do it again. I'm flexible."

A giggle pushes up my throat. "What if it changes things between us?"

"How so?"

I take a breath, unsure if I'm ready for the answer. "What if we're done? How do we stay friends after sharing that? I know you do it all the time, but I don't know how."

He rolls onto his side. "I'll teach you."

I don't know what I wanted him to say. We won't stop having sex. He doubts he'll be done with me. *I'll teach you*, wasn't it, though.

I pull my hand away and move it to my stomach. It seems childish, but I'm not emotionally equipped for this.

"What's wrong, Sadiecakes?" He rests his head on his hand, his elbow bent. "Is it Dash?"

"It's a lot of things." My body tenses, and sadness creeps over me.

"What do you want?" he whispers.

For him to want me the way I want him. For him to want to try to date me, not just mess around. For him to take me right now, making the decision for me, and make me feel good in the way only he can. I hate myself for thinking and wanting these things. It wasn't part of the deal. The deal was kisses and a payment plan with sexual trysts. Somehow, I surpassed that and caught feelings for him, real feelings, while he sits back, comfortable with his single status. It's not fair to be angry at him, but I am, and I hate myself for it. I hate myself for ruining this beautiful night that could have been so romantic had I just stuck to the damn plan.

A tear slides down my cheek.

He catches it with his finger and pulls me on top of him, holding me in his strong embrace. "Why are you crying?" He strokes my hair.

I let my cheek rest on his firm chest and cry a little more. Once it's out, I'll feel better. "It's nothing."

"It's not nothing. You're upset. What can I do to help?"

I cry harder. "You can't. No one can." This is a me problem. One man wants to marry me, but I'm not sure I can marry him. Another man wants to be my friend and please me sexually in the best way I've known, but he doesn't want anything else.

How did I get here?

"Sadie, baby. I'm here. I'm here for you." He kisses the top of my head and rolls me onto my back, his arm behind my neck. His side hugs mine, and he caresses my cheek as I cry. "Please tell me what's wrong?" He kisses my tear-soaked cheek. Then the other, and the corner of my mouth, and the other corner. When his lips gently brush mine, I'm gone.

I slide my fingers into the back of his hair and hold him to me for more kisses. His tongue sweeps the seam of my mouth, and I open, letting him in. Our tongues touch and tangle, tasting of tears and bourbon.

It's delicious, like salted caramel. His kiss unravels me the way it always does. I moan into his mouth and snake my hand under his sweater. If this is all I can have, I'll take it because I need it. I need him in a way he'll never understand.

He pulls his sweater over his head. I drink in his sculpted tanned chest, the muscles corded and flexing. Has there ever been a more beautiful man?

Easton removes my sweater. The tank-top bra I'm wearing comes off with it. My nipples harden, but I'm not cold. I'm burning up, desperate for Easton to consume my every thought and need.

"I'm on birth control," I murmur as he kisses a trail down my neck, his fingers playing with my hard nipples. Tingles erupt inside me, shooting straight to my core. I'm drenched and writhing my hips, ready. "I want to have sex."

He chuckles. "I figured."

"Are you...clean?"

"I never have sex without protection, but I didn't bring any, Sadie." He kisses the top of my breast. "Sorry, baby."

"Sorry, my ass. We're both clean. I'm protected. It's settled." I arch my back and move his head to my nipple.

He chuckles again. "Demanding. I like it."

"Shh. Less talking, more action."

"Very demanding." He lifts his head. "That deserves a spanking."

My core clenches with need and the memory of what it did to me the last time. "What are you waiting for?"

"Shit, Sadie." He sits up next to me and stares into my eyes. "I want to spank and fuck you so hard right now, but I don't know if I should."

Oh hell no. Standing, I remove my boots and undo the button on my jeans. Before taking them off, I turn and slide them down, making sure my ass is in his face.

He hisses and grabs my hips, holding me still. He kisses my left cheek, then bites and spanks it.

I squeal at the sudden attack, even though the sting is minor. This is what I want from him. Dominance. I don't want to think or make decisions. I want to be seduced, screwed, and sated.

"This ass is mine." He spanks the other cheek and then gives the muscle a deep massage. "Say it?"

I'm soaked and panting. "This is yours."

"What is?" He rises to his knees and kisses me between my shoulder blades.

"My ass."

"*My* ass, Sadie. It's mine." He kisses and bites my other cheek. The bites are never hard, more territorial. "Get on all fours."

I do, as he says, my blood racing toward the part of me that wants to feel him the most.

I hear him remove his clothes, then he's on his knees behind me, his legs outside of mine. He bends over me, his chest warming my back, and kisses the side of my neck. "Turn your head."

I do and he claims my lips, his tongue teasing as his hard erection pushes between my cheeks.

He slides away and kisses my shoulder. "Good girl."

His hands skim my sides all the way to my hips as he straightens onto his knees. "Does my girl like to be spanked?" He slaps my ass.

"Yes," I pant.

"Does my girl want me to fuck her now?"

The anticipation is as much a turn on as his touches.

He rubs his hand along my soaked core and hisses. "Yes. My girl does. She loves it." He spanks me again and spreads my legs.

I can't take it. "Easton, please. I need you now."

"Almost." He slides two fingers into my sex.

I moan, thankful to have something inside me.

I rock into him, needing to feel him deeper.

"You want more, baby?"

"Yes?" I can barely breathe. My muscles are tight, my body pulsing and begging for all he has to give.

He fucks me harder with his fingers and adds a third. It slips right in and isn't as filling as it was before.

"Damn, baby. You're soaked."

"Easton, please. I want you inside me. I *need* it."

He pushes my head to the blanket, my forehead resting on the floor, my ass up in the air. He spreads my legs farther, slipping between them, and rubs the tip of his huge cock at my entrance. I moan and try to push back.

"Easy, Sadie. You're going to feel this."

"Good." I can't believe I'm acting like this, but I don't care. I'm out of my mind with desire.

He pushes in the tip but meets a bit of resistance. "Relax, Sadie. Let me do the work."

He rubs my ass with his big hands, then slides them to my folds and opens me. At the same time, he pushes in again. His width fills me, but I force myself not to tense.

"Fuck, you're tight." Slowly, he eases in more.

I go limp, feeling every inch of him stretch and fill my body to the point where there is no more room. The slight pain his size causes makes it that much better. I wouldn't have thought so, but it does. Like the spanking, it's a mild sting but followed by so much pleasure.

I doubt he's in all the way, but it feels like he is, and it feels divine.

"You did good. Took me deep." He leans forward, his chest to my back, and brushes my hair aside to kiss my neck. "I'm going to fuck you now."

Remaining over me, he takes a moment to caress then pinch my nipple, flooding my core even more.

"God, Easton," I groan.

"Just me, baby. Just my name." He straightens, grabs my hips, and eases out.

I moan at the loss of his girth until he stretches me out again by shoving back in. He does it again and again. He's so big and invading, consuming my every thought and replacing it with only need.

"Faster." I rock my hips backwards.

He pulls almost all the way out and slams into me, his body slapping into my ass and sending me forward. I push to my hands to keep from getting a face-burn from the blanket. He slams into me again and again, stealing my breath with each thrust.

"Oh, God."

"Easton."

I can't think. I am a vessel for the taking, and I like the taking.

He leans over me while he thrusts his big size into my hypersensitive body. His warmth and his sweaty skin touch my back. In my ear, he says, "If you want me to keep fucking you, you better call my name."

"Easton," I murmur. "You. Only you."

"Fuck, I like that. I need to see you. I need to see that pretty face when you orgasm and call my name." He pulls out and flips me onto my back.

I barely have time to register what's happening.

He sits on his heels, his knees bent, and grips my waist, pulling my lower half onto his thighs.

I'm naked on a lake in a glass shed, half covering him, my nipples aching, and I don't care. I want his lips on me and his dick back inside me. That's all that matters.

My wish comes true the moment he shoves the tip of his big cock into my heat and fills me with one thrust. He secures me to his lap and fucks me hard, the way I like, the way I need. My boobs bounce, and his gaze goes from my face to my breasts. He licks his lips.

"This is mine, Sadie." He pounds into me. "Do you hear me? This is mine."

I hear him, but I can't speak. I'm on the edge of an orgasmic cliff, ready to fall over. I open my eyes right before I orgasm and see the stars, so bright against the black of the sky.

"Easton!" I cry his name as pleasure swarms me, carrying me off on a cloud of ecstasy, where nothing else exists.

"That's my girl." He stills. "Give me it all." He waits until I stop moaning, then hammers his cock inside me again.

At first, I'm too wiped out to participate, then he lowers me to the blanket and plunges into me again. His mouth covers my nipple. He sucks, drawing desire to the surface in an instant. My body recharges with a need I can't believe is possible so soon.

This has never happened before.

I slide my fingers into his hair at the back of his head and wrap my legs around his torso as he feasts on my breasts.

"Oh, G—Easton."

I feel him smile against my nipple. He lifts his head and runs his hand down the sides of my torso to my ass. He smacks my cheek.

I moan and orgasm again, shooting up like a rocket and coming back down.

Easton groans, and with a final thrust, he comes inside me, cursing and calling my name.

Chapter 24

Easton

I roll Sadie's naked body on top of mine, then cover her with the fur blanket, pulling it up to her bare shoulders. I kiss the top of her head.

Her cheek rests on my chest. She's been quiet for some time, answering my questions with few words.

Me - "How are you?"

Her - "Fine."

Me - "Am I crushing you?"

Her - "A little."

Me - "Are you cold?"

Her - "No."

Now, I'm wondering if something is wrong.

She's on me but not snuggling against me. Her body is more like a blanket I placed a certain way. I can't believe we had sex. It was the best sex of my life, and it was with Sadie. Never had I imagined she'd be this way. Never.

"Sadiecakes?" I stroke my hand down her clammy back. "We shouldn't stay out here for too long. I'd hate for you to get sick from the cold."

She nods against my chest and then pushes herself up, taking the blanket with her.

"I didn't mean right this second." I grab another blanket from the other side of me and cover my naked body from the chill.

"It's okay. We should go." She avoids my gaze and gathers her clothes.

Dammit. Something is up. She couldn't have hated the sex. It was obvious in many ways that she enjoyed herself. A worse thought comes to mind. I tense. "Did I hurt you?"

"No," she snaps, as if the question is absurd.

It isn't. We had rough sex and I'm big. She's dainty. It wouldn't be a surprise if she were sore considering how tight she is.

I get my phone, then turn on the flashlight so she can find her clothes in the blankets. She collects her sweater and pants. I watch her dress, checking for any marks or bruises on her body. The wood floor is hard, even with the layers of blankets. Nothing stands out other than how glorious she looks naked. Her body is perfectly proportioned for her size.

Realizing I'm staring, I quickly grab my clothes and get dressed. She collects our jackets, then hands me mine as I gather the blankets. I need to say something to ease her or find out what's wrong, but I haven't a clue how to go about it.

She slips on her boots and eyes me. "Ready?"

I tie my shoelaces, then gather the blankets in my arms. "Yep." What the hell is wrong with me? Why can't I think of something more or better to say?

With anyone else this sudden distance and desire to leave would be normal. I wouldn't think anything about it other than we did what we came to do and now it's over. But this is Sadie. My closest friend. My houseguest. My brother's wife's best friend. She's different and an important part of my life.

We climb into the boat. It rocks slightly. Sadie takes the blankets from me and sits on the back bench, holding them on her lap. Probably to keep warm. The colder temperature and the wind on the ride back will be chilly. Before turning on the spotlight so I can steer us back to shore, I catch Sadie taking in the stars. Thousands twinkle above us and reflect on the surface of the lake. The peace and beauty almost take my breath away. The fact that I'm sharing it with Sadie makes it that more special.

"Beautiful, isn't it?" I say.

She nods, her gaze still toward the sky. "I love the stars. When I was little me and Everleigh would sneak onto her roof and watch the stars. Sometimes, if we were brave, we'd go down to the lake up the street and watch them from the grass with our feet in the water."

"You weren't afraid of gators?"

"I was young and not afraid of much."

"What changed that?"

She inhales a deep breath. "Honeycomb is small, as you know. Everyone knows everyone. News travels fast. A woman who worked with my mom at Mimi's, the consignment shop downtown," she adds like I'd know it.

I shrug, clueless.

"It's the big store on the corner," she explains. "It's historical and pretty famous to the locals. My mom worked there all through my childhood and up until she met Tim. Anyway, the woman's husband was walking their dog by the lake downtown and the dog got attacked by an alligator. It snatched him from the water's edge and dragged him under. They never found the dog. It scared me to death because the day before I'd been at that lake, skipping rocks and splashing. That could have been me." She shivers and hugs the blankets tighter.

"That's scary. I'm surprised you let me take you out here." Amazed really. "If I'd known what caused your fear, I wouldn't have suggested it."

"I'm glad I came. I'm glad I got to see this." She gazes at the stars again.

"It's pretty brave of you, Sadiecakes."

She giggles and shakes her head.

Feeling a little better now that I've got her talking and smiling, I start the engine and then drive us to shore.

We exit onto the dock. I take the pile of blankets, and I offer her the less bulky, empty basket to carry.

"Do you want to talk?" I ask on the way up the slight incline to the house. Small lights line a stone trail, leading the way.

Hooting sounds in the trees, drawing Sadie's gaze. "What was that?"

"An owl."

"I've been in the city for too long. I forgot what it's like to be surrounded by nature. I miss it."

"Maybe you should move back." *Maybe you should move here.* The thought throws me off balance. I stumble but catch myself before she notices.

She draws in another deep breath and releases it out slowly. "It's something to think about."

She gets quiet again, and I can't help but wonder if she's thinking about Dash and his offer to move to a small town outside of Atlanta. It won't be like this. She won't get what she wants most. This is what she wants. Maybe I could build her a house on part of the property. Would she like that? Coming from me, probably not. She'd think I'm taking pity on her. Coming from Everleigh though, she might be open to it.

I should talk to my sister-in-law, ASAP. But wait. How does that fit in with my lifestyle? Would bringing women back to the house make things awkward if Sadie ran into us or noticed? After the sex I had with Sadie, the thought of other women is a complete turn off. I can't imagine sleeping with anyone other than her. Hell, I'd take her to my bed and have my way with her right now if she seemed interested in round two. I can't get a read on her though, unusual for me.

"Let's go in through the basement." I lead her around the side of the house to the entrance.

We enter a hallway, where I dump the blankets in a laundry room.

"So this is where this is," she says.

"One of them. I prefer the laundry room on the second floor." I freeze. "Wait. Did I not tell you where they are?"

She lets out a breathy giggle. "No, but I wouldn't have needed to use them. I'm leaving—or I *was* leaving this Friday." She sighs. "I wish I had more clothes now. I need to make sure Reva can keep watering my plants, too. At least I was smart enough to bring DP. I should check on him." She takes a step then pauses. "Which way to the stairs?"

"I'll take that." I retrieve the basket from her and point down the hallway. "The stairs are halfway down on the left."

"Thanks." She walks off, leaving me dumbstruck and uncomfortable in a way I've never known. I'm not a closure guy. I'm an upfront guy. But with Sadie and this situation, I need closure. More importantly, I need to know how she feels about us having sex and if we can continue to have more. I've never been in this predicament. The uncertainty is a mental torment I'm not familiar with.

I empty the basket, then set it on the counter. Once I'm upstairs I glance around the empty great room, my gaze landing on the kitchen. I'd planned to make coffee or cocoa. I ordered hot chocolate for her after she mentioned it the other night. The delivery arrived yesterday with an assortment of flavors: dark chocolate, milk, peppermint, hazelnut, and s'more.

I need a shower, but I'm not yet ready to leave in case she comes down. Screw it. I text her.

Easton: Do you want hot cocoa?

Sadie: We don't have any.

Easton: I got some.

Sadie: You did?

Easton: Surprise.

Sadie: That was sweet, but I need to shower.

Easton: Me, too.

Want to join me. I don't text her that.

Sadie: Maybe after.

Not an invitation for me to join her. Damn.

Easton: Okay. Let me know.

None of this is okay. I want her in my shower and in my bed. I want to know what she's thinking, and I want to hold her while she falls asleep. I've never wanted that. Ever. It could be because we're so close. The women I sleep with regularly are friends. I know them. I know their bodies, but I don't know them personally, like I do Sadie. I don't care to know more. If they need to vent, I listen but, typically, they don't. Our arrangement is mutual. When I pick up a woman at a bar or meet one from a dating app, I don't know the person other than what I learn from small talk. We have a mutual understanding that we're going to have sex. I was so concerned with how Sadie would handle being with me in a sexual capacity that I didn't stop to consider how I'd be affected.

I shower and then change into sweats and a t-shirt. When I leave my room, the house is quiet. I listen for movement upstairs. Hearing nothing, I head downstairs. A murder crime show plays on the flat screen above the fireplace, but I don't see Sadie. I glance at the kitchen. Two coffee mugs sit next to the variety pack of cocoa I left on the counter for her. Was she waiting for me? Warmth fills my heart, the sensation is as strange as it is enjoyable.

Where the hell is she?

The bathroom maybe? I stroll to the couch to wait and find Sadie curled on her side asleep. Her damp hair falls behind her, the maple color darker. An oversized sweatshirt bares one of her shoulders, and matching pants cover her legs. Her bow-shaped lips are slightly parted. The sight of her cuddled on my couch sends more of that warmth to my heart.

I brush a finger across her cheek. Her eyes flutter open, and she lets out a sexy sleepy moan.

"Were you waiting for me?" I ask.

She nods, then snuggles her head into the pillow. "I'm so tired."

"Let's go to bed," I say, a plan in mind.

"Okay." Her eyes close.

A chuckle escapes my throat. I scoop her into my arms, then carry her upstairs to my room. Other than murmuring, "I can walk," she doesn't try to get down or even open her eyes.

I put her in my bed, then slide in beside her, and cover us up. She turns onto her side and snuggles her face in the pillow like she had on the couch.

I'm about to pull her to me when she murmurs, "Too hot."

She pulls off her shirt and pants and then tosses them on the floor.

Well, this is going better than I planned. I'd already removed my shirt, but now I want to join her in the no-pants-department. I consider leaving on my underwear, which I never do so she doesn't think I'm trying for round two. Crazy thinking given the sex we had less than two hours ago and how she encouraged it—initiated it. Not that I'm complaining. I loved every second, especially when she pulled down her pants and stuck her plump little ass in my face. As if summoned by the memory, my dick stands at attention. Not going to happen, buddy.

Ignoring my hard-on, I strip bare, then tuck Sadie against me, her back to my chest. I hold her there with my nose buried in her sweet apple-scented hair. A peace I've never known settles over me. Why did I ever think having a woman in my bed is a bad idea? This is amazing. But then this is Sadie. Everything with her turns out amazing.

* * *

My phone dings, waking me from the best sleep I've had in a long, long time. Early morning light scatters through the trees outside the windows.

Sadie's body is still tucked against me, where I'd moved her last night. Carefully, I lift my arm, then turn to get my phone from the nightstand. She stirs a little but doesn't appear to wake.

I read the text. It's from Steven. He has information about Sadie's attacker. Equal parts of concern and anxiousness tumble through me. As desperate as I am to know what he found out, I fear how the news will affect Sadie.

Should I wake her and we call Steven together, or should I find out the facts and then present them once she's eaten and had coffee? Option two sounds much better than disturbing her slumber.

I inch from the bed, careful not to disturb her and then put on my clothes. Once I'm dressed, I head to my office and close the door, separating the space from the bedroom where she sleeps.

Steven picks up on the first ring.

"That was fast," he says instead of a greeting.

"How bad is it?"

"I found who the stalker is, and I have some dirt on her ex-boyfriend, Dash."

"Dash? He's involved?" My fingers ball into tight fists. I'll kill him.

"Not regarding her stalker. That's separate, but my digging uncovered secrets he's been keeping from her. I figured you'd want to know everything."

"You figured right. Give me the details on the stalker first."

"Wait until you hear this." He tells me a story I know will leave Sadie in shock. Hell, I'm in shock. As for the dirt on Dash, I'm going to kill the piece of shit.

I end the call and stare at the closed door, my heart in agony, my arms shaking with barely checked rage. This information will tear Sadie apart. It's a lot for anyone to handle.

Suddenly, I wish I wouldn't have slept with her. I'm not reliable like Daire. And after this, Sadie will need someone she can depend on. I've never been that person. As much as I'd love to try to be that for Sadie, I don't know if I can trust myself not to mess up. Even though the thought of being sexual with other women does nothing for me and how Sadie is the only person I want to sleep with at this time, who's to say I won't get bored and eventually let her down. She needs a friend in me, not a friend with benefits who has the potential to hurt her should I fail.

Shit. Neither of us thought this through, but how do we go back to what we were before? Everything she does makes me want her more than before because I've had her. I know how amazing it is to be with her sexually. I may never find that kind of connection with anyone else. But that's not enough for her. She wants the fairy tale. She deserves it.

I've had this conversation with myself. Already, I've complicated things between us and for that I'm ashamed. From now on, I'll only do what she wants and what I can to make her life easier. No matter how badly I want her, especially if she throws herself at me, I'll resist. It will be the hardest thing I've ever done, but I'll do it for her.

Chapter 25

Sadie

I wake from a peaceful slumber to an empty bed. Easton's bed. Why am I here?

Last I remember, I went downstairs for cocoa with him. I was tired and almost didn't go to meet him after my shower. I was also a bit embarrassed about how I acted.

Easton being Easton thought nothing of my behavior. Why would he? For all I know that kind of sex is vanilla for him. For me, it was insane. In the best way.

I stretch and notice I'm a bit sore between my legs. My cheeks heat and I cover my eyes, embarrassed again. I went for it with him last night. I wanted him, and for the first time ever, I acted on my desire—there was so much. Easton turns me on in a way no man ever has. And the sex... My cheeks scorch.

I roll to my side and bury my face in the pillow. I never knew sex could be so exhilarating and pleasurable. Dash and I never had sex like that, not even close. We never connected in the way I do with Easton. It's like he knows my body and what I like better than I do. How is it possible?

Have my past lovers been that bad or is Easton that incredible?

He brings out a side of me I didn't know existed. I like to be spanked. Who would have thought? But then, he's not a brutal spanker. I don't know that it would count as BDSM with how playful and painless it is. Only, in the moment, I don't feel like playing with anything except his dick.

Oh my gosh. I cover my mouth to smother a squeal. I'm out of control. The worst part is I like it. Would that make it the best part then?

Sadly, I believe my pleasure-seeking time with Easton has come to an end. He's done with me. Why else would he not be here to face me? Of course, he did put me in his bed last night—a bed he never lets anyone else sleep in. It could be his way of smoothing things over with me. He knew I was upset after we had sex. His comment that we should leave set me off. I tensed and figured he was ready to head back, so I jumped up. Having never slept with a man who isn't my boyfriend, I don't know what the protocol is. I hadn't figured he would want to leave the little house on the dock so quickly. It made me nervous. What do you say after casual sex? How do you act? I don't have a clue, so I stayed quiet. What I wanted to do was stay in his arms for the night, even if it meant sleeping on the hard floor of that dock. I suppose I got my wish in that way but in his soft bed.

Water turns on in the en suite bathroom. So that's where he is. And is he showering again?

I scramble from the bed and stand. Where are my clothes? Did I remove them? Vaguely, I remember taking them off. Oh God. He probably thought I was trying to get him to sleep with me again. I would have. I want to again now, but I know it won't happen.

It's for the best. Any more sex like that and my heart

will belong to him. A part of it already does with how close we are. All my friends have a piece of my heart. It's how I am. Easton has a little more than a piece, and that scares me. I need to be careful. I need distance.

In a hurry, I pull on my clothes and patter from the room, closing the bedroom door quietly behind me.

I head upstairs to my bedroom and lock the door. I haven't locked it once since I got here. I'm being silly, but I've gone into protective mode regarding my heart. This is how it needs to be.

I check the time. 10:00 a.m.

Everleigh should be awake, and I could use the distraction and actual physical distance from Easton.

Sadie: Want some company?

Everleigh: Sure. Daire is checking to see if everything is ready for Thanksgiving dinner at the farm next week. Now that you're staying for longer, I assume you'll be joining us.

My shoulders drop. I'd forgotten. If I hadn't slept with Easton and still desired him, I'd probably say yes. Now…

Sadie: My mom hasn't seen me in a while and wants me to join her and Tim. I'll be staying with them as soon as they get back.

Everleigh: Oh. For some reason I thought you were staying here. Pregnancy brain. I hear it's a real thing. Well, I'll make sure to send you one of our famous apple pecan pies.

Sadie: I will happily accept. Where do you want to meet?

Everleigh: The estate.

I scurry to the bathroom, brush my teeth, my bedhead hair, and then wash my face. Faster than seems possible, I throw on jeans, a sweater, and boots. Easton hasn't texted me. Maybe he left?

Where is the book with instructions on how to have one night of casual sex?

I open my bedroom door slowly and listen. Nothing stirs. With light steps, I make my way to the second floor. Still no sounds, and his bedroom door is closed. I don't see him over the railing that looks down into the great room. Continuing to the first floor, I head for my purse and keys by the front door. Still no Easton.

Maybe he really did leave.

It hurts that he did without saying goodbye. I don't know that for sure. He could be in the bathroom still. But I'm growing attached, clearly, bothered by what he has or hasn't done and reading too much into things. I'm so out of my element in this situation.

I've always found it best to leave when I'm confused or scared. I did it to Dash when I broke things off with a vague text, and I'm doing it again with Easton. Not that Easton wants anything from me. He could want me gone, and he only brought me to his bed to sleep because he thought it was what I needed or wanted.

Ugh. This is so confusing.

Footsteps sound from the stairs to the basement. I freeze for a moment, then race out the front door to my car. I'm such a chicken. Unable to face him and this new reality we created, I start the engine and drive away without looking back.

I haven't even made it to the gate when Easton texts me.

I don't play his message in my car. I don't want to hear it. What if it's awkward? What if he makes excuses for leaving me in his bed this morning? I can't handle this right now. Since I don't want to be rude either, I hit reply on my dashboard screen and say, "On my way to meet Everleigh. Will be back later."

In record time, I pull through the gate to the estate and park near the front door. Another text from Easton comes through.

I put my phone on silent. I can deal with him—us —later.

One of the housekeepers lets me in and directs me to the breakfast room.

The space is a semi-circular shape with windows over-looking the parklike backyard. Daire officially proposed to Everleigh in this room. It was covered with hydrangeas and a magnificent charcuterie board. Easton and I were hiding, waiting for her answer, before we jumped out and congratu-lated them. I have so many fond memories with him, which makes this even harder.

"Hey!" Everleigh rises from her chair.

"Morning." I hug her and we both sit.

"I have pastries and coffee, but if you want something else, I can make it for you."

Like I'd have her do that. "This is perfect."

She points to one of two coffee pots. "This one is decaf tea. This one is the organic coffee you like."

"Thank you." I help myself to the coffee.

"What's the emergency?" She sips her tea. Remnants of a croissant are on a plate in front of her.

"What makes you think that?" I lie, knowing she'll see right through it. To keep from saying more, I get a cinnamon pecan muffin and nibble on a piece.

Everleigh stares at me, the message in her vibrant blue eyes as clear as day. *I know you and I'll wait for you to fess up.*

I sigh and think of something to say that sounds believable. I can't tell her I slept with Easton. "I need to talk to Dash and give him an answer."

"About getting back together?"

I nod and sip the coffee. It's strong and delicious.

"What's causing your hesitation?"

"What if the chance to get married never comes again? What if he's the one I'm meant to be with?"

"*What if* wouldn't be a part of a meant-to-be relationship. You would know in your heart without question if he was the one."

"But how do you know?" Geez, I sound whiny, even to myself.

She tucks her long black hair behind her ear and turns toward me, her belly rounder than the last time I saw her.

"You feel it. Every part of you knows. Denying it to yourself doesn't change what you know to be true in your soul."

Her words trigger one name. Easton. It kills me to think this way about him. It isn't fair. He didn't promise me anything more than friendship and sex. But somewhere along the way, I fell for him. I wouldn't have acted the way I did last night if I hadn't.

Everleigh studies my face, and I hate how I'm unable to hide things from her. "Who are you thinking about?"

"No one. Dash. I... I'm scared, I guess. Of being alone. Of not getting what I want more than anything. A happy marriage and a family."

"In a small town like here," she adds. "Dash can't give you that. He doesn't want it. Even if he bought a house somewhere outside of Atlanta for you, do you think he'd be happy?"

"No." It spurts from my mouth. "He'd hate it. His

friends are all in Atlanta. His job is in Atlanta. He loves his life in the city."

"You'd be settling and so would he. That's not what you want."

"No." I lower my head and pick at my muffin. "I want what you have."

No, I don't. It's the first time I've thought that. I want what Easton and I have. The problem is, he doesn't want it back.

"Call him."

My head springs up and I meet her gaze. "Who?"

"Dash. Who else?"

For a stupid second, I thought she meant Easton.

"Call him," she says. "Tell him you're not getting back together. Tell him why. Because he wasn't there in the way you needed. And despite having a wonderful past with him in high school, you want different things for the future."

"You make it sound so easy."

"It is easy. Besides, you know this. I know you do. He doesn't. He's holding on, and you've always been a bit of a people pleaser when it comes to guys."

"Always?" I ask, uncertain and scared. "That's not good."

"Even when you warn people about murderous danger, it's your way of pleasing them. Caring for them. It's an anxious behavior you grew into. I get it. I've had my share of anxiety. When you're in it, it's harder to see. When you take a step back and breathe, it comes to light."

"What comes to light?"

"Everything. What you have. What you want. What you need. It becomes clear. Maybe you need to take a step back."

"I thought I was." I set my elbows on the table and rest my cheeks between my hands.

"Maybe you need a bigger step so you can look at your life as a whole. See what you have, figure out what you want, and determine what you need to make it happen."

"What if what I need is impossible?" I murmur.

Everleigh giggles and touches my forearm. "You sound so dire. Nothing is impossible. Look at how my life turned out. Did you ever once think I'd marry Benedict's best friend?"

That draws me upright and my gaze to hers. "It's so easy to forget about him and all that happened. So much has changed."

Even more from when we first met Benedict in Savannah for my college graduation trip. Everleigh came with me. We met some super rich guys at a rooftop bar and partied with them for the days that followed. I kissed and did a little messing around with one of Benedict's friends. He was cute and fun, but when I asked him what he expected to get out of this and he answered, "a summer fling," I did what I do best and friend-zoned him. Benedict was sneaky and gorgeous in a villainous way. Little did we know he was an actual villain.

"I'm so happy that Daire put Benedict in his place and did what was right by you." A warm smile pulls at my lips. "He really is perfect for you."

"I didn't think so at the time, especially when I learned they were friends. I ran, remember? But then I let him explain, because of you, and I forgave him. Think of every-thing that had to happen for us to get here." She rubs her belly.

A bigger smile curves my lips. "You're right. I need to call Easton."

Her brows bunch together. "Easton?"

"Dash," I correct. "I need to call Dash. Then I need to step back and look at my life. I should do that from my mom's house when she returns this weekend. It'll give me a chance to think about what I want without distractions, and I'll be safe there, too."

Everleigh knows Mom and Tim live outside the city in Sandy Springs and that the neighborhood is gated with cameras.

Everleigh frowns. "I'll miss having you here, but if that's what you feel you need to do, I'll understand."

"Thank you." I cover her hand with mine. "And I'll be back soon to visit before for your baby shower."

With Easton as my helper, I'm not sure how I'm going to manage. Hopefully by then, the distance will help us find our way back to our friendship and give me time to fall out of love with him.

"And for the grand opening of the inn," she adds with a bright smile.

"And to meet baby Livingston." I pat her belly.

She laughs. "Baby Livingston. I need a onesie made with that on it."

A tall man rushes into the breakfast room.

At first, I think it's Daire, only it's Easton.

His hand covers his heart. "Thank God you're okay."

Everleigh stands, her attention on him. "What's wrong?"

Yeah. Why is he so upset? I stand, too. "Did something happen?"

"I've been calling you." He glares at me.

I get my phone from my purse and turn on the sound. "Sorry. I had it on silent."

"Sadie, I swear to God, if you ever do that again..." He

runs a hand through his disheveled hair. "I thought something happened to you."

"I told you I was visiting Everleigh."

"And then you didn't answer your phone."

"She's fine, Easton." Everleigh gestures to me and walks to him, touching his arm. "You look sick. Do you need to sit?"

"No." He continues to stare at me with a mix of anger and relief.

Everleigh glances back and forth at us, her brows pulling with concern again. "What's going on?"

Her question is valid, more so because of the intensity in Easton's eyes.

"We need to talk," he says.

Once more, Everleigh looks at both of us. "I think we need to talk more, too," she says to me.

She knows. How can she not with the way Easton's gaze won't leave my face?

"Steven called."

The PI. No wonder he's upset.

Daire walks into the room. "You found her," he says to Easton. He puts his arm around Everleigh and kisses her lips. "Hey, beautiful. How's the baby?" He rubs her belly.

"Good. Want to tell me what's going on?"

Daire's eyes meet mine, and he nods. "Sadie. Glad you're okay." His tone isn't as friendly as usual.

I stiffen, worried he knows about me and his brother. Is that what this is about? Not what the PI does or doesn't know?

"I have news about your stalker," Easton says, his tone grave. "You should sit down."

Cold fear slithers down my spine.

Everleigh's eyes widen on me. "Let's go into the other

room. You'll be more comfortable." She separates from Daire and takes my hand, guiding me into the huge living room.

"Is it bad?" I murmur to her.

"I don't know." She sits next to me on the couch, near the fireplace. Daire takes the chair beside Everleigh, and Easton sits in the chair beside him.

For some reason I wish Easton was beside me, holding my hand. I hold his whiskey gaze and will myself to be strong. "Tell me."

"Steven knows who the man is."

I draw in a calming breath and nod for him to continue.

He glances at Everleigh and Daire before bringing his gaze back to me. "Are you sure you want an audience for this? I would have done it at the house, but you'd already left."

Oh God. I slump, feeling stupid. That's why he kept calling me. Is it why he was avoiding me, too? Was he talking to Steven? That doesn't explain him taking a shower or not waking me. All things I could have asked had I stayed and faced him.

"I'm her best friend," Everleigh says. "I know everything about her. I want to be here for her." She turns to me. "Unless you want to do this alone with Easton?"

The confusion in her eyes kills me. I should just come clean about Easton and me here and now. Rip off the Band-Aid.

I look at Daire. "Do you know already?"

"No. I was sent to find you. That's all." He studies his brother the way Everleigh had studied me and Easton in the breakfast room. "Maybe we should give them a minute."

"No. It's okay." I squeeze Everleigh's fingers, her hand still holding mine.

"Okay." Easton agrees with reluctance. He leans forward, his elbows on his thighs, his hands clasped between his spread legs. "The stalker is a man named Alejandro. He's the bodyguard for Lola Novarro."

I shake my head, confused. "I have no idea who these people are."

"You wouldn't. They're from your father's side of the family."

"Tim?"

He pauses and visibly swallows. "Your biological father."

My stomach drops to my feet. "What—how?" I don't understand this at all.

"Lola Navarro is your father's other daughter. She's been trying to reach you. In secret, is Steven's guess, because of her stature in Spain. Your father was prominent and influential. He has a fortune. Steven assumes that's why she wants to talk. That's why her bodyguard grabbed you."

My brain reels, trying to process this astounding information. My father was Spanish. Influential. I'm part Spanish. "I have a sister?" I don't know why that comes out.

Everleigh puts her arm around my shoulder.

"A half-sister," Easton says. "But she's not... Steven doesn't think she's here to be friends. She's here to settle something with her father's estate. Without talking to her directly, we can't be sure if that's the only reason. Steven suspects either your father left something for you, or she's here to make sure you don't try to stake a claim on Gabriel Navarro's fortune."

"Gabriel? Is that his name?"

Easton nods.

Tears spring to my eyes.

"Oh, Sadie." Everleigh hugs my side, knowing what that means.

Finally, after all these years, we know his name. My mother never did. She met him at a nightclub in Atlanta on a girl's weekend trip. He was in the VIP section. She said they locked eyes, and that was it. He beckoned her over, and she went. He was the most beautiful man she'd ever seen. Bronzed skin, chocolate hair, full lips, and bright blue eyes. She knew he had money from his suit and watch alone.

He invited her to play a game where they made up names and pretended to be whoever they wanted for the night. She had so much fun and just enough to drink that when he invited her to his hotel suite, she didn't say no. In hindsight, she says, it could have gone badly had he been a horrible man. He wasn't.

They spent the evening drinking Champagne, and eventually, they slept together. When she woke in the morning, he was gone. A single rose rested on the pillow beside her with a note about what a wonderful night he'd had. He signed it with his made-up name, Roman. His accent had been so slight Mom never knew if he was Italian, or Spanish, or something else, but she'd assumed he was American.

It had been the most romantic night of her life, until she met Tim. Not once did she regret conceiving me with the man of mystery. She only regretted not being able to contact him about the pregnancy or share with me who my father was.

It haunted her for a long while, until Tim helped her let go of the guilt. I never held anything against her. She was an amazing mother who did the best she could. She never lied to me about the night I was conceived, although the version I got when I was younger was more fairytale. For a long time, I wished for him to appear at our house and whisk us away to his castle. It was the wish of a child. As I got older, I resented him for what he did, but never my mother. Then Tim became a part of our lives, and I stopped caring about what might have been. To learn about him now, after all this time, is bittersweet.

Tears of joy and heartache spill down my cheeks. Everleigh cries too as she clings to my side. "I have to tell my mom. She deserves the truth."

"Now?" Everleigh asks. "While she's in Greece?"

My stomach knots. "You're right. It wouldn't be fair to do that to her while she's on vacation. I already dumped the stalker news on her. But this is huge and something she's wanted to know for so long."

"She's also moved on from that time in her life. I think if you wanted to tell her, she'd be okay. She has Tim with her if she needs support."

"Yeah." He knows everything about our past, too. "That doesn't mean it'd be fair to either of them." I fight a fresh wave of tears at the heartbreak this could cause my mom. When I was younger, I cried for my father at times, begging to know who he was, and she hated that she couldn't even give me his name. "I don't know if I can tell her and risk ruining her vacation more. I don't want to upset Tim, either. He's been amazing to both of us. Accepting me as his daughter and being the man Mom always wanted. I don't want to hurt him."

"You won't." Everleigh says, her tears subsiding as she combs back my hair from my tear-soaked face.

I get myself together and calm my crying. Daire hands us tissues. Everleigh separates from me to blow her nose. Daire embraces her. I use my tissue to wipe my face and feel a strong arm go around my shoulder. I give a small gasp, surprised to find Easton beside me on the couch.

When did he move here?

He pulls me against his body in a sideways hug. "Sadie, I'm so sorry. I knew this would hurt you and hated having to tell you."

"It's okay." I nod, wanting to crawl onto his lap and straddle him, chest to chest, my face in his neck, as he holds me until I'm ready for him to let go. We can't do that here. We couldn't do it even if we didn't have an audience. This is us as friends. He kisses the top of my head, but it's nothing more than a sentimental gesture.

"What am I supposed to do now? Do I have to talk to her? Lola? And settle this?"

"I'll go with you," Everleigh says.

"*No.*" I pull away from Easton enough to look at Everleigh. "I don't want you or your baby anywhere near her. You know what her bodyguard did to me. I have to do this alone."

"Like hell you will." Easton tightens his hold on me. "I'll go with you."

A half-laugh-half-cry escapes me. "No offense, Easton, but this guy is massive. I'd need a bodyguard of equal size, and I wouldn't be okay if you got hurt, either."

"Because this is a tough time, I'll ignore how you just shredded my manhood and remind you I fight dirty. But in the interest that I want to keep you safe, I'll have a bodyguard of equal gigantism come with us."

I meet his misty gaze. Was he crying, too? "I don't want anything from her other than some information about my... biological dad." It feels weird to say. "If he left me something small, I'll take it. A momentum. A picture. I don't know. Do you think that's what it is?"

"I don't know, Sadiecakes. We'll have to wait to find out."

"When can you set it up?"

"Steven will make the arrangements. He'll want to go, too, and he'll get the bodyguard."

"I'll help," Daire interjects.

For a moment, I forgot they were there. That's what happens when I'm cocooned against Easton's body.

I clear my throat and straighten away again. My gaze goes to Everleigh.

Red veins streak her glossy eyes. She's as taken aback as I am, too emotional to have noticed anything beyond friendship between me and Easton. She's also holding her belly as if she's in pain.

"Are you okay?"

She nods, and Daire rubs her back. "She's okay."

I should have heeded Easton's tone and let him tell me this alone. I had no idea what to expect, though. Had I stayed home this morning, this could have been avoided.

I touch Everleigh's belly. "This needs protected more than I do. No more tears for you. You've shed enough throughout your life." She lost her parents, then her grandma, and a year ago, her grandfather. Daire and I are all she has.

Daire sends me a thankful grin.

"I'm in good hands with Easton. Okay? No more worrying about this. We have a plan. I'll be fine. But I won't be fine if something happens to you two." I pat her belly gently.

"I should take her home," Easton says.

Home. My temporary home until my mom gets back. Only now that we know who the stalker—stalkers—are and their intentions, maybe I could return to my condo.

239

Chapter 26

Sadie

Three days have passed since I learned the truth about my stalker. Easton and I have been busy separately—or possibly we're avoiding each other. He's kind and caring and attentive, but other than warm gestures, like rubbing my back or kissing the top of my head, he hasn't flirted or tried to do anything more with me.

He spends a lot of time in his office or on his laptop in the kitchen, while I've been working in my room and creating more book covers to keep my brain busy. If I let my thoughts stray, they lead to my biological father and my half-sister, which sends my heart hammering and turns my palms clammy.

I can't allow myself to go there until I have more facts. I searched his name, though, and saw pictures on the internet. I have his lips and hair color, but that's where the similarities stop. Everything else about me is my mother, and I'm thankful. I couldn't have handled looking like a man who wasn't there for me.

As much as I thought I was over feeling abandoned like I did during my teen years, that anger has returned. Why did he only care to be with my mom for one night? Why did he use a fake name? Why did he disappear before she woke up? What was he afraid of? Was he married? Engaged? Was he a cheater and that's why he wanted to use fake names? Turns out the answers aren't pretty. According to Steven, Gabriel was married when he met my mom, which is a betrayal to both women.

I slam my fists on the bathroom counter with a small grunt. No more thinking like this. I have to keep my cool. In a few minutes, I'm going to meet my half-sister.

It's been set up for a day now. Easton and I flew in the helicopter to Daire's Atlanta penthouse this afternoon. We met up with Steven and a hulking ex-military bodyguard, then we all went to the penthouse.

Easton thought it'd be safer and give us the upper hand if I met Lola and her bodyguard here. It definitely made me feel more comfortable.

Two knocks sound on the door. "Sadie? You ready?" Easton asks from the hallway.

"Yeah." I smooth down my cream sweater and cream corduroy pants. It was the nicest outfit I had packed. It's also silly for me to want to look nice for this woman. I shouldn't care about what she thinks. She didn't consider me when she sent her bodyguard to grab me that one night.

I saw some pictures of her, too. She doesn't look much like our dad either, other than having his blue eyes and bronzed skin. Her hair is long and black, and she looks regal.

We couldn't possibly have anything in common. After Steven spoke with her and arranged this meeting, he informed Easton, who then informed me that his initial assumption about her was correct. Lola doesn't want to be my friend. She's here on business—getting me to sign a document stating I won't try to gain money or power by legitimizing myself as my father's biological daughter or sue her for any part of his estate now or in the future.

I exit the bathroom and walk into the family room. Gregory, *our* bodyguard, stands near the foyer, as if ready for anything. Steven, who's also fit but much leaner, sits in one of the leather chairs near the sectional. His laptop rests on the coffee table. Easton watches me like a hawk as I cross to sit on the L-shaped couch, where Steven said we should conduct the business.

Steven looks at his phone. "They're on their way up now."

Easton slides in beside me on the couch. He takes my hand in his. He must notice how clammy my palm is, but he doesn't let go. I tap my foot at a vigorous pace. Easton presses his hand to my leg to stop me, and I'm thankful. I don't want to look as frazzled or as weak as I feel.

Gregory lets in my stalkers. Lola's bodyguard, Alejandro, leads the way with my even more-beautiful-in-person sister trailing behind him.

Wow. For some dumb reason, I glance at Easton to see if he's ogling her tall figure. Apart from the dark hair, she's more his type than I am. His hawklike gaze is on her in the same way he had tracked me a moment ago.

Steven stands and greets Lola with a handshake. "Miss. Navarro. I'm who you spoke with on the phone." He gestures to me. "This is Sadie."

Like she doesn't know who I am. I stand and raise my hand to her. "Nice to meet you." Why did I say that?

She shakes my hand, but it's awkward the way she positions her fingers downward, as if she wants me to kiss her leather-gloved hand. Her grip is lax, too. Her blue eyes roam over me, taking stock as she sizes me up. A tight smile curves her lips. Snotty is the best way to describe it.

Other than making a "hmm," sound, she doesn't say a word.

Her gaze shifts from me to Easton, and her expression changes to a sultry invitation. Unbelievable. He could be my boyfriend, for all she knows. Wait. She knows a lot about me, so she'd know he isn't.

Steven gestures to the couch. "Please have a seat."

She snaps twice, and Alejandro appears behind her. He helps her remove her coat and gloves, holding them while he stands behind her like the protective brute he is. Her red dress hugs her body like a second skin and has an extremely high slit. When she sits it's with grace and a sex appeal I could never possess.

She's clearly used to being waited on. She removes a gold-encased tablet from the huge leather purse at her side. "As per our discussion, the documents are all here," she says, in a rich, slightly accented voice.

"May I verify they are what we agreed upon?"

If she says no, this whole deal will be off, per Steven's advice.

Lola nods.

Taking the tablet, Steven opens it and proceeds to read. The way he sinks in the chair makes me think this will be a while.

Easton placed bottled water on the table earlier, but she hasn't made a move to take one.

Instead, she eyes me, her expression emotionless. "I didn't know you existed until my father passed," she says to my surprise.

My jaw drops a little. I wasn't expecting her to say anything to me, least of all that. It takes me a moment to find my voice. "Did he know I existed?"

"Yes."

Yes? I expected her to say no. I was prepared for no. But this, knowing he was aware of my existence and chose not to participate in my life or to help my mom, makes it hard to breathe.

I fight the burn in my eyes. "He knew?"

"At some point in his life, he learned of you. My father had money and means at his disposal. I'm sure there were precautions in the event you discovered who he was and wanted compensation."

The sting of those words buries into my heart. I suppress a shudder and compose myself.

"You're not the only half-sibling I have." Her jaded tone shows how little empathy she has regarding the situation. She crosses one leg over the other, her slit revealing the top of her toned thigh.

I can't help it. I peer out of the corner of my eye at Easton to see if he's looking. It's too hard for me to tell without turning my head and giving away what I'm doing.

She notices though because she shifts her attention to him, sizing him up the way she had me, only with a glint of approval in her eyes. "We haven't been introduced." She holds out her hand like a duchess.

To my surprise, he doesn't rise to take her hand. "Why did your bodyguard attack Sadie?"

Not at all offended, she lowers her hand and smirks as if she likes that he rebuffed her. "I needed to speak with her alone."

"Why not have him ask her? Why not go to her condo in private or approach her outside of her work?"

She tilts her head to the side, her pleased grin in place, and shifts her weight to show even more of her thigh. "That was a blunder on Alejandro's part. The brute doesn't know his own strength." She waves gracefully at the man behind her, who seems none the wiser. "That and she's not an easy woman to catch. She's in and out. She doesn't linger."

True. Lingering invites danger, and I'm always rushing around, stopping only in the evening for ID shows on the couch.

"I didn't want to draw attention to myself, and risk being identified," she continues. "No one can know about this exchange. My father's personal life should not corrupt his memory or his legacy—*my* legacy."

I ground my molars together, hoping my anger isn't showing on my face. "Was he a kind man?" Can a cheater be kind? I need to know something nice about him. I couldn't have come from a monster.

Easton puts his hand on my knee.

"In general, or as a father?"

"Both?"

She takes a moment before answering. "He was charming, and he knew it. He was kind when it served him. He provided a luxurious life for my mother and me. He took pleasure when and where he wanted it." She waves her hand at me. "He had a temper, though I rarely saw it, and when I was a child, I remember him making me laugh and spoiling me in the way only a father can."

I didn't expect what she said to hit me with sadness, but it does. A selfish, unresolved piece of my heart wishes I could have known him as a father—as my father—when I was a child.

"Don't feel bad," she says, reading the frown on my face. "Had he known you existed, he would have made sure no one else did. He wouldn't have been the father you hoped for or dreamed about. He and his people would have erased you for the sake of his image. His reputation was what mattered the most to him."

Her words hit me like a blast of cold air. I shiver, and Easton puts his arm around my shoulders. In my ear, he whispers, "Don't give her anything else." He kisses my temple, but it could be to cover up what he whispered to me.

"Aren't you two adorable," she says in a mocking tone.

Part of me wants to say we're not a couple. Another part doesn't want to give her anything more, like Easton said.

Steven sets the tablet on the coffee table and slides it to me. "It all looks good. If you're still not interested in suing for a portion of Gabriel's estate, which is within your rights as his biological daughter, you can sign here and send her on her way." He nods at Lola without glancing at her, as if she isn't worth his full attention or even the respect of him using her name.

"A word of warning." She leans forward, showing us her bountiful cleavage. "I will not only fight you with an arsenal of top attorneys; I will assure your name is tarnished beyond repair, leaving no doubt that you are nothing more than a bastard child desperate for money and willing to steal it from the only true heir to my father's estate."

Easton exhales sharply and shifts like he's about to stand. He doesn't need to clean up my messes.

"Even if I were starving and homeless, I wouldn't want a penny from a family that breeds such arrogance and disrespect. You are your father's daughter in every way." I push to my feet, my shoulders back, a chorus of cheers erupting in my mind over how I stood up for myself.

Before I can stroll out of the room like the hero in a movie who gets the last word in, Easton grabs my hand. "Sweetcakes, you still have to sign."

Well, shit. That didn't go as planned.

Lola snickers.

Hot embarrassment rolls through me. Why didn't I sign first before delivering my bad ass retort? Now I look like a fool. Ugh. I lower to the couch and sign where Steven points on the tablet. He has me sign a few more pages and then takes the tablet and hands it to my bitchy half-sister.

She tucks it into her purse and stands.

Steven stands, too.

So badly, I want to leave the room and forget this ever happened. To avoid looking like a coward, I force myself to stay put. I don't glare at her. That would show anger or resentment, and she doesn't deserve either. She would like it, I have no doubt. Instead, I turn my attention to Easton, who's still sitting. I catch his gaze, which is easy because his whiskey eyes are already on me. Pride shines in his eyes and understanding for how I don't want to give her a moment more of my time.

I don't notice Lola walk over. Only when she bends near Easton's ear and slips a business card in his hand, do I realize her presence. "Call me when you're in need of a real woman," she says loud enough for everyone to hear.

A new wave of heat crashes over me, this one burning with rage. How dare she?

Instead of showing her my anger, I give her a smirk of my own and calmly say, "In your dreams."

Then I take Easton by the face, a hand on each cheek, and kiss him as if we're alone, as if I'm the only woman in his life. As if I'm his and he's mine. As if I desire him above all others and he feels the same. As if I love him, and he loves me.

Like always, when our tongues meet the kiss is magic. His lips mold with mine in the way I love, and he devours me, making it clear I am all the woman he needs. If only that were true. I finish the kiss with a playful nip to his bottom lip and hold his gaze when we separate.

His eyes are wild with emotions. Desire, anger, surprise. The anger throws me.

I glance over just as Alejandro helps Lola into her coat. "Oh, you're still here?"

She shakes her head and tsks. "Cheap displays of affection do little to deter me. Like you said, I am my father's daughter." She moves her gaze to Easton. "Call me."

My fingers ball into fists. I've half a mind to throw a pillow from the couch at her head, just to see the shock on her face. I'd love to mess up those glossy locks, too.

I don't realize I'm standing until Easton grabs my waist and pulls me onto his lap. At least he didn't shove me onto the couch like I'm an out-of-control child.

"I'll see you to the door," Gregory says.

Alejandro and Lola follow him, her heels clicking on the floors as she goes. If I had magical powers, I'd cause her heel to break. They leave without looking back, and why would they? She got what she came here for.

"You did the right thing," Easton says and shifts me onto the couch.

"I know." I keep my gaze on the closed front door. "She didn't have to be such a bitch, though."

Steven packs up his laptop. "In my experience, people with that much wealth and public status are often entitled assholes. The good news is you never have to see them again."

Finally, I pull my gaze from the door to look at Steven. "Thank you for all your help."

He nods and clutches the handles to his bag.

To Gregory, I stand and say, "And thank you for your part and being so intimidating."

He cracks a small smile. "Happy to have helped."

Easton stands and shakes his hand. "Thanks, Steven." He walks with him and Gregory to the door.

I follow but stop at the opening to the foyer.

Steven turns to Easton. "I trust the information on Mr. Pritchard was helpful, as well?"

My heart jumps. Mr. Pritchard, as in Dash?

Easton stiffens and shoots a quick glance my way before regaining his composure.

What does he know? What don't I know? And why didn't he tell me?

I wait for Steven and Gregory to leave. Easton closes the door behind them and turns to me but keeps his distance.

I cross my arms. "What was that about?"

His eyes close briefly with a sigh. "I wish he wouldn't have said that."

"I don't," I snap. "What are you keeping from me? And *why* are you keeping it from me? That's not a good friend move, Easton." I stomp off. Not the best way to get him to confess. Forget this. I turn around. "Tell me what you know. It's about Dash, isn't it?" What are the odds of him knowing another man with the last name of Pritchard?

"Sadie." His tone sounds heavy. "I wasn't keeping anything from you. I was waiting for the right time." He walks to the bar and pours two glasses of bourbon.

"I don't want a drink. I want the truth." I cross my arms again and stare at the back of his head as he downs the glass. He holds the other out to me. "Trust me. You're going to want this."

Nothing about his demeanor shows he's angry or irritated. His morose concern is what chills me to the bone.

"Is it bad?" Obviously, it is. I walk over and take the bourbon. A sip is more than enough. It's not smooth and sweet like Easton's pecan bourbon. It's potent and burns my throat. I set the glass on the counter.

"Let's sit."

"I'm tired of sitting."

He cups my cheeks and plants a gentle, chaste kiss on my lips. "You should sit."

He's preparing me for something big, and that scares me most of all. I swallow my fear and ask the first question that comes to mind. "Is he dead?" He hasn't texted me in the past three days.

"Dead?" Easton's eyes widen. "No. But say the word, and I'll make it so."

My brain struggles to comprehend his statement. He hates Dash? He wants him dead?

"It's too soon," Easton murmurs and shakes his head, his features pinched with torment. "I wanted to give you more time."

Dread curls in my stomach. I down the rest of the bourbon, cough, and walk to the couch to sit in the spot where we were before.

Easton follows and sits beside me. Perched on the edge of the cushion, he turns toward me. "Please know that I'm here for you. Okay?"

"What the hell, Easton?" I whimper, fighting tears because I'm afraid. "Just say it."

He runs his hand through his hair, looking at a loss for words. "Dash—" He clears his throat. "Dash has a baby."

I don't say anything. I can't. Because it can't be true. A baby? Not possible.

"Did you hear me?" He touches my cheek.

I shoo his hand away. "I heard you. It's not true. He can't have a baby. He has friends and works all the time. He barely has time for me, let alone a baby." Unless this whole time he's been gone caring for the—I can't think it. "No." It's another whimper. Talk about a fool.

"I'm sorry, Sadie." He rests his big hand on my knee. "I feel like that's all I say to you, but I'm so sorry."

"When?" I lift my burning eyes to his, my heart shredded. "Who's the woman?"

"It's someone he dated in college. They've been on and off since graduating, but four months ago they got serious again during her last trimester, and she has a three-month-old baby now."

I let out a sob. "You're sure the baby is his?"

"Steven is."

Oh God. I curl in on myself and pull my arms close to my chest.

Easton embraces me in a hug. "I didn't want to tell you until later. When this ordeal with your father and half-sister was less fresh. That's why I didn't say anything."

"I get it," I murmur through tears. "I do." It doesn't change the facts or the pain. "I needed to know before I talked to him. I just can't believe it. All this time, he's been lying. He's been cheating on me, making a baby, and pretending I'm the only one in his life. The only one he wants to marry."

"He isn't with her. He ended it after you broke up with him."

"After?" I laugh without humor and lift my head. "Steven is sure about this? It doesn't make sense that he'd dump her after I dumped him."

"Steven talked to her. Mara something. I can't remember her last name. She was really upset. She wanted to marry him, but he made it clear he only wanted to marry you."

Oh God. I cover my mouth and run to the bathroom to vomit. The bourbon burns worse coming back up.

Easton appears in the open doorway and hands me a towel. "I'll get you some water."

I might throw it up, too. I can't believe he dumped this woman to marry me. What kind of man does that? When was he going to tell me? *Was* he going to tell me? That poor baby. My stomach churns again.

Easton sits on the floor and holds out the water.

I take small sips until I feel a little better. I wipe my eyes. Black mascara stains my fingers. What a mess. "I can't believe he did that. I don't know him at all. I almost married him."

"I know. But you didn't." He brushes strands of my hair behind my ear.

I move away, not wanting him anywhere near my vomit breath. "I need a toothbrush." I need my own things.

"I can get one for you." Easton stands. "Daire has extras somewhere."

I slowly push to my feet. "I need to go home. It's time."

Fear and concern radiate from his eyes. "I don't know, Sadie. You shouldn't be alone."

"Why not? I'm safe now. I was never in any real danger." So much worry for a spoiled brat who wants to keep her fortune. First her, then Dash. Have I ever felt more used? "Please don't tell Everleigh. She doesn't need to know this. Not now. I can tell her later. It doesn't matter, anyway."

"I won't tell her. But I don't know if I can leave you alone."

"Why? We're done now, too. We had sex. You can go back to being you, and I'll go back to my life."

He doesn't say anything, just stands there like he's

confused.

I push past him and get my jacket from the foyer closet.

He follows and lingers by the entrance to the room, still seeming dazed.

"It's okay, Easton. We'll figure it out." Maybe. I walk to the breakfast room. "I'll get an Uber home." I get my purse from the table.

When I turn, Easton is behind me, blocking my path. "No."

"No, what?"

"No. I can't let you go. I don't want to. I don't want to be with anyone else. I want to be with you." He cups my cheeks.

"No, you don't." He doesn't know what he's saying.

"I do. I want to be who you want, and I need you to give me that chance."

More tears spring to my eyes. It's what I wanted to hear from him, but I can't.

"I'm sorry. It's too risky. After everything I've been through, I can't get hurt anymore. Not right now. Not for a while. I need to play it safe. My heart can only take so much, and it's overloaded. As much as I want to try this with you, I just can't. You could change your mind or get bored, and I'd be...I'd be—" My voice catches. "Please understand." I slip away from his hands and run to the door, praying he doesn't follow me.

The elevator is private to the penthouse and arrives quickly. I get in and watch the doors close. Easton doesn't try to stop me. Even though I'm thankful he doesn't, not seeing him come after me hurts. Knowing I hurt him with my rejection kills me. For him to offer to try to be what I want is huge, and I ran away. I'm such a mess. I cover my face and cry in my hands.

Chapter 27

Easton

Aday has passed since Sadie left. I'm still at Daire's penthouse. I spied on her condo last night to make sure she was okay. The guard at her complex loves me or else it wouldn't have been possible. He thought I was picking something up from her. I doubt he would've agreed to spying.

The lights were on in her condo, and I watched her shadow pass behind the sheers of her window. I wanted to beat on the door until she let me in. She felt so far from my reach, even though she was only one floor away from where I stood in the courtyard. Thankfully, none of her neighbors came out or noticed me staring.

Now I'm on the phone with Daire in the kitchen of his penthouse. All I wanted to know was if Everleigh had talked to Sadie and if she was okay. Instead, after an hour of being questioned, I'm spilling my guts in a way I never thought I would.

"I told her I wanted to try to be who she wants, and she left." I finish the story, surprised at how tight my chest gets when I recall how small she seemed as she ran away.

She was destroyed, heartbroken by what her half-sister had said, and I dumped the news about Dash on her lap, then expected her to fall into my open arms. Mr. Unreliable. Mr. Never-Had-A-Long-Term-Relationship-Never-Wanted-To. Never gave the impression I wanted one with her.

In my defense, I didn't know I did. It hit me in that moment. Seeing her so broken and devastated triggered something inside me. The whole exchange did, with her half-sister and how she stood up to her. How hard I knew it was for her. Dash's betrayal had been tough to deliver but not as difficult as it was for Sadie to hear. She'd trusted him.

I hated the pain I saw in her eyes. I hated that people had hurt her. I wanted to kill them all. More than that, I wanted to take her in my arms and never let go. No one has ever made me feel that way. I didn't know it was possible. I didn't care about myself or my desires. I wanted Sadie to have the world and I wanted to be the one to give it to her.

"How do I fix this, Daire?"

Everleigh's soft voice sounds in the background. I'm on the phone with Daire, but it's like I'm on with Everleigh, too.

"It's okay if she's mad at me," I say. "You, too. I expect nothing less."

They said they weren't, but how can they not be? Everleigh loves Sadie, and I've made things worse for her.

"If you'd have used her, we'd be upset. But it's clear you love her."

He's been saying that ever since I gave him a sugar-coated version of my secret relationship with Sadie. My initial response was to lie to him until I found out Everleigh had talked to Sadie, and she'd told her enough to validate what Everleigh and Daire had already guessed. That we were hooking up. Daire said that for me to be with Sadie intimately, I would have had to have fallen for her. In fact, he had the nerve to say I had fallen for her a long time ago, but I was too hardheaded to see it.

Nice older brother. Yet here I am asking for his advice.

"Can you admit you love her?" Daire asks. "That's the first step."

"I'll admit it to her if I get the chance." I'm still working that word out for myself. Love. It seems so mature and certain. Two things I've never been.

As if Daire knows my thoughts, he says, "You're not the irresponsible man you were a year ago. You've proven that you are capable of dedication and true compassion. That is huge progress. I don't think you see it fully. I'm beyond proud of the work you've done and who you've become. You are capable of so much more than you realize. Sadie would be lucky to have you and you to have her. You're different with her. I've noticed it for a while—Hey!"

"Easton," Everleigh says, clearly having taken the phone from Daire. "I've never seen Sadie trust anyone the way she does you. You're not the only one who's grown. She's come a long way, too. Before, she wouldn't have opened herself to you at all. You remember how she shut you down when you first met? That was her protecting herself. It's what she does. Dash was safe or so she'd thought, but she never had any passion for him. The way you two look at each other is like a fire erupting in the room. The way you both help each other and want what's best for each other shows how deeply you care. And you do, Easton. I wouldn't be okay with this if I didn't believe it with my heart. You are more than capable of being the man she wants and needs. I know it."

"What if I don't?"

"Then you'll tell yourself you're capable of it until it's real," Daire chimes in. "That's what I did with Everleigh."

"It is?" She gasps.

"It is?" I echo her in surprise. Daire never comes across as unprepared or insecure.

He chuckles. "Yes. To both of you. Everleigh, you were the first woman to make me think I wasn't good enough."

"You were always good enough," she assures him.

"I'm going to let you two continue this without me as a third party."

Daire laughs again. "Easton, wait! I meant what I said. I'm proud of the man you've become and honored to be your brother."

"Well, shit, now you're going to make me cry. I can't show up at Sadie's looking like a pussy with tears in my eyes."

"She might like it."

"She'd love it," Everleigh says.

"Shit, sorry, Ev. I didn't know you were listening."

"You're on speaker. Now, go get your woman and tell her you love her."

I laugh, even though the idea scares me to the core. "In all seriousness, thank you for what you said. Both of you. I appreciate it."

"Love you, Easton," Everleigh says.

"Love you, brother," Daire says.

I end the call with a smile, despite my stomach twisting with dread about telling Sadie how I feel after she rejected me. That shit stung like salt in an open wound, but I have an idea.

Chapter 28

Sadie

Loud voices reach my ears. If the TV were on, I wouldn't be able to hear them. I haven't been in the mood for murder shows, though. Usually, I play them as background noise when I work or do anything.

I set down the plant mister bottle next to Detective Pickles's cage. His travel cage is still at Easton's house. I asked Everleigh to get it from Easton and watch DP for me until I can get back to the farm. I'll have to use the helicopter because my car is at Easton's.

I wasn't thinking when I left Daire's penthouse yesterday. My emotions were heightened and all over the place. When Easton asked me to give him a chance, I was confused. Did he mean what he said, or was it brought on by pity?

I couldn't bear trying to work things out with him when my emotions were so raw.

The ruckus grows louder and what sounds like a fight breaks out. I race to the window and peer outside.

Two men fight in the courtyard below. One is in a suit

and the other is tall and sexy—Easton! And is that Dash? No!

I fly out the door and down the stairs. "Stop!" I raise my hands and repeat myself until they listen.

Easton has Dash on the ground, his jacket torn and his eye red and swollen.

"Did you punch him?" I ask Easton.

"He punched me first. Tried to." With his hair a disheveled mess and falling over his eyes, he stands, then hauls Dash up by his suit jacket.

"Thank God, you're here." Dash fixes his coat, his plastered hair only slightly out of place. "Call off your guard dog. He's out of control." He touches the corner of his mouth where there's a streak of blood.

A few neighbors have gathered. One of them rushes over with the security guard.

"It's okay, Mr. Campbell," I say to him. "You know these men, and they're done fighting."

"They better be." He raises his phone. "I'm a second away from calling the cops."

"I promise. They're done. They're leaving, in fact."

"Like hell I am." Dash walks toward me.

Easton puts his hand on Dash's chest, stopping him from reaching me. "Did she invite you to go near her?"

Mr. Campbell tenses and raises his phone. "Do you boys want me to call the police?"

"No, sir. I apologize." Easton uses his southern manners to persuade Mr. Campbell. "I'm just protecting my friend." He glances at me. "Do you want to talk to him, or do you want him to leave?"

Dash glares at Easton. "I'm her fiancé. Of course, she wants to talk to me."

Ignoring him, Easton stares at me. "Whatever you want."

To start, I don't want an audience for this. I'm also not ready to hear more lies from Dash. But I can't let him leave without telling him I know the truth.

I step to Easton's side and eye Dash, my hands shaking. "I *know*. Don't say a word. I won't believe it, anyway. Just listen. I know about the other woman and the baby. I know you're a cheater and a liar, and now you know. You're a rotten person and we will never be together again. Leave and don't ever come back."

His face pales, and his eyes widen. He opens his mouth to speak.

Easton pushes him back a step. "You heard her. Leave."

"Sadie?" Dash implores.

"Do you want me to carry you out?" Easton says calmly. I notice his knuckles are cut and swollen.

Dash backs up on his own and straightens his shirt from where Easton's hand wrinkled the fabric.

"Good boy." Easton smirks.

Dash's eyes catch mine, and then he turns on his heel and stalks away.

Good riddance.

"I'll go too if you want, but first..." Easton walks to a nearby bench and picks up DP's travel cage from where it was safely hidden. "I got him for you. I knew you'd miss him."

"You brought me Detective Pickles?" My heart swells with warmth. "How?" I take the cage.

"I flew there and brought him back. Your car will take longer, but I'll get it for you, too."

"You don't have to do that.'

"I want to, Sadie." His whiskey gaze bores into mine. "How are you?"

This is the caring, thoughtful friend I know. The friend I went and fell in love with. The friend who just yesterday asked me to give him a chance. Did he mean it?

The neighbors have scattered and returned to their condos. Mr. Campbell left with Dash.

I glance at Easton's beat-up knuckles. "You should come upstairs and wash those cuts." I turn and let him follow me to my condo.

At the front door, I shift DP's cage to one hand.

"Let me." Easton opens it and waits for me to enter.

"Thank you." I walk in and set DP's cage on the counter. I check his water and food and stick a finger inside to pet him. He's quite alert. "Hey little guy. Are you happy to be home?" He sniffs my finger, then walks around, maybe taking in his surroundings. Being outside during a fight might have scared him, and it's cold. I scoop him up and hold him long enough to kiss his furry head before putting him in his warm cage.

"Anything I can do to help?" Easton watches me.

"You can clean your hand." While he does as he's told and washes his knuckles in the sink, I give DP fresh water and food.

Once that's settled, I join Easton at the sink. He dries his hands with a paper towel. "Let me see." I take his hand and inspect the injuries. They look much better already. "Do they hurt?"

"No." A crooked smirk tilts his lips, and his eyes dance with amusement.

"What?"

"This is nothing. Well worth it."

I take ointment and a Band-Aid from a nearby cabinet.

"Why did you get into a fight with him? Did you know he'd be here?"

"Did you?"

"No. I haven't talked to him since before we left the farm."

"That's what I thought." He leans against the counter.

"How did he know I was back?" I rub ointment on his knuckles and cover the cut with a Band-Aid.

Easton's jaw tightens. "He better not be spying on you."

I pause in the midst of putting the medical supplies away. "How else would he know?"

"He won't be back," Easton says with confidence.

"I hope you're right." I toss the wrapper into the trash. "I don't want to see him ever again."

"I could stay here for a while in case he comes back."

I turn to him, my brows raised. "You'd stay here?"

He nods, his gaze unwavering. "Sadie." He closes the few steps between us and brushes his fingers across my jawline. "I know my timing was bad, but I meant what I said yesterday."

I swallow and shiver at his nearness and gentle touch.

"I take that back. I meant it, but I didn't fully understand why I meant it until I talked to Daire and Everleigh. They helped me realize several things."

My brows pull together. "When did you talk to them?"

"This morning."

"About us?"

He nods and smirks. "It's part of the reason why I'm here. To be clear, though, I would have come regardless."

"What did you tell them?" My pulse spikes. If he mentioned the spanking, I'll die. But he wouldn't tell his brother that, and certainly not Everleigh. When I talked to her yesterday, I spoke more about my feelings than the sex I had with Easton. She didn't have anything good or bad to say. I assumed she needed time to process.

"I didn't tell them anything they hadn't already figured out for themselves or learned from you." He runs his hands down my arms to my hands.

I shiver again, despite my confusion and racing nerves. "And they told you to come here? *Everleigh* told you to come here?"

"She insisted, but like I said, I was already planning to come and tell you I meant what I said yesterday. You don't have to decide anything right now or even this week. I'll wait."

"Wait for what?"

He gives me a sexy grin. "For you to realize that you love me and can't live without me. That you need me and my body. And that no one else can give you what I can."

I roll my eyes, even as my heart flips in a way it never has before. "You're not the waiting type."

"I wasn't before you."

"I've been in your life for a year," I point out. "Why now? The sex can't be that good."

He grabs his heart and gasps dramatically. "You wound me, Sadie."

"I meant the sex can't be that good for you. For me, it's incredible. The best I've ever had."

"The best you've ever had *so far*. I have plans for us, Sadiecakes." He backs me against the counter.

"What exactly does that mean? Sexual plans?"

"Sex is always on the table. When you're ready." He lifts me onto the counter and moves between my thighs. "I said I'd wait. I mean it."

My breathing turns shallow as heat and energy radiate

through my body. His touch undoes me, his undivided attention even more so. Still, I ask again, "Why?"

"Because there's no place else I want to be. There's no one else I want to be with. I was too dense to realize what that means. What everything about us means. You and I fit, Sadie. In all ways, we fit. I never had that with anyone before. Because they weren't you. You said it yourself, we were destined. Written in the stars." He takes my chin and brushes my bottom lip with his thumb. "And because I love you."

My breath catches and tears burn my eyes. "I didn't think you'd ever fall in love."

Another sexy grin. "See what you do to me?"

"You love me?" I whisper, unsure.

"And lucky me, I get to spend the rest of my life showing you just how much."

He bends to kiss me.

I lean away, cold panic slicing through me. "I'm sorry. I'm scared. I've been hurt so much lately. I'd never recover from losing you."

"Oh, baby." He kisses my forehead. "I'm not going anywhere. I'll stay right here, wedged between your sweet thighs if you let me. I know it's hard to believe, but all I can do is tell you what's in my heart and what I've realized I can't live without. You." He kisses my nose. "My sweet, Sadiecakes." He kisses my eyebrow. "My little spank kitten."

I giggle.

He kisses my other brow. "My best friend. My everything." He tilts my chin. "May I kiss you? Nothing more. Just a kiss. You can say no." The words are a whisper across my lips.

How can I say no to him? He's everything I want, and

he's offering to be mine. What am I waiting for? I close my eyes. "Easton?"

"Yes?"

"I love you."

He exhales and chuckles. "I was starting to wonder."

"You can kiss me now."

With that, his lips meet mine with a tender kiss—a kiss I didn't think he had in his deliciously sexy body. "I'm going to screw up sometimes. Don't hate me for it. And don't run. But, if you do, I'll catch you."

I put my arms around his neck and slide close to him, more at peace than I've been in a long while.

"I promise not to run...too far," I tease.

His eyes spark with light. "That kind of talk will get you a spanking."

"Promise?"

Epilogue

bout a year later

Christmas decorations shower every inch of the estate. The inn side has a traditional theme of red and green, but Everleigh chose pastels for her side of the house. I don't know which I like better.

My and Easton's tree is fifty shades of pink in honor of our baby girl's first Christmas—celebrated from the womb. It was his idea. He didn't want to wait until next year. He's so excited to be a dad it blows me away. He continues to surprise and impress me around every turn. How he ever thought he couldn't commit is beyond me. The man is a natural at being a boyfriend and now my fiancé.

His mom walks over with a glass of bubbly liquid. I can't believe she's serving me. It's a Christmas party, Daire and Everleigh have it every year for the farm employees. Servers galore walk the place, but Mrs. Livingston insisted on getting me this herself.

"One glass of sparkling apple cider." She hands it to me and sits on the chair next to mine.

I'm on bedrest. At eight months, I pulled muscles in my

back and was ordered to stay off my feet until the baby is born just after the New Year. Could be the New Year, though, if she comes early. "How do you feel? Are you comfortable enough?"

I'm propped up on a huge, wingback chair with pillows surrounding me, my feet on an ottoman, and nestled near the roaring fire. I'm as snug as can be.

"I feel great, thank you."

She sits on the couch beside me. "I've been told Easton is carrying you up the stairs in the house."

The entire farm knows, it seems.

I refrain from rolling my eyes because this is his mother, and I don't want to seem disrespectful. "I told him I'm fine living on the couch on the first floor, but he's a stubborn man."

"That he is." She sips Champagne from a tall skinny flute. "I believe he's stubborn for all the right reasons now." She smiles warmly. "I have you to thank for that."

"I didn't do anything. He's done this himself. I'm as shocked as anyone by his transformation. Did he send you a picture of the Christmas tree?"

"So much pink." She rolls her eyes.

I almost fall out of my chair. Easton's proper, classic, pearl-wearing mother rolled her eyes. That's a moment I'll never forget.

"I always thought he was born to have fun. I was happy for the carefree life he lived, but I see now he's even happier settled." She rests her hand on my knee. "We—me, Daire, and his father—are elated that he found such contentment in you. I think he'll make an amazing father."

"I know he will. He's so protective and caring. He'll dote, I have no doubt, and our daughter will be a daddy's girl."

The thought of my child having a father who will cherish every precious moment of her life is a dream I never knew I wanted. Easton has changed me, too. He's shown me that if you have faith in someone, they can prove to be the best gift you've ever received. But you have to be willing to take the risk, like Everleigh said, and believe it will work out.

Easton and I did that with each other. We chose to have faith in us, and our love and the most beautiful relationship blossomed as a result. And a baby.

I never could have foreseen this for our future. A year ago, we were on different journeys.

I rub my huge belly. I swear it doubles in size each week. But I heard that's common during your last month.

Everleigh walks over with Daire Evans Miles Livingston the IV. Miles is after her grandfather. It is the sweetest contribution to his memory.

Apart from a head of black hair like his mom, Daire is the image of his dad. The boy will be a heartbreaker like every other Livingston son.

He arches his back as if to escape her arms as soon as she sits on the couch. "Na, Na, Na, Na." He chants his version of Nana and reaches for his Mrs. Livingston.

Her face brightens in a way only baby Daire can bring out in her. I hope our little girl, Hayley—Hayleycakes according to Easton—has the same effect.

"Gentle," Everleigh says to baby Daire as he mauls his nana's face with his little hands.

She giggles. "It's okay. Daire used to do the same thing. Isn't that right, my beautiful grandbaby," she coos.

Something else I never thought I'd see. I guess she's not as prim and proper as I'd always believed. I need to stop being intimidated by her.

"Hey, sweetcakes." Easton knees beside me and kisses my belly. "How are my two favorite girls doing?"

"Better now that you're here."

I'd be lying if I didn't say it still amazes me how well he's handling this surprise pregnancy. I remember the night we made Hayley. It was spring, and we visited the floating dock. We hadn't been back since that one night that started it all for us. That's not accurate, though. It started between us the day we met.

But this night was warm for spring. The water was too cold for swimming, so we took the kayaks out during the day.

I didn't know he'd prepared a picnic and had flowers inside the cabin for our four-month anniversary. He celebrated every month to show me how much he embraced being in a committed relationship and loved being a doting boyfriend.

"How could I have known I was made for this when I'd never tried it," he said.

"Maybe I'm the reason you're made for this," I'd teased.

"You are the reason I breathe," he'd replied, and I melted, in the way I did so many times when he said such sweet things or looked at me like I owned his heart.

We'd made love out there under the sun, birds flying above. I'd told him I had messed up my pills that month and he should pull out. Had I known we were having a romantic lunch, I would have brought a condom. In the midst of round two, where we got a bit wilder, he didn't pull out.

I'd reminded him, too, but he'd held my gaze and said, "You've ruined me for anyone else, Sadiecakes. I'm all yours, only yours, even after death. Marry me. Be mine eternally."

I'd cried, then came so hard I thought I'd clench his dick off. True story.

After, when we lay on the blanket and snuggled, I asked, "What if we just made a baby?"

"Then we become a plus one couple. A family. I wouldn't mind that at all as long as it's with you." He kissed me tenderly, savoring the moment, and I believed our hearts fused together in that moment. Perhaps that's also what led to the conception of Hayley. Who knows?

I'd never felt so loved or fulfilled. Easton gave me that. We gave it to each other, and now we'll get to share that love with a baby girl.

Baby Daire squeals, drawing me from the memory. He plops down on the couch suddenly and makes a serious face.

"What's got the little guy focusing so hard?" Easton eyes him. We all are. One minute he was bouncing all over Nana, and the next, he's motionless.

"That would be the pumpkin pie Daire gave him earlier. I told him not to let him have more than one bite." She scoops him up. "Time for a diaper change."

Daire walks over the moment Everleigh stands. "Everything all right?"

"Remember when I said don't give him too much pumpkin pie?"

Baby Daire's stomach erupts with gurgles, his expression still intense.

"Oh no," his father says. "Come on. I'll help."

Easton looks at me and his mother. "I don't get it. He went number two. So what?"

Daire's mother says, "That wasn't number two."

"More like number four," I add.

Mrs. Livingston laughs deeply and points at me. "She's

a funny one," she says to Easton. "Excuse me." She rises and joins her husband in the other room.

Not many people are in this less formal part of the house. They're mostly mingling in the living and dining rooms, whereas I'm in the more casual den.

Easton scoops me up, like he does so often—the additional twenty-five pounds of baby weight nothing to him—and cradles me on his lap. "Much better, don't you think?"

"I always love being in your arms. It's my favorite place."

"As it should be. These babies were made to hold you."

Aw. I kiss his soft lips. "I love you."

"I'll never get tired of hearing that." He kisses under my jaw line. "Damn, sweetcakes, you smell good enough to eat."

"It's the cocoa butter. I might have put too much on my belly. I don't want stretch marks." So far, I'm good.

"I don't care what marks you get from this. You're making our baby in your little body. That deserves awards and respect and maybe some light spanking. Very light. The doctor said sex could help induce labor. We want this show on the road, don't we? So we can meet our beautiful baby and get married."

I smile, my heart warmed and my insides alight with desire. He's conditioned me with that word like Pavlov conditioned his dogs. "I could use some light spanking as long as it doesn't set off my back."

I never want to experience that again. The spasms were horrific. Soon, I'll endure a kind of pain that could make or break me of ever wanting a baby again. We have a birthing plan, and Everleigh said the epidural made labor much easier.

"You won't have to do a thing but lie on the bed. I'll do

all the work and make you feel like you're flying. How does that sound?"

"Mmm." I nestle my face in the crook of his neck and kiss his warm skin. I wasn't sure that I would want to have sex once my belly got huge, but Easton's attraction for me hasn't faded one bit. In fact, it's grown stronger.

"Is my sweetcakes ready to go home?"

"I'm ready for all of it." I smile.

Home, the baby, and to get married. This isn't at all how I planned my life. What I've learned about planning is that you underestimate fate and what the universe might have intended for you. I promise I'll teach our daughter to be open to the world and what it sends her way. That fear can be restricting. And that love can surprise you if you let go and trust your heart. Her father and I are proof of that.

Other Books by Tara Gallina

Want more steamy romances set in college or just after
graduation?
Check out the couples in The Forever Series.
Heat level varies in each book from 3 to 4 out of 5

THE FOREVER SERIES
Steamy New Adult Romances

SERIAL NOVELLAS
Risking Forever: vol 1
Daring Forever: vol 2
Claiming Forever: vol 3
Sebastian – Risking Forever: vol 4
STANDALONES
The Forever Series (Serial Romance Collection)
Waiting Forever: vol 5
Losing Forever: vol 6
Hiding Forever: vol 7
Finally Forever: vol 8

Other Books by Tara Gallina

<u>PRETTY GEORIGA PEACHES</u>
small town steamy romances

Sugar Coated Lies
Sugar Coated Secrets

<u>WHERE REALITY MEETS FANTASY</u>
Young and New Adult Romances with magic

Fated To Die
A unique twist on *Beauty and the Beast* based on the
Scottish folktale about the Washer Woman

Enchanted Kisses
(A twist on The Vampire Diaries original book with a mix
of Greek mythology)

Enchanted Kisses: Extended & Uncut Edition 18+
(The steamier version with explicit scenes not included in
original.)

For new releases, giveaways, ARC team sign ups, and my
other novels visit: TaraGallina.com

Acknowledgments

This book was so fun to write. I feel like I wrote it for the fans of Sugar Coated Lies.

I got so much love for that book and the reviews were amazing. Readers even got creative with their poetry skills, adding key elements like pecan pie and bourbon to the reviews. Seriously, they were inspiring.

So I had to give you all Easton's story—and Sadie's, to be fair. It's more about her than Easton. While Daire and Everleigh's story was a true slow-burn, and heartfelt, the brother's book is more angst and fun with extra spice. I hope it delights you as much as it did for me to write.

I can't thank you (the readers) enough for your love and support. Writing is hard. It takes a lot of time and dedication. Authors want to fulfill you and transport you to a fictional place that feels real. We want to make you happy. No one does this to disappoint or leave you frustrated—unless it's a cliffhanger with a promised sequel. Then we might frustrate you for a little while.

If it weren't for the readers and love of the romance genres, my books would be stuck in a laptop or in a drawer. Thank you for going on this journey with me.

I can't thank my family enough for their constant love and support. My hubs only reads books for work—if forced. He's never read an entire book of mine, and that's perfectly fine. I talk about the stories so much, he knows the plots and characters already. He knows the struggles, the high and lows, the doubt, the imposter syndrome I—we all—suffer from now and then. And he knows how to make me happy. That's why he's still around. Oh, and I kind of love him a lot, lot! Can't imagine my life without him.

One of my sons, my youngest, is super talented and creative when it comes to storytelling. He blows me away and one day, maybe he'll share his writing talent with the world. I will be right by his side if and when he does.

To my social media peeps. Thank you for sharing my books, your thoughts, your creative content, and sending random love and support my way. So thankful! A big shout to my mom for liking all my stuff, even the steamiest, most embarrassing content. Not embarrassing to me, of course. I left shame behind long ago. For her, that's dedication and support at it's finest.

Also, I have to shout out to Margie from my Facebook group. Sometimes, it's only me and you, and that's just fine. Thank you for always popping in to like a post and share the love.

I can't leave out some other important people, like my book designer. Ana Grigoriu-Voicu with Book-designs.com. The cover you created blew me away! It is the perfect match to Sugar Coated Lies but with it's own unique feel and style. I love it so much! Katie, from Kaye Kemp Book Polishing, thanks for making sure my manuscript looks its best. My beta readers are such a helpful part of this process. Sometimes I get to share my ms with new readers who impress me. A big shout out to Kaitlyn Slowik!

I also have a tight circle of trusted friends who in one way or another are with me for each book. They listen, encourage me, grovel and gripe with me. They keep me going, lift my spirits, support my stories, and journey with so much love, I can't imagine my life without them. Ladies, you know who you are!

Tawney, my constant sunshine provider and romance reader companion. Karen Marie, my soul recharger and wine-night bestie. Shelly, my right hand, my organizer, and my everything all at once lady. Lizzy, my random long conversations about life, books, writing, and creative arts friend. Summer, my we'd-rather-be-shopping buddy. Jen, my longest ever friend from freaking elementary school. Braces, bad clothes and hair choices, bad guy choices. Dancing at parties. Those are my favorite memories. My reads-all-my-books-and-is-so-proud-of-me friend! Trinity, my we-wrote-the-same-name series, new adult romance. My you're amazing, and I can't wait to see where life takes you friend!

Women need other women. Men can't possibly comprehend the silent understanding that goes on between us. Women also need panty-melting book boyfriends. I hope I've delivered a few or more over the years with my stories.

About the Author

Tara Gallina is the author of The Forever Series vols 1-8, Pretty Georgia Peaches book 1 & 2, Fated to Die, and Enchanted Kisses.

She believes in fairies, true love, and happily ever after. When she's not writing or spending time with her husband and two older sons, she loves to visit gardens, European castles, and Caribbean beaches.

She's passionate about interior design, obsessed with throw pillows, addicted to vinegar, favors the color pink, and only drinks wine that tastes like melted sugar.

Daily needs: sunshine, laughter, coffee, family.

Daily wants: castle, English accent, princess hair, anti-age venom.

taragallina.com